6/94

D0464186

Missing at Tenoclock

Missing at Tenoclock

Arthur Williams

Walker and Company
New York

First published in the United States of America in 1994
by Walker Publishing Company, Inc.

Published simultaneously in Canada by Thomas Allen & Son
Canada, Limited, Markham, Ontario

Library of Congress Cataloging-in-Publication Data
Williams, Arthur, 1930–
Missing at Tenoclock / Arthur Williams.
p.   cm.
ISBN 0-8027-3185-6
I. Title.
PS3573.I44745M57   1994
813'.54—dc20   94-38034
CIP

Printed in the United States of America
2 4 6 8 10 9 7 5 3 1

Author's Note

Readers who know Colorado may notice that slight tinkering has been done with the way the legal system operates there, for the sake of the story. Those familiar with the San Juans will recognize the names of some real places, but will be wasting their time if they look in the atlas for Tenoclock, a town that does not really exist.

Similarly, a few real-life celebrities will be found in cameo roles here, but the major characters don't exist either.

Missing at Tenoclock

▽

Wednesday, September 26

THE ASPEN HAD turned to gold on the higher mountain slopes around Tenoclock, Colorado, and the evening sun made their color blaze. To the south, Killdeer Mountain had its first traces of snow above 12,000 feet, and at lower elevations the ponderosa pines and Douglas firs stood vivid dark green. Since it had started being famous, people came from everywhere to admire the scenic beauty around Tenoclock.

Scenery was the farthest thing from Henderson Gregg's mind.

Carrying the telephone with him as he paced back and forth in front of the glass deck windows of his second-story motel room, Gregg felt almost out of his mind with frustration.

"I *know* his number is unlisted," he said. "But I've got to get through to him now, right away. This can't wait! How can I make you understand that?"

A small, wiry man in his forties, with thinning gray hair and granny glasses, Gregg listened to the response. He gritted his teeth so hard they ached sharply.

"All right," he snapped. "If you won't give me the number, then at least call him yourself and give him my name and number. Will you do that much for me?"

Again Gregg paused, freezing in midstride in front of the patio doors, listening again.

"Goddamn you, you won't even do *that* much for me?" He threw the telephone against the wall.

So angry his heartbeat felt irregular, Gregg paced again, then stopped to look at his wristwatch. They weren't going to let him get through on the telephone, and he couldn't wait. He had no time left. It might already be far too late. His panic made him feel crazy. If I had gotten here just one day earlier, he thought. But he had not come earlier, and there was no more time for trying to check further into what he now—with dawning shock and anger—suspected. He had to act.

Pacing again, his mind filling with ghastly imaginings, Gregg might have been mistaken on the street for any of the other tourists flocking in for the turning of the aspen. His plaid wool shirt and worn Levi's were not unusual, nor were his scuffed and dirty hiking shoes. But his trip to Tenoclock had nothing to do with vacationing. How he wished it did!

No one could—or would—help him. All the fruitless telephone calls he had made from Texas should have told him that before he came here. He doubted now that they had even made note of his calls. They didn't care. No one cared.

It was up to him.

Outside, far to the west beyond the rambling shake-shingle roofs of Tenoclock's rustic downtown, a dust-colored sun slipped below the 14,000-foot crest of Red Mountain. Instantly it was twilight. In a few minutes it would be dark. Insanely, a line he had read in a college poetry class leapt into his mind: Hurry up please, it's time.

Opening the soft-sided Tourister suitcase on the rack at the foot of his bed, he rummaged beneath clothing items and brought out a heavy object wrapped in a wine-colored bath towel. He carefully unfolded the towel on the bed. A Colt army .45 automatic pistol tumbled softly onto the covers along with a blue metal cartridge clip, shiny with oil and already loaded with ugly, brass-nosed bullets.

Gregg's hands shook as he rammed the clip into the butt

of the .45. He worked the action of the weapon, loading a round into the chamber. He carefully lowered the hammer and fumbled with his thumb on the side safety. Slipping into his dark blue peacoat, he buttoned it and pulled on a navy stocking cap. Night was coming on, and it would be cold.

He dropped the gun into the right-hand pocket of the coat. He checked in the full-length mirror. The .45 didn't show.

It was almost dark when he walked to his rental Ford in the parking lot and backed out to drive away. He felt dazed and crazy. Maybe his guesswork was all wrong. He hoped to God he was wrong. A part of him didn't want to know—wanted to run away. But he had to do this.

9:10 P.M.

In HIS DANK basement headquarters at the Tenoclock County Court House, Sheriff James "Big Jim" Way looked up from his latest issue of *Colorado Country Life* and studied the clock on the far wall. With a heavy sigh, as if he had been working hard all day, he opened the middle drawer of his scabby military-surplus metal desk, stowed the magazine on top of a copy of *Penthouse* and fifty or sixty unexamined incident reports, and got ponderously to his feet. An extensive paunch sagged over the silver cowboy buckle of his belt as he stretched, stifling a yawn. He had been a good-looking man once—an athlete—but the years had turned a granitic profile to lazy pudding and ballooned his weight from 210 to 260, if you didn't adjust the bathroom scales quite up to zero before you stepped on. Most people liked Jim Way; it was often said that he never gave anybody any trouble.

Yawning again, Way walked slowly around his desk and down an aisle of similar ones, all deserted, toward the front counter.

Deputy Johnelle Baker, the only other person on duty except for the jailer in the back, looked up from the antique

Motorola radio console behind the counter. A tall woman, thirty-two, with ash-blond hair and features that were extraordinarily attractive if not classically beautiful, she was wearing a red flannel shirt and faded old Levi's, and an old-fashioned green eyeshade against the glare of the decrepit overhead fluorescents, which always flickered. She seldom wore her gray deputy's uniform on late shift because she seldom got out of the office. Tenoclock, despite its extraordinary boom in recent years, had little crime. After the sheriff completed his routine evening rounds, there wouldn't be anyone else out there to call in on the county frequency, and telephone calls after dark were unusual.

"Everything quiet?" the sheriff asked as usual.

She gave him a small, friendly smile. "Everything quiet," she said as usual.

"Well, Johnnie my girl," he added as usual, "I'll be heading out."

"See you tomorrow," Johnnie said, again following the routine.

"I'll cruise around awhile, show the flag, you know. You hold the fort here, keed. I'll try to beat back the forces of evil one more night out in the boondocks."

It was an old departure line. Jim Way liked things routine, familiar, and predictable. Johnnie responded in kind: "If you need reinforcements, Sheriff, call 911." Tenoclock, despite its status as Colorado's newest tourist-celebrity boomtown, didn't have 911, and never would at the rate things were going.

The sheriff grunted and ambled up the stairs and out into the night. Moments later, Johnnie heard the heavy outside door to the parking lot slam closed, and within another few seconds the distant cough of Way's big Bronco engine. Then headlights splayed momentarily over the high side windows of the office, the sound of engine and tires on gravel faded, and Johnnie was left alone.

She turned to the old Motorola console and waited.

Way's call crackled in: "Sheriff's unit one to base."

Johnnie's antique swivel chair creaked as she keyed the desk mike: "Unit one, headquarters."

"Radio check?"

"Loud and clear, one."

"Ten-four. Out."

Johnnie glanced at the clock. "Roger. Twenty-one-four-teen."

Sheriff Big Jim Way would cruise a few county roads, shine his spotlight into a few darkly wooded spots, make sure the patrons saw him go by the Sawmill Saloon and a couple of other late-night spots outside the city's jurisdiction, then meander on higher up the mountain to park and have a drink or two, usually bourbon, neat from a pint he always had in the glovebox of his truck. Around eleven, he would call in to report all quiet. That was the signal that he was headed home. Soon afterward, Johnnie would shut down the radio and switch the telephone line into the back end of the basement, where the jailer, old Jason Ramsey, would be the county's sole law enforcement officer on duty until 7:00 A.M.

It all felt quite normal. Johnnie turned back to her desk behind the counter and the latest routine reports from the county's other two deputies. They would go to Way for action, but unless she marked them with a bold red under-liner, she knew they would go in his desk drawer unexamined.

Less than five minutes later, the routine shattered.

First bright headlights glared against the high basement windows on the parking lot side, followed closely by pulses of red and blue—rotating gumball machine roof lights of a city police car. Moments later, the upstairs security door banged open. Loud, angry male voices racketed down the staircase along with heavy footfalls.

Sliding her billy club out of the tray under the counter just to be on the safe side, Johnnie headed for the frosted glass back door. Before she could reach it, it swung open and one of Tenoclock's city policemen, an officer named Schwartz, came in, pushing two tall, disheveled college-age boys. Both were handcuffed behind the back.

"We weren't doing a damn thing!" the taller youth, a redhead, protested loudly.

Schwartz ignored him. To Johnnie he said, "Couple of customers for you. They need the county jail's hospitality real bad."

Johnnie pressed the under-counter button that would summon Jason Ramsey. She opened the big booking ledger on the counter. "Drunk and disorderly?"

"Who'sh drunk?" the redhead slurred.

Schwartz, not much older than the two prisoners, looked weary. He had been in a scuffle, judging by the rumpled condition of his dark blue city uniform and the dirt stains on the knees of his trousers. "Let's start out with public drunkenness; disturbing the peace by starting a riot in the Silver Dollar Saloon; outraging public decency by gross and offensive behavior—"

"Outraging what?" Johnnie looked up from the ledger.

"Outraging public decency," Schwartz repeated tiredly, "by urinating in the goldfish pond in the municipal rose garden. Oh, and resisting arrest. We might as well put that down, too."

The second kid, considerably dirtier and more mussed up than the redhead, shook his head violently and hawked up spit that gobbed onto the front of Schwartz's uniform shirt.

Schwartz pulled out a handkerchief and mopped at the mess. "And assaulting an officer. Add that."

"Bastard!" the blond boy said, violently angry.

"Cut it out," Johnnie told him amiably, "or we'll gag you. Now. You, Mr. Redhair. Name, last name first?"

By the time she had gotten their names and hometown as well as local address, Ramsey had shuffled in through the back doors that led to the jail. Somewhere between sixty and eighty, he had been the county's jailer since the days when Tenoclock's permanent population was less than three hundred. Lean and bent, with wiry gray hair and rich brown skin heavily furrowed by the years, he came to the counter at a gait that suggested he might be breathing his last.

"Yassum?" he croaked, looking ignorant.

"Cells four and eight," Johnnie told him.

"Yassum," Ramsey murmured, doing his best shufflin' Mose act. "Guess you better come along with me, boys, real nice 'n' easy, ain't that so, Miz Deputy Baker, ma'am?"

Johnnie almost lost patience with the old man. He had two college degrees, a B.A. in English from Langston University and a master's in sociology from Indiana, he was working on his third book tracing the role of black men and women in the settling of the West, and he was studying Hebrew in his spare time. He planned never to retire from his night jailer's job because, he said, it paid his grocery bill and rent while giving him plenty of time to do his research. But he insisted—until you knew him quite well—on acting like an embarrassing old movie stereotype.

Seeing the look of contempt that crossed the face of the blond kid at the counter, she wished more fervently than ever that the old man would drop the act.

"Four and eight, Mr. Ramsey," she repeated sharply. "Well separated."

"Yassum," Ramsey drawled, showing two gold crowns on front teeth. "You jus' come along with me, now, boys."

"Want me to help?" Schwartz asked.

"I guess I can han'le 'em," Ramsey murmured sleepily.

"Let me get my cuffs, then." Schwartz turned both youths to the wall and unlocked the metal bracelets. They rubbed sore wrists and turned back to glare. They looked crazy-drunk enough to try something again, but they didn't move.

Ramsey made a hand signal. "Now jus' come along nice 'n' easy with me, boys, an' we'll get your valuables in a good safe place an' give you a spot to sleep it off."

Johnnie thought the redhead got a dangerous, violent glint in his eyes for an instant, but then it was gone and he walked unsteadily beside his blond friend ahead of Ramsey toward the back door. City officer Rick Schwartz watched them go out of the office. With a deep breath of resignation, he signed the booking sheets.

"We'll get the incident reports to the assistant DA's office first thing in the morning, Johnnie."

"Okay, Rick. Thanks for the business."

Schwartz looked startled, then got the joke. "Yeah. Right. Well, good night."

He left the room, and in a few moments the flashing lights went out and his cruiser could be heard pulling away.

Johnnie started to finish the booking report. A sharp yell, followed by the crash of something heavy against a wall back in the cell block area, brought her to her feet.

Grabbing her billy club, she went over the counter and ran to the back. Rushing through the staircase hall, she jerked the jail section door open and ran into the small office where Jason Ramsey kept his desk files. Ramsey lay sprawled on the linoleum floor, his mouth bright red with blood. The blond kid stood over him with a heavy glass ashtray in his hand, and the redhead was rifling the personal property envelopes Ramsey had just used to collect their valuables.

"Hold it!" Johnnie said sharply.

The redhead turned, grabbing Ramsey's nightstick off the desk. He started toward her with the stick in his hand. The blond boy, ashtray still in hand, moved with him.

Oh shit, Johnnie thought. "Stop!"

They didn't stop. The redhead swung the nightstick at her. She sidestepped and jammed the end of her billy club into his midsection, stepping into the motion to give it extra force. He yelled with pain and doubled over. The blond boy grabbed her, trying to get the club. She twisted out of his grasp and brought the billy club around in a backhand motion that caught him across the forearm with a sound like a tree branch breaking. He yelped and went to his knees. The redhead, still bent over, grabbed at her legs. She tapped him on the skull and he stretched out peacefully on the linoleum. She whirled to face the blond boy again.

"Enough!" he cried, holding his hands together in supplication. "Don't hit me again! I give!"

"Are you going to behave, you little shit?"

"It's police brutality! I think you broke my arm!"

"On the floor, facedown," Johnnie snapped. "*Move!*"

He scrambled to obey. "I didn't mean it! I was just kidding!"

Johnnie knelt beside Ramsey, who had struggled to a sitting position on the floor. "Are you okay? Let me look at that lip."

The old man gently pushed her away and staggered to his feet. He fished a red bandanna out of his hip pocket and pressed it against his mouth. "I'm fine—I'm jus' fine." He seemed to rally a little. "You know, Miz Baker, you can't hurt a man like me by hittin' him in the *haid*. . . ."

"If you don't *stop that*," Johnnie snapped, "I'm going to hit you myself."

Ramsey chuckled through the bandanna. He turned to his desk and produced some old handcuffs. With surprising speed and deftness he got them on both the boys. "I really must be getting old," he said with perfect diction. "Saw it starting, but the reflexes simply wouldn't fire."

"I'll help you get them in their cells."

The redhead groaned and sat up. Ramsey smiled. "You sho picked on the wrong lady this time, boy."

After they had the boys securely locked up, Johnnie insisted on examining Ramsey's lip. It did not appear to be a bad cut. Johnnie's hands trembled as she accepted a cup of the vile jailhouse coffee.

"Look at me," she said ruefully. "Some people think I'm tough, and I'm shaking worse than an aspen in a high wind."

"Guess you're a little like me," the old man told her.

She studied his dark face. "What do you mean?"

His teeth gleamed. "Outside, one thing. Inside, something else."

9:22 P.M.

An AMAZING NIGHT sky full of stars dimly lighted the twisting mountain road. Gregg, his stomach a knot of tension, drove as fast as he dared over the unfamiliar curves and switchbacks of the narrow paved road. He had it all to himself, hadn't encountered another vehicle since leaving the gas station. Now the distant lights of Tenoclock glittered far below, and a spooky gibbous moon glowed behind thin, distant clouds that hung low over mountains far to the southeast. Not much farther, Gregg thought.

He negotiated another sharp, ascending curve. His headlights picked up the beginning of an eight-foot rustic stone wall on the right. The road went along beside the wall. Evenly spaced small red signs said PRIVATE—KEEP OUT.

The trip odometer showed 7.1 miles from town, just what the man at the Texaco station had said it would be. The man had acted bored as he gave Gregg the directions. Many tourists asked about the location of celebrity chalets near Tenoclock. It was not likely, Gregg thought, that the Texaco man would even remember him.

Ahead was a gravel driveway leading up the mountain to where three or four house lights shone dimly through the dense woods. At the mouth of the gravel drive, high gates made of ornamental wrought iron blocked the way. Beside the gates, light glowed from inside a small guard shack. The sign on the shack said SKY ESTATES—NO ADMITTANCE.

Gregg drove past, proceeding up the road another two hundred yards to the spot where the high rock wall cornered. He turned around and drove back past the guarded gate. Going downhill now, he poked along until he reached the lower corner of the wall. The shoulder here was wide enough to allow him to pull off the pavement. He parked, cut the engine, put the transmission in park, and doused his headlights.

At first he felt almost blind. Trying to control shallow, nervous breathing, he waited. Within a minute or two his eyes began to adjust. The combination of starlight and the cloud-shrouded moon made the adjustment fast and easy. He reached back and switched off the car's dome light so it would not flash when he got out. Checking to make sure the .45 was secure in his pocket, he reached under the seat and pulled out the tool he had brought along. He opened the car door and stepped out onto weedy roadside gravel, shoving the tool into the back of his belt under his coat as he did so.

The chill night air began to penetrate his clothing as he crossed the road and hurried through knee-high brush to the stone wall. Hitching up his pants and making sure the .45 was deep inside his coat pocket, he reached up, grabbed hold of protruding rough stones, and heaved himself up, the rubbery soles of his boots holding strong on other stony protrusions.

Fear made him stronger than usual, quicker. Within moments he was at the top of the wall. He had expected barbed wire or broken glass or something on top, but the thirty-inch concrete cap was smooth and featureless. Gregg pulled himself over the lip and let himself down on the far side, feeling for foot- and handholds.

When he felt tall brush rubbing against his pantlegs, he let go and dropped the last eighteen inches to the ground. Expecting barking dogs, a shouted challenge—anything—he froze where he was, sweaty hand slippery on the weapon in his pocket.

Nothing happened.

Well off to his left, Gregg could just make out the light of the guard shack through the dense timber. He couldn't see the house from here, but he knew which way to head. He started up the slope. His movements through the brush seemed to make an ungodly racket. But no challenge came.

The first house he came to was low, with stone walls and a rambling wood roof with shingles that looked six inches thick in the pale moonlight. No lights showed inside; its celebrity owner probably was in Hollywood, Gregg thought, possibly New York or Miami. He skirted this property and kept working his way fast uphill.

Another hundred yards or so on, he came out of the woods and underbrush onto a smoothly clipped lawn. Ahead of him, the moonlight shone pale on a neatly edged gravel driveway. To Gregg's right, close enough that he could have hit it with a well-thrown rock, was the house he wanted. In the moonlight it was enormous—a massive contemporary structure with winglike extensions north and south, swooping curvilinear roof lines, well-tended shrubs and trees. Lights blazed from several tall windows on the first floor and from others on the second, but he could not detect any sound.

A single automobile, an elderly compact, sat parked in the curved area of the driveway in front of the soaring main entrance.

Gun in hand now, Gregg scuttled across the driveway to the shadows of big evergreens. Crouching, he hurried around the side of the house, looking for a place to break in. The windows all looked too high and difficult.

At the back he encountered a wood stockade fence with a four-foot gate. He tested the latch, and to his surprise the gate swung back freely. He went through. In the moonlight he saw decking and patios, covered cabana areas, the gentle rippling reflections of a swimming pool. The house was to his left, and there was a large redwood deck with wide doorways leading into the house.

His footsteps made no sound as Gregg moved along the patio and then across the deck. The French doors leading into the house were black—no light inside this part of the mansion. Gregg tested a handle. It didn't budge, locked.

Reaching behind himself, he dug the heavy Vise-Grips out from under this coat. He locked the teeth of the tool on the doorknob and threw his weight down on the tool's handle. There was a soft crunching sound inside the door mechanism and the knob broke free.

Nerves shrieking by now, Gregg left the Vise-Grips on the ground, swung the door open, and stepped into the house.

It was dark in the large room, but in the faint light coming from a front hallway he could make out a pool table, chairs, a corner bar. You can still turn back. But that was cowardice speaking. He could not turn back.

He skirted the pool table and went down a long interior hallway, the light becoming brighter with every step.

He emerged at the back of a colossal entry foyer, brightly lighted doorways opening into silent, unoccupied rooms as big as his whole house back in Texas. A beautiful, curving white staircase led to the second-floor balcony.

Hesitating, Gregg heard the faint sounds of music coming from the upstairs. Then he heard the voices.

A man's voice, one many Americans would have recognized.

Then the other voice. Gregg recognized it, too, and for a second he thought the pain would make his heart stop.

A towering anger overwhelmed everything else. Gregg rushed up the staircase, taking it three steps at a time, the .45 gripped firmly in his right hand.

9:28 P.M.

DAVE DICKENSEN HAD just shoved a new compact disc into his cabin stereo system when the emergency telephone rang. In the three years he had owned and operated DD Security Systems, he had had someone at the downtown office test the line by calling him once every month. It had never rung at any other time, signifying a real emergency.

Dickensen had not ordered a test tonight. Flicking his stereo off, he rushed across the broad expanse of the cabin's living room and grabbed up the phone before it had a chance to ring a second time.

"Dickensen," he said.

"Dave?" a recognizable male voice said tightly. "This is Hinson, out at Sky Estates."

"What's happened?" Dickensen demanded.

"I'm in the guard shack and I just got a silent burglar alarm from up at station six. I'm headed up there to check it out."

Dickensen did not have to ask who lived in the property designated station six in the elaborate Sky Estates security system. "I'm on my way." He slammed the phone down.

Hurrying into a back room of the cabin, he pulled on his wool coat and grabbed a 12-gauge pump shotgun off the wall rack. Pocketing a handful of shells—no. 4 shot— he hurried to his front door, paused only long enough to arm his own burglar alarm system, and ran to his Dodge Ram pickup.

The big modified engine fired at once, and Dickensen sprayed gravel as he backed away from his cabin and started down his driveway at high speed. If it was a real break-in at Sky Estates, why hadn't the perimeter alarms picked any-thing up to give Hinson more advanced warning? Of all the places for a possible break-in! Sky Estates was the showplace for DD Security Systems.

Dave Dickensen's arrival in Tenoclock five years earlier had been timed almost perfectly, although that had been an accident. Shortly after he left the Denver police force during a bleeding-heart investigation into alleged police brutality, he picked Tenoclock as a nice place to buy a cabin and have time to fish and hunt. His original intention had been to join the small local police force, or possibly run for sheriff. It had not occurred to him then that Tenoclock might be transformed almost overnight into a booming tourist vaca-tionland, once the state finished a decent road through the mountains, and the latest "in" spot for some of Hollywood's prettiest people as soon as two fine ski lifts were completed and the county commissioners floated a bond issue to complete a 7,000-foot runway for celebrity bizjets.

Even with the first signs of the coming boom—and the building of the first half-dozen mountainside mansions for the rich and famous—Dickensen had not tumbled to the idea that was to turn into a gold mine. Only when the county failed to expand its sheriff's force, and spring blizzard burglars ransacked the house of a famous old jazz singer, did the idea bloom.

What Tenoclock's famous needed, Dickensen realized then, was a private security firm that could alarm-wire houses deserted much of every year, inspect seasonally vacant properties on a regular basis, and provide security for the most famous, who needed protection not only from criminals but from curious celebrity seekers as well.

Since that time it had been almost all gravy. Yes, Dickensen's continuing investments in security equipment, weapons, office management, and vehicles kept his debt far into six figures. But he could see it coming now—the day when his company would turn the corner and make him a millionaire. The Tenoclock city council and county commissioners were only too happy to have "colorful Dave Dickensen" hiring out to provide the security that otherwise would have required huge increases in taxes to support expanded police and sheriff's departments.

He had been lucky, too, in how things had gone in the first years, Dickensen knew. Tenoclock hadn't grown into city-level crime yet. There had been only two serious break-ins at DD client residences since the company started, and one of those had been thwarted. The other had involved kids, apparently, who took only some beer and food.

"Never a successful break-in at a client home!" Dickensen's colorful advertising brochure boasted.

But all that would be changed if someone had gotten past everything at Sky Estates—even inside the house where the famous Brandon Warner was enjoying a few weeks' retreat to study scripts in search of a new film.

What, Dickensen wondered, could have gone wrong? Could it be an electronic breakdown? How could anyone have gotten past the guarded gate, past all the perimeter devices, actually into the mansion? A system failure seemed unlikely; Dickensen had only this week checked everyone's alarms because a flood of celebrities was due in the next few days as Tenoclock filled up with people in to see the turning of the aspen.

Had Hinson screwed up?

Dickensen reached the mountain road, spraying more dust and rocks from his truck tires as he swerved off the gravel and onto narrow blacktop pavement. Christ, if somebody successfully got into *this* chalet, the resulting publicity could really hurt—make DD lose face and clients wholesale, get knocked on its financial ass.

He knew the road like the inside of his own cabin. Foot down hard on the accelerator, he pushed the pickup as hard as he dared, tires screaming around the curves. Fifteen minutes, he thought. He could make it in fifteen minutes, unless he hit a deer or missed one of these curves and made like a two-ton bungee jumper instead.

9:28 P.M.

The antique Motorola console at Johnnie's desk made a crackling noise, as if clearing its throat.

"Sheriff's unit one to base."

Johnnie keyed the mike. "Unit one, headquarters."

Sheriff Jim Way's voice sounded a bit gargly, showing he'd had a nip or two: "Johnnie, everything quiet out here so far. Anything to report?"

Johnnie decided not to mention the drunk kids right now. "Everything quiet, one."

"Okey dokey, then, I'm on old Route 16. I figure on going on up as far as the cutoff for Engineer Pass, and then come on back in the other way, ten-four?"

This, too, was routine. "Ten-four," Johnnie said.

"One out."

"Headquarters out."

Johnnie stretched. A nice, quiet night, also as usual. In another hour and a half she could start home.

9:40 P.M.

FEELING MORE MELLOW and self-satisfied by the moment, Jim Way trundled his Bronco along the gravel streets of a small mountainside subdivision, spraying his spotlight this way and that, briefly illuminating trees, underbrush, the small log cabins that dotted the addition on half-acre tracts. Most of these cabins belonged to working stiffs like him— were occupied only a few weeks each summer at most, and maybe for a few days around Christmas, for the skiing. Most had been closed and winterized now, their owners gone back to wherever their full-time homes might be. But lights glowed in some windows—enough to ensure that word would go out that dependable old Big Jim Way had been on the job, checking for security.

Way reached the far end of the addition and drove the Bronco slowly down the steep slope toward the paved road at its bottom. He stopped there, reached across the seat for his pint bottle of Jim Beam, and had another snort. The bourbon felt nice and hot going down. Way reflected that it was a pretty night—lots of moonlight and stars, brilliant in the high mountain air. He really loved it in Tenoclock. He was a happy man. Maybe, when he got home tonight, he would see if mommy would give him some nookie.

Recapping his pint, he pulled onto the pavement and headed west. The cutoff for the Jeep road to Telluride was not so far ahead now. He would park there, as he often did, and enjoy the night sky for a while . . . have a few more little nips before heading back.

9:44 P.M.

GRAVEL SPRAYED IN all directions from the locked wheels of Dave Dickensen's pickup as he jammed on the brakes in front of the closed gate to Sky Estates. Setting the parking brake, he jumped out and ran to the gate lockbox, using his master key to open up. He slipped through the small crack he could shove open in the steel gates and rushed into the lighted guard shack. He pushed the button to activate the electric motors that would swing the gates wide.

As he did so, he glanced over the alarm system control panel. The red house-intrusion light still blinked rapidly. So did five of the amber alarm lights that signaled tripped perimeter sensors around the house. But hadn't Hinson said there had been no early warning of an intrusion?

There was no time to think about it. Hurrying back to his truck, Dickensen floored the accelerator, making the pickup practically leap through the gates up the drive in the direction of the house. Driving like a maniac, he took the first two wooded curves on squealing tires.

Suddenly a bright light flared across his windshield. Taken by surprise, he almost didn't react in time. Spinning his steering wheel to the right, he hit the edge of the narrow estates roadway. Just as he did so, the glare in his windshield became blinding for an instant as some other vehicle careened past him in the opposite direction.

Dickensen's brightness-stunned eyes couldn't make out more than dim outlines. In the rearview mirror, all he could see was the flare of pink-red taillights as the other vehicle—it was a small car—braked for the last curve in front of the gate. Then the red lights vanished behind trees.

It had been an older car, Dickensen thought fleetingly as he retook the middle of the lane and gunned on up the hill toward the house. Maybe an old Toyota hatchback, or maybe a Datsun when they still called them Datsuns, or possibly something American like a Mustang. He had no idea what anyone else was doing here at this hour, but he didn't have time to think about that, either.

He skidded the pickup to a halt in front of the sprawling contemporary home. Hinson's car stood in front with the driver's side door open, no other cars in sight. The front door of the house stood open, letting light from the entryway spill out onto the concrete slab of a front porch.

Dickensen shoved shells into his pumpgun as he hurried up the front steps to the entrance, worked the slide to chamber the first shell as he moved into the foyer. The silent mansion looked empty, every light ablaze. Dickensen slowed down, defensive instincts taking over. His breath rasped in his lungs.

He took the living room on the right first, found it deserted. Behind that room was another one almost as big, but the lights were off here. He found the switch and turned on the overhead tracks. Seeing no one, he pressed on, into the game room at the back. It was dark, too. The light switch activated a gorgeous red and green cut glass light fixture suspended over the beige pool table.

Turning through the utility kitchen, leaving more lights in his wake, Dickensen worked his way back toward the front, coming out again in the soaring entryway after checking four more rooms. He considered calling out Hinson's name, but this was no drill; the intruder or intruders might have taken Hinson out, and just because a car had roared down the driveway, it didn't mean all of them were out of here yet.

A movement up at the head of the staircase made him whirl, crouching, shotgun ready.

"It's me!" Hinson, his gate guard, croaked.

Hinson looked like hell, no color in his face, eyes at pinpoints of shock, thinning hair standing straight on end like a cat's hair will do when it has been thoroughly spooked.

Hinson waved at him. "Up here!"

Dickensen ran up the stairs. Hinson, shaking, gestured for him to follow. They went down the hallway to where bright light flowed out of an open doorway.

"What the hell *happened?*" Dickensen demanded hoarsely.

Mute, Hinson ducked through the open doorway into the room beyond: the master bedroom, Dickensen thought, unless his memory of the security system blueprints was faulty.

He followed Hinson inside, took one look, and involuntarily moaned.

10:00 P.M.

THE UNLISTED LINE into the dispatcher's position rang, slightly startling Johnnie Baker. She picked up the phone. "Tenoclock County Sheriff's Office, Deputy Baker speaking."

"I love it when you talk dirty like that," the voice said.

Johnnie grinned. She could picture Luke Cobb, six feet tall, curly dark hair messed up and blue work apron spattered with reddish pigments after his nightly stint with the clay in the workroom behind his gallery and store on Silver Street.

"You'd better watch it," she told him. "If we were an up-to-date department, we'd be automatically taping every telephone call for the record."

"But you're just an old-fashioned girl in an old-fashioned department," Luke replied. "I guess that's why I love you; you remind me so much of my sainted mother, God rest her soul."

"Luke, have you been glazing pots again with some of that stuff that gives off the funny fumes? Never mind. Don't answer that. What do you want?"

"Coffee. I've got some news. How about meeting me at the Pick & Shovel after you get off work?"

"Sure. What's the news?"

"If I tell you now, there's nothing left to tell you over coffee."

"Luke!"

"Okay, okay. You remember the pair of big azure-glazed urns I did last winter? The ones that have been in the window all this time?"

"The ones you've got priced at twelve hundred for the pair? Sure."

"I sold them."

"You're kidding! That's great!"

"Lady from Fort Collins, in to watch the aspen turn. Came in and took a look, said she'd be back with her husband, and I thought, Oh, yeah, sure. But she did come back with her husband. Bought 'em on the spot."

Johnnie felt glad for him. Luke Cobb's art and pottery store never ran very far ahead of financial disaster, even in these boom times for Tenoclock. For one thing, his pots and other ceramics were considered truly fine by people in the art world who knew about such things; they did not sell cheap. For another, every time Luke saw a comfortable balance in the store checkbook he closed for a few days. Sometimes he went fly fishing in the high country. More often he went to New York or San Francisco, where he renewed contact with other artists.

"So you're in the bucks again," she said.

"Paid cash, no dickering. We sold that huge coffee set today, too. I feel like a millionaire. I think it's time you and I finally made that trip to the Big Apple."

Johnnie hesitated. They had gently clashed before over the idea of taking a trip together. It seemed like taking trips together signified more than she thought the relationship meant right now.

She said carefully, "You know there's no way I could get away from the job right now, Luke."

He paused a beat, and then his voice sounded different— flatter, perhaps tinged with bitterness. "Right. Well, we can talk about it, anyway."

"See you a little after eleven."

Replacing the telephone on its cradle, Johnnie leaned back in her swivel chair, experiencing a mixture of happiness and worry. Luke Cobb was a wonderful man. Five years her senior at thirty-seven, he had come to Tenoclock a decade ago after a divorce. He had never discussed details. She understood wariness and old hurts; her own divorce in New York—the last straw that convinced her she would never make it big as an actress or dancer, and it was time to go back home to Colorado—was old history now, but it still hurt, too. So while her relationship with Luke had grown closer and nicer all the time in the past year, both of them had been stung badly before. Neither of them felt like charging into something that might spoil how nice it was as it stood—no vows, no demands, as few expectations as possible.

She had been in bad shape emotionally and just about every other way when she returned to Tenoclock six years earlier. The divorce was a fresh raw wound at that time, of course, but it had seemed everything else was sour as well. She was twenty-six then, and had reached the end of her five-year plan to make it in New York. At first some people asked her why she had come home to the mountains after stints in both New York and Los Angeles, and she had usually replied flippantly that she had learned she was "not quite pretty enough and not quite talented enough." Friends clucked at that, saying they knew it couldn't be so.

But it was. She had given her best shot, and simply hadn't been able to quite make the grade. Oh, there had been jobs in a couple of short-lived musicals, and a couple of illicit propositions from scummy Hollywood types who said they could make her a star, just lie down, baby, and let's talk about it. Beyond that, nothing had worked out. She had managed to save some money from a number of modeling jobs—outdoor wear, jeans and jodhpurs and things like that, which her rangy good looks appeared just right in—but she had returned to Tenoclock lecturing herself twice a day that she wasn't really a failure just because she had failed . . . that she had *tried*, and that was the main thing, and now it was time to get on with the rest of her life.

So, still shaky inside, she had built a new cabin on the old family ranchland northwest of town, out in the higher country. The family house had burned down only months after her father died . . . only months before her mother followed. It had felt eerie and sad, moving back onto the long-familiar land. But she had always loved it.

She had bought a small flock of sheep. Dad had always had a flock of sheep, and there was money to be made with them. But the terrible winter of 1988, climaxed by the May blizzard, had killed most of the flock and had taken the last of her money reserves.

After that, the job working as dispatcher and part-time help for then-Sheriff Butler "Butt" Peabody had seemed a straw to grasp most eagerly. Butt had been there to make the offer only a few days after the blizzard. He had been a good friend of her parents, pioneer stock, maybe as old as fifty now, although he looked and acted younger. As sheriff he had done an honest job in a thankless job.

Starting to work for Butt Peabody had really been when some of the healing began. Johnnie could look back and see that now. Butt had been such a grand guy to work for. So tough inside, yet such a gentle man in spite of his attempts to act like a cobby old cowboy. It still pained her, thinking how the local power-brokers had gotten him defeated for reelection. But he had been first in line to tell her she ought to hang on to her deputy's badge if the new man, Big Jim Way, asked her to stay on.

That was like Butt, she thought. Did he ever think of himself?

The honk of a horn on one of the streets outside brought her back to the present. She looked at the clock. It wouldn't be long now, she thought, until the old Motorola belched again, and she would get the sheriff's nighty-night transmission. After that she would close the office at eleven or so, having switched the incoming line to Jason Ramsey's desk in the back, and it was a short drive to the Pick & Shovel Cafe, and Luke. She hoped they wouldn't have an argument, because she knew she wasn't going to New York with him—or anyplace else, for that matter.

10:05 P.M.

O N THE TWISTING North Mountain road into Tenoclock, Donna Smith fought her panic and kept the speedometer of her venerable green Mustang at a steady twenty-five, except on the curves where she rode the brake to go even slower. Everything in her said to hurry, get back to the boardinghouse, hide. The drive back to town from Sky Estates already seemed to have taken forever. But Donna was stoned, and knew her time sense was screwed up. Take your time, take your time. My God, the worst thing in the world would be to have a wreck right now.

She had no idea what had happened back there. Shocked awake by the noises, she had panicked, knowing only that she had to get away as fast as possible. She had packed a lot of thrills and excitement into her nineteen years, but had never experienced anything like this. She was scared through and through.

Creeping along at fifteen, she rounded the last bend in the narrow road and saw the lights of Tenoclock scattered across the valley floor just ahead. She was going to make it, she thought. She could slip into the parking lot and park in the back and then use the rear entrance to the rooming house, and no one would ever be the wiser.

Had she told anyone besides Barbara about the special invitation? If she had, she could still be in trouble. But she couldn't think of anyone else. No one else could know.

God, what had happened out there? What might be happening now? Was Barb all right? Maybe I should have waited for her. Yes, Donna thought, she should have waited. But how was she to know that Barb wasn't right in the middle of whatever had broken loose in there? She'll be all right. She's resourceful. She'll handle it, whatever it is. Take care of yourself; that's rule number one, isn't it? Just because I took her out there doesn't mean I'm her nursemaid.

In the morning, Barb would be at work at the cafe just as

she would be. Barb might be pissed, but she would get over it. She had wanted to go. The noises probably hadn't been at all as bad as they sounded. As she struggled to clear her brain, Donna began to convince herself that she was only imagining something bad might have happened. It had been dynamite dope, and good stuff like that made her feel a little paranoid sometimes.

Nursing the old Mustang along a bit faster, Donna drove into Tenoclock, taking Silver Street and then the back way, where even at this hour there was little traffic, not much chance of anyone seeing her and recognizing the car. Her head went around in dizzy circles as she hunched over the steering wheel, squinting at the street ahead.

When she came to Orchard Avenue, she turned left, went as far as the alley, and turned in. She cut her headlights as she drove under the back security light of the parking area. She pulled into a back spot and turned off the engine, grabbed her purse off the empty passenger seat, and got out quickly, locking up. She hurried to the rear door of the rooming house and slipped inside. It was quiet. No one saw her go up the back stairs and walk to the door of her room. Her hand trembled, making it hard to get the key in the lock. Finally, in a silent frenzy of desperation, she managed it.

Once inside her own familiar room, she relocked the door and turned on the bed lamp. The unmade bed and clutter of clothing on the floor looked so normal, so dull. Everything as usual, no problem, and now she was safe.

Donna sank to the edge of the bed and experienced a violent case of the shakes. Oh Jesus, Barb, oh God. Be all right. I feel like shit for running out on you, but you would have done the same thing, wouldn't you? Wouldn't you?

10:50 P.M.

Out on the notch in the mountain that marked the cutoff to Engineer Pass and Telluride, parked well off the side of the gravel road, Sheriff Jim Way sat in his dark Bronco and admired the moon and the stars, thinking back to the days when he had almost gotten in on the big money in the National Football League. He often thought back to his NFL days when he'd had just a little too much to drink, which meant such thoughts came to his mind almost every evening about this time.

Looking out through the dirty windshield, Way studied the stars, picking out Orion and there, way off, Mars. There had been a time in college, back at Utah, when he took a course in the mythology of the heavens because everybody said it was a pudd course, a sure B at least if you showed up. The professor had been a mousy little man, bald, with a shaggy mustache, baggy dark suits, really a sweet old queen, Way realized now. But at the time you didn't know as much about queers as everybody did these days, and it would never have occurred to Way to realize Dr. Anderson was that kind of man, or that maybe that was why he liked all the jocks so much, because there must be some kind of fantasy in it for him.

Way had gotten mildly interested in the course, although taking any coursework seriously had been considered a weirdo thing for an athlete to do. He had even memorized the names and locations of a lot of the constellations and all, enjoying being able to pick them out in the night sky and tell some neat little coed the mythological stories behind them. You fascinated a lot of coeds by taking them out in the bushes somewhere and talking poetic, like that sweet old queen did in his lectures. Girls thought you weren't just another jock when you talked that way, they thought you were "sensitive," or even "sweet." You got a lot of tail that way.

That had been long ago now, though, Way thought with

a certain sadness. Then the seven years in the NFL, an inside linebacker first with the Cowboys and then, after his knees started to go, with the Redskins. Good old George Allen, taking the castoffs and making respectable teams out of them. An asshole, really, with all that rah-rah shit, but he had given Big Jim Way three more years that he could not otherwise have had, enough to qualify for the pension plan.

Dead now, George was. A lot of the old guys were dead now. Way felt sadder as he thought about some of the ones already gone. He wondered, not for the first time, why so many good old boys died young, and assholes seemed to live to be a hundred.

Way sighed. Fuck it, he thought. This wasn't a bad life. People respected you around here. They didn't know how close you had come to becoming a truly big star—a candidate for the Hall of Fame—in the NFL. They thought it was a big deal, just playing in the NFL. That showed how stupid they all were, but their respect made Way feel good anyhow.

He reached across the seat for his pint, uncapped it one more time, and tipped it up. The dregs—maybe a half jigger—drained into his mouth. Shit. Rolling the window all the way down, he tossed the dead soldier deep into the bushes.

He realized then that he had to pee. Getting out, he walked around to the back of the Bronc, dug out his thing, and watered the bushes. His knees ached. He wondered if he would have to have another operation, or if that Denver doctor had been right when he said more operations were just horseshit anyway, the knees had been ruined by playing hurt too many times, and they would just get worse and worse, more arthritic and all, until finally the only place they would see Big Jim Way was in a wheelchair.

It seemed to take a long time to finish peeing. Way had noticed that lately. Something about his prostrate. Or was there an *r* in there? Well, who cared anyway? Just as long as he didn't let Myldred know about it. Good wife that she was, she would start yammering and nagging his ass constantly about seeing a doctor. He wasn't about to see a doctor; a doctor would want to cut on him, and it would cost a fortune besides.

Way wiggled his thing back and forth between his fingers to get the last drops off, then stowed it back away. He felt a slight pulse of sexual sensation. I know, hon, I know. You want some pussy. We'll get you some sometime soon. Maybe even tonight, if mommy doesn't have a headache.

Thinking about his wife was sort of depressing, good woman though he recognized she was. Sometimes the last thing a man wanted was a *good* woman. But you couldn't just pick up some cunt at a truck stop locally when you were the sheriff. You had to be careful. Real careful.

Which made Jim think again about his deputy, Johnnie Baker.

Oh boy, oh boy, oh boy. Would he like to have a piece of that. She was his kind of woman: rangy, with some muscle on her, but not too much. And that pale hair drove him bananas sometimes.

Way buttoned up his pants and walked stiffly back to the driver's side of his Bronco. No sense thinking about Johnnie, he told himself. She had made that clear the first time he told an off-color joke, just kind of testing her out. Man, beside that stare she had given him, a glacier looked like a summer resort.

Way liked her, though, even if these occasional fervent thoughts sort of bothered his mind. She was the only smart deputy he had, actually. Billy Higginbotham might have had the IQ of a jackass in his prime, but he was into his fifties now and could really make you believe in early Alzheimer's. How one man could be so goddamn stupid and slow was more than Way could understand. But the fucker had friends among the county commissioners—had spent his whole life sucking around people in high office—and you had about as much chance of firing him as you did getting in Johnnie's pants.

Way's other deputy came to mind. Dean Epperly. Dean

was young, just twenty-six, and he wasn't really very stupid. What he was was lazy. And slow. And insolent. But he looked handsome in his uniform and enjoyed strutting around town, serving court papers and making all the tourist ladies get wet pants. And how were you going to hire anyone any better for the kind of salary this county allowed you to pay a man?

It was far better, Way reminded himself, to just not think about it. Three deputies was all he was ever going to have. He was lucky, actually, that even one of them was smarter than a turnip. As long as things stayed nice and quiet, it would be fine.

He got back into the Bronc. His watch said it was time to head home. Starting the engine and turning on the headlights, he backed around in the pull-off and started back the way he had come.

Picking the microphone off its hook, he thumbed to transmit. "Sheriff's unit one to base."

Johnnie's fine, sort-of-husky voice came back quickly: "Unit one, headquarters."

"Anything up, Johnnie?" Besides my pecker, I mean?

"All quiet, one."

"Ten-four. I'm heading in."

"Roger. Have a good one. Headquarters out."

"One out." He put the microphone back on the hook on the dashboard.

He took it slow and easy heading back down the mountain, aware that he was snockered. He was in no hurry and not really looking for much of anything.

After a while he came around a curve in the road and could look down on his right-hand side at the glint of moonlight, now and then, on Rock River, rushing down the gorge. Trees broke up the reflections and made them almost stroboscopic, Way thought. Then he thought that he had just made a really neat comparison, the moonlight on the river like a strobe light. He would have to remember to wax poetic about that to Johnnie tomorrow. For all the good it would do him. But at least it would show her he wasn't just a dumbfuck former football player.

Nearing the lowest point on the gravel road, Way drove along close to the river, which tumbled along some one hundred feet below the road level. His headlights picked up high Cyclone fencing, well maintained, with "No Trespassing" and "Danger" signs posted at regular intervals along it. Dangerous place, despite all its colorful history.

It must have been neat in the olden days, Way thought. Gold and silver coming out of here, people getting rich overnight. The ore trains had hauled more than two million dollars of silver out of here in 1889, and even as late as 1895, two years after Congress passed the Silver Act, lowering the price from $1.29 to $.50 an ounce, production had been almost $700,000.

Way sighed. Those had been the days! The Denver & Rio Grande Railroad linking Tenoclock with Ouray, Telluride, Lake City, and Silverton, telephone service all the way down to Durango, more than five thousand permanent residents. What it must have been like to be here then.

Nearing the precipitous dirt turnoff that led down to the river level, and the black clutter of old mining structures down there, Way slowed down. How he wished he could have seen all this when it roared!

At that moment something caught his eye, something down there beyond the fence. He quickly touched his toe to the brake pedal and peered again, more intently.

Had there been the flash of a light down there?

No, shit, impossible. The place was wired up tight. Everybody knew what assholes the present owners were about trespassing. They—

But a second glint of light caught his eye, and this time he was sure—he had been looking right at the spot where it came from.

He braked to a complete stop on the road. He hadn't imagined it. He felt intense curiosity. What was that down there? A flashlight? No. Impossible.

What, then?

Probably just kids farting around.

But it wouldn't hurt to check.

Feeling absolutely sober, he backed up to the mud-slick driveway that plunged down to the level of the river. He cut the engine and lights.

Jerking his shotgun off the ceiling mount, he opened his door and climbed out into the soft grayish mud of the shoulder. After quietly closing the door, it occurred to him that maybe he should call Johnnie. But then he glanced at his watch. She would be gone by now.

Of course, she had a radio in her Jeep, but it didn't always work. Besides, no sense bothering her or anybody else. And whether she got his transmission or not, it was a sure bet that half the permanent population in town would hear him on their scanners. He could just imagine the shit he would take about that. "Find any ghosts out there last night, Jim?" or, "Hey, Jim, that was real exciting, listening to you go down there to take a leak."

Nope, fuck it. Too hard. This was probably nothing anyhow. But check it out just to be sure, then get on home.

Boots slipping slightly in the gray gumbo of the steep driveway, Way transferred his shotgun to his left hand so he could pull his flashlight off its belt clip on his right-hand side. His boots made a considerable slurpy racket in the mud as he descended.

11:20 P.M.

LUKE COBB HELD a Marlboro between his perpetually clay-darkened fingers as he sat at the corner table in the Pick & Shovel Cafe, waiting for Johnnie to appear. She was a little late.

Her lateness irritated him. Once he would have been worried, but by now he had come to realize that nothing ever happened around the sheriff's department, especially since Big Jim Way's election. She could just as easily close up promptly at eleven and be here on time, Luke thought. He would never understand why she was so devoted to such a crummy job.

The front door of the cafe swung open and the lady herself strode in, long-legged and lithe in her jeans and sweater, her sand-colored hair loose on her neck. She spied him, and her smile lighted the room. She walked over and sat opposite him. "Hi."

From the serving counter, where two late-hour customers sat hunched on stools, owner Mabel Murnan called over, "The usual, Law-Lady?"

"You got it," Johnnie called back.

Mabel came over with the coffeepot in one hand and a mug dangling from the pinkie of her hand that carried a plate with two small sugar doughnuts on it.

"You're working late," Johnnie said.

Mabel was a woman of about sixty, medium height, gray-haired, with enough lines in her outdoors-woman's face to corrugate a roof. She shook her head in disgust. "All my damn help abandoned me today. First a couple of the kids missed the afternoon shift, so I had to rush around and call in my evening help. Then, did you ever try to track down college-age kids after suppertime to try to get 'em to work an extra shift? My aching back!"

"Just about all of them have already headed back home for fall classes," Johnnie observed.

Mabel sighed heavily. "Well, thank goodness for dropouts, locals, and runaways. I'll get by until the snow flies, even with the rush that's starting now for the aspen. When ski season comes and *all* the celebrities descend on us at once, I ain't sure what I'm going to do. Finding good help gets harder every season."

"Some of the movie folk are here already," Luke said.

"Yeah, and there'll be a lot more tomorrow and the day after that. Honest to Pete, sometimes I wish we'd never started all this crap to make Tenoclock like Vail and Telluride and those other places."

"Cher is up at her place, and we heard Warren Beatty and his bunch got in," Johnnie said.

"Yep." Mabel nodded. "There was durn near a riot down the street at the Cadillac today; he and his sweetie were down there to try the rainbow trout special."

"He should have come here," Luke said.

Mabel put her hands on her hips and glared. "Listen, if the celebs want to come in here, fine. I'll wait on them in their proper turn. But if they want to go someplace else, that's fine, too. I was making a go of it in this joint when our permanent population was three hundred, and that was only if you counted real slow. Just because we've got a good road in now, and that fancy-schmancy airstrip for the Learjets and all, the Pick & Shovel is still the same place it was before the boom, and it'll be the same if the whole bubble bursts, too, you can count on that." She turned and stomped back toward the kitchen.

"She never changes," Johnnie said, biting into a doughnut.

"Thank God something doesn't."

It was Johnnie's turn to sigh. "Yeah, I know. All this new construction—they might have zoning laws that require all the new stores and buildings to have bric-a-brac fronts, like in the old days, and it's great for local businesses to have all the stars and star gawkers pumping money into the economy. But it sure isn't the Tenoclock I grew up in."

"We're the new Vail," Luke pointed out. "*Newsweek* said so."

Johnnie groaned.

They, like most older residents of Tenoclock, had talked endlessly about the boom. Tenoclock would never be a lazy little town again. It had passed some critical mass and now seemed to feed on its own momentum. At a glance the streets downtown looked "quaint" enough, lined with newly built but old-appearing "frontier-style" structures by fiat of the county commissioners and the town planning board. But the town was no longer anything like it once had been. The glitzy showbiz people had changed all that, and so had the boom in construction of smaller cabins all through the wooded mountains. An outsider might think this was all just wonderful. But locals like Luke and Johnnie knew that the commissioners and town board alike were just plowing all the tax revenues back into still more attractions for further growth—additional runway length at the airport, street- and road-widening, underwriting loans for more ski slopes and lodges out on North Mountain and even beyond, in the Snowmass and Emerald areas. Sometimes it seemed that everybody here was racing around and around like a lab rat in a circular running wheel, going faster and faster, to go faster and faster.

"So how was your day?" Luke asked now.

"Routine," Johnnie told him. "We've got a ton of subpoenas to deliver for the next court term that starts next week up in Gunnison."

"Does that mean you'll have to work all weekend?"

"Sure. Why are you glaring at me like that?"

"I was hoping maybe *we* could have some time together for a change."

"Oh, hell, Luke. We've been over this a hundred times."

"You could take some time off if you wanted to."

"You know better. We're too shorthanded."

Luke struggled to stay cool. "You don't *need* this job. You could get something a lot better."

"Luke, dammit, being a deputy sheriff isn't something every woman can do! I love the challenges . . . when they come."

"No other job would challenge you?"

Johnnie's jaw stiffened the way it did when her stubborn streak came to the forefront. "Not the way this one does. I've explained all that. I need to prove I'm not just some has-been entertainer who came back to spin stories of the might-have-been, and spend the last of her folks' inheritance after blowing her own savings on a bunch of sheep she couldn't keep alive through a snowstorm."

Luke puffed out his cheeks and blew. She had beaten him again. He almost wanted to lean across the table and slap her. Instead, he forced himself to smile. "Okay, then. If we can't have the weekend, what would the lady deputy think about coming over to my place for the night?"

"Tonight?"

"Why not?"

Grimacing, she reached across to put her hand over his. "The lady would love to, Luke, but the lady has some office paperwork to catch up on yet after she gets to her own cabin tonight."

Luke stared into her remarkably clear eyes, really trying to understand. But he knew with a sinking feeling that he would never understand her.

Johnnie finished her doughnuts and coffee, then leaned back with a small sigh of contentment. "I better scat."

Luke picked up the ticket, but she quietly snatched it out of his hand and carried it to the cash register. It would be really terrible, Luke thought bitterly, if I was allowed to pay for her coffee. He said nothing.

Outside, Johnnie gave him a brief, fond hug and hurried toward her Jeep. Climbing inside, she saw Luke stride around the far corner, shoulders hunched angrily, heading back for the store. With a mental sigh she started the engine and backed out.

As she pulled away from the curb, a battered pickup truck trundled down the deserted street, headed south, and went slowly through the blinking amber at the intersection. Johnnie recognized Butt Peabody's vehicle and touched her horn, but he didn't hear her. She got a glimpse of his chiseled profile through the side window glass, and he looked angry.

Wondering what her old boss and even older pal was doing out so uncharacteristically late at night, she put her Jeep in gear and headed in the opposite direction.

▽

Thursday, September 27

OUT ON THE side of the mountain, the *Starlight Special* chuffed down the long grade from Breakheart Pass, headed back to Tenoclock. The little narrow-gauge train was late, highballing for home, trailing a long, silvery plume of smoke in the moonlight.

Up front, in the cab of an ancient Whitney Excello engine, a beautifully restored old 2-4-0 built in Baltimore in 1888, they were pouring the coal to it because the 10:00 P.M. run ("The 10 o'clock to Tenoclock") was already more than fifteen minutes late getting back. Behind the engine came the little coal car and behind that the two red and gray and green passenger coaches, windows yellow from the battery-powered lantern simulators inside. Last came the bright red caboose, nobody in it, but two red lanterns aglow on each side anyhow, for the effect.

There were twenty-three passengers back in the two coach cars, well below the capacity of sixty-four. It was unlikely that any of them cared if the special was a few minutes behind schedule, but a schedule was a schedule, and engineer Lyle White wanted to make up as much time as possible.

"Give me one more shovel of coal," White bellowed into the wind, his head stuck out the side window so he could watch the track ahead in the feeble glow of the old engine's headlight.

"Aw, Lyle," fireman Bert Marcus complained, "we got up plenty of steam. It's just a few miles more now."

White ducked his head back inside and ran a bony big hand through his wind-wild gray hair. Fiftyish, with thick features permanently windburned, he tapped a blunt finger on the steam pressure gauge. "I want her past the black mark, Bert, goddammit. We're going to highball the rest of the way."

"Boss will be pissed if we waste coal," Bert Marcus sighed, reluctantly reaching for the scoop.

"Boss is already pissed about us being late again," White replied. "You heard his tone of voice on the radio when I called in from the top and told him we'd had trouble with the turnaround."

Using a long-handled iron tool, Marcus swung open the door of the firebox. Bright orange light and heat spilled out into the drafty cab. "Damned if we do," Marcus said, swinging his shovel into the coal tender and digging out a scoop of finely broken low-sulfur coke, "and damned if we don't." The scoop of coal seemed to explode as it hit the flames inside the boiler.

"That'll do her," White said, nodding with satisfaction.

"Yeah." Marcus slammed the door shut. "If we don't rock right offa the tracks."

"No problem, man, no problem." White reached up to the cord hanging down from the overhead and gave it several tugs, making the steam whistle cry mournfully into the mountain night.

The little train chuffed on down the grade, rocking on the narrow track as it reached the start of a long, sweeping outside curve over the Sacramento River gorge, the big river for which both the Rock and the Tenoclock were tributaries. Lyle White, satisfied that the pressure gauge was where it ought to be, stuck his head out his side window again into the freezing night breeze. The rush of cold air made water stream from his eyes and his face tingle with pain. But he loved it. Where else in the whole country anymore could a man run a *real* railroad train, except on a damned few automated passenger runs that never ran right, or those mile-long freight trains grunting along at twenty miles an hour because the trackage was in such sorry shape? And they were all diesels anyway; this little dude was a *real* train, by gadfrey. Coal and steam, and ain't she a dream! He loved it.

Looking out ahead, White admired the starlit sky and the moon, beginning to near the horizon now, and how the combined skylight made silvery splinters on the down-rushing waters of the Sacramento. The vast woods looked silent and empty, but White knew there were deer in there, and moose and elk, skunks and possums and beavers and squirrels and coyotes and marmots and wolves, maybe, and bears, by gadfrey, fer sure, fer sure. Thinking about all the critters, he reached out blindly and found the whistle cord, and gave it another couple of long pulls. A good evenin' to you, critters. And stay outta my way.

White returned his attention from the scenery to the long, curving sweep of steel up ahead. They had come around the tightest part of the bend now, and swept more swiftly down the milder part of the downhill curve toward the level of the Tenoclock Valley, and the town itself only a few miles away now. In another minute or two they would round the last part of the curve, run alongside the Sacramento below the level of the highway high up on the right, and begin to slacken speed a bit for the last five miles in.

The old engine's single ornate headlight provided adequate illumination, but nothing to brag about. Coming off the long curve on the downhill run, White was looking far ahead down the track, really outside the maximum effectiveness of the headlight, when he thought he saw something.

Reaching behind himself, again without looking, he yanked the whistle cord repeatedly. The steam whistle racketed. But the object near—or on—the tracks ahead did not budge.

What was it out there? White squinted, but couldn't tell. He wished it would move. He yanked the whistle cord again.

At first he thought it might be a deer, but then as the headlight's illumination improved at closer range he saw it wasn't a tall animal like that, but rather something down across on the tracks, not moving.

It didn't look like any animal he had ever seen.

"Shit!" White grabbed for the brake.

"What is it?" Marcus yelled.

"Something on the track—durned boulder or something."

"Are we gonna hit it? Are we gonna hit it?"

White hauled on the brakes as hard as he dared, if the passengers in the back weren't all to be thrown ass over teakettle to the front of their cars. The wheels all almost locked up, and the train was going too fast to stop in time. Geezus, if it's a boulder . . . !

The headlight glared down on the thing on the tracks for just an instant—it was some kind of big white plastic trash sack or something—and then both White and Marcus felt the sharp, heavy thump and felt the train stagger ever so slightly as engine wheels ran over the object.

"What was it?"

"I dunno, but we better find out."

Still lugging on the brake handle, White got the train slowed and then stopped, steam billowing from the escape vents on both sides, smoke pouring from the stack. His heart was hammering like a drunken woodsman's ax.

He pulled the intercom microphone off the hook, swallowed, and tried to speak normally as he keyed the button that sent his voice back to the tourists in the coach cars.

"Please remain in your seats, ladies and gentlemen. Please stay in your seats. We have not yet reached the Tenoclock depot." He released the mike button for a moment to gulp air. "Folks, you're extra lucky tonight. You get to stay in your seats—just stay in your seats, please—and enjoy the view onto the Sacramento River down there on our left, and the rise of the mountain on our right. That's Jumbo Mountain on our right, and if you watch close in the trees, you might get a glimpse of a deer or even an elk or something."

White unkeyed and gulped more oxygen. "The reason we've halted for a minute here, folks, is that we thought we saw a tree back yonder that had about half fallen down the slope, and might be getting ready to slide on down too near the tracks for safety." What a liar! he thought. "Nothing to be alarmed about at all, but we're going to take a two-minute break here and hotfoot it back down there a hundred yards or so and note the position, so our work crews can come out in the morning and chop 'er up if she's really in a position to cause a problem on some later trip.

"We regret the delay, folks, but let us assure you again that it'll only be a minute or two, and it's a precaution for the added safety of folks who'll be making this same run tomorrow. Please stay in your seats. We'll just be a minute."

White slammed the microphone back into its cradle.

"You sure can lie," Marcus said admiringly.

"Let's get back there."

"What do you think it was we hit?"

Not replying, White grabbed a big, battery-powered train lantern and swung the heavy iron door open on his side of the cab. "Double-set that brake and come on with me."

It seemed vaster and scarier out in the chill black of the night, hiking back up the track, their boots slipping in the gravel alongside the steel rails. Neither man spoke. They hurried. The curious faces of their tourist passengers looked out at them from the lighted coach windows.

"Was it a coyote, maybe?" Marcus wondered aloud, panting as they left the red lanterns of the little caboose behind and hurried on into the dark.

"I dunno," White rasped, breathing hard. "But I don't think it was a coyote. It was too big for that." He licked dry lips. "I just hope to shit it wasn't what it *looked* like, right there at the last second."

"What did it look like, Lyle? Huh?"

"Shut up, Bert. Just shut up."

Ahead in the dim starlight was the spot where the object had been on the tracks. Whatever it was no longer had the same form it had had before being hit. It was sort of scattered now. Chunks of stuff, and the biggest part . . .

The light of Lyle White's battery lantern reached it. He held the lantern high, bringing it all into clear view for the first time.

"Oh, no!" Bert Marcus moaned. "Oh, my God!" He fell to his knees onto the sharp white trackage rocks and began rocking back and forth, making sounds like an injured animal.

Lyle White bent over from the waist and threw up.

1:05 A.M.

NUMBED BY WHAT she already knew, Johnnie spotted the area of the accident when she was still more than a mile away, her Jeep laboring under heavy acceleration on the steep grade up the road across Jumbo Mountain. Rounding a bend, she had a momentary glimpse through the tall firs of bright headlights on the side of the road far ahead, flashing red emergency lights, amber flashers, the metronomic blue and red pulses of an ambulance and wrecker. Then the road bent sharply again, blocking her view. This can't be happening, she thought.

Rounding another tight turn, she saw what a traffic and rubbernecking mess she already had on her hands: Besides the medical center ambulance, a wrecker, and the ominous dark bulk of the hearse from John Lemptke's funeral home, there were at least eight or nine more cars and small trucks parked haphazardly on both sides of the narrow strip of pavement. She spotted a couple of Tenoclock's permanent residents scurrying across the road from their just-stopped car to gain a vantage point for gawking.

Bringing her Jeep to a halt behind a dirty, elderly brown Oldsmobile that she recognized as belonging to Deputy Dean Epperly, the first person she had been able to reach after she got the terrible news, Johnnie hoped Epperly was following her stunned instructions, but it didn't look like it.

Hopping out, flashlight in hand, she hurried along the narrow gravel shoulder. She saw the brown Dodge pickup belonging to the other deputy, Billy Higginbotham, and the gleaming white Taurus wagon that belonged to Niles Pennington, editor of the Tenoclock *Frontiersman*. Just what they needed, she thought, Pennington already running around and creating chaos with his camera and questions. But she should have expected it; the *Frontiersman* paid twenty-five dollars for news tips, and this had been a good one for someone to call in.

Reaching a spot beside the A&A wrecker, she peered down through a rent in the firs and pines to the scene below, where the narrow-gauge railroad track bisected the hillside between road and river. Someone had set up a portable emergency light, and it bathed everything and everyone in a vivid yellow-green glow. It looked like as many as a dozen people down there, some of them with lanterns, some just milling around. Johnnie spotted Billy Higginbotham's gray uniform for a second, but then the movement of the crowd swallowed him up again.

Somebody tugged at the sleeve of her jacket. "Is it true, Johnnie? Is it poor old Big Jim?"

Turning, Johnnie realized she had a small crowd of gawkers all along the shoulder of the road. She knew the face of the middle-aged man questioning her, but couldn't pull out his name. "I don't know anything yet for sure," she told him.

Another man farther back called out, "We heard he flang himself right in front of the *Special!*"

"Made mincemeat of him!" another voice chimed in.

"Let's git down there!" someone else suggested. Several shadowy figures started to move.

"Just hold it!" Johnnie called out sharply. "Stay up here. Better yet, get on home. You can't help and you might cause another wreck."

Nobody replied, and nobody moved, either.

"All right, then," Johnnie called out, her voice carrying.

"If you won't leave, just stay put. That's an official order." Wondering if they would pay any attention to her, she turned and started down the steep, rock-and-fern-studded slope into the gorge below, slipping and sliding and only precariously maintaining her balance.

She had been back at her cabin brushing her teeth for bed when the telephone jangled at twelve-thirty. Her telephone never rang at that hour, not on the nights she and Luke had already chatted as they had tonight. Reaching for the instrument, she had known already that it had to be news of trouble.

But she had in no way been prepared for the voice of J. Maxwell Copely, mayor of Tenoclock and owner-operator of the narrow-gauge rail line. She was even less prepared for Copely's first words:

"Johnnie? This is the mayor. I'm afraid I've got awful news, just awful. The *Starlight Special* was coming back from Breakheart Pass a while ago and it hit something on the tracks. It was the sheriff. It was Big Jim himself. It happened up there on the Jumbo Mountain curve. My engineer couldn't have prevented it, Johnnie. Honest to God. He said old Jim was passed out cold, right across the tracks. The engine hit him and then one or two of the cars ran over pieces of him. He was killed instantly. The train just chewed him all to shit!"

Johnnie couldn't believe it. "How could that *happen?* Doesn't that old engine have a cowcatcher on the front?"

"Yes," Copely said, his voice shallow and burry with emotion. "But Lyle—you know Lyle White, our engineer—he said the catcher thing tried to toss Big Jim aside, but it only sort of flipped him around, or something, and the big wheels of the engine went right on over him."

Feeling sick with shock, Johnnie made emergency calls. Then she called the mayor back at his little train station office.

The *Special* had just pulled in with the news, Copely said. Everything he knew, Lyle White had told him over the radio

inbound from the scene. White had left his fireman, Bert
Marcus, out there with a battery lantern and a rifle, to stand
guard. The passengers didn't know what had happened.
Copely had called the police and ambulance service, and
then before he could call Johnnie, Niles Pennington, from
the *Frontiersman*, had called *him*. Pennington had heard all
about it on his scanner. Oh, this was a mess, Johnnie, this
was terrible, this kind of PR could set Tenoclock back with
the tourist public; imagine—your sheriff so drunk he falls
asleep on the tracks in the middle of the night and gets sawed
in half by a train.

Johnnie hadn't heard a lot more after that, because by this
time her other telephone was alive with calls. She had
rousted Billy Higginbotham out of bed and told him to get
to the scene to help Epperly, and then contacted Jason
Ramsey at the jail to fill him in on developments. People she
didn't even know had then made her phone jangle continu-
ously with their questions until she ignored the ringing and
rushed out.

Now, sliding almost out of control down the steep slope
toward the bright lights and total confusion below, Johnnie
braced herself.

Onlookers and emergency workers milled around in total
chaos under the painful glare of portable floodlights. Johnnie
heard Higginbotham's squeaky voice pleading for people to
get out of the way. She pushed through the melee just in
time to be blinded momentarily by a stab of light from
Pennington's camera strobe unit. He grabbed her arm and
started saying something about Jim Way's Bronco being in
a ditch not far away, and Johnnie didn't have to worry, the
Frontiersman was a booster all the way and would never
mention the fact that Big Jim must have been drunk out of
his mind to do such a stupid thing. Two or three other voices
yammered at the same time.

"Okay, okay," Johnnie muttered, pulling away from Pennington. "Let me see what we've got here first, all right?"
Shading her eyes with her hands, she peered up the shiny

tracks. Beside them, a dozen paces away, gleamed the orange
rubberized folds of a body bag. It was tied closed at one end
and there were dark, wet smears all over that end, as well
as along the track and gravel. Johnnie fought to stifle her
gag reflex.

"What do you make of it, Johnnie?" someone piped up.
"Did he fall down the hill, or what?"

Pennington's strobe unit blinded her again. "Look this
way, Johnnie. How about taking out your pad and pencil,
like you were making notes at the scene. If you could get just
a little closer to the body bag—the rest of you stay right where
you are, it's a great shot."

"That's enough," Johnnie snapped, anger jerking her out
of her stunned passivity. She raised her voice: "Everybody
not a county or health official, out of here! Now! I mean it!
That means you, Charley, and you, Rick. Mr. Burns? Isn't
that your name? Outta here!"

Startled looks gave way to scrambling movement as most
of the men moved obediently. Johnnie began to lose some of
her momentary feeling of panic that she had no control here
whatsoever.

She grabbed Billy Higginbotham's uniform shirtsleeve.
"Billy, get these people back up that hill. Then you get that
roadway cleared, and I don't mean maybe. Get that traffic
out of here."

Higginbotham blinked and slowly started to move. "I
don't know if I can get 'em to drive away, Johnnie. . . ."

"Just do it!"

Higginbotham jolted into unaccustomed action. "Aw
right, folks, you all heard what the deputy said. Come on . . .
come on . . . let's get moving, there. Back up to your cars.
The show's over."

The mob started to melt as if by magic. Johnnie was left
trackside with John Lemptke, the owner of the ambulance
and Tenoclock's only mortician; a stoop-shouldered boy who
always helped him; a thoroughly ashen little man in a
railroad cap, who must be the one left behind to guard the

body; Mayor Copely, in rumpled corduroys and unlaced hunting boots and a floppy red mackinaw, and Pennington, who chose that moment to shoot another picture.

"That's enough, Niles," Johnnie said firmly. "You too. Out of here."

"Me?" Pennington gasped. A tall man, bone-lanky and permanently hunchbacked, the local editor opened his eyes so wide with surprise that his glasses slid far down on his extraordinarily long, skinny nose. "I'm the press!"

"Out." Johnnie jerked her thumb over her shoulder.

"You can't do that!"

"I just did. Beat it."

Muttering something about the First Amendment, Pennington scrambled up the hill after the others.

Johnnie heaved a breath and turned to Lemptke. "You've, uh, done all you can do here?"

Lemptke nodded. Rotund, and with a cherubic pink face like the one on old-fashioned pictures of Santa Claus, he pointed at the ghastly wetness on the gravel on both sides of the track. "We've collected all the, ah, body parts. There really isn't anything more to do, unless possibly go over the earth on our hands and knees, with tweezers, but even then it would be better to do that after daylight, because with these shadows . . ."

Johnnie shuddered. "You'll take the body to your mortuary?"

"Why, yes, I thought so, of course."

"And you're the county's appointed coroner, right? So you'll do an autopsy?"

"Why, yes, of course. But I can't see that it's going to be difficult in this case. Cause of death is perfectly clear, isn't it?"

"I want a thorough job, John."

Lemptke's face stiffened. "I'll do enough."

Johnnie wondered how thorough "enough" would be. "Exactly how did this happen?"

The slope-shouldered youth with Lemptke pointed up-slope. "Somebody said Jim's Bronc is back up the road thataway. In the ditch."

"I heard that. But—"

Lemptke cut in morosely, "Speculation is that his radio wouldn't operate, and it's a lot shorter walk back into town if you come down here and follow the tracks, rather than follow the road all the way around the other side of the mountain."

"You know how he liked his nightly nips," Mayor Copely said.

Johnnie turned to face him. "Is that what you think?"

"Drunk," Copely said, shaking his head. "Had to be. His clothes are saturated with whiskey. They found an empty fifth of Maker's Mark on the front floorboards of his truck."

"Jim never drank an expensive whiskey like Maker's Mark in his life! He was a Jim Beam man. In pints."

Copely ignored her comment. "Ran his truck off the road, came down the hill to walk the tracks as a shortcut to town, fell asleep or passed out on the tracks."

"That's ridiculous!"

"Ask Bert, here. He was in the cab. Ask what Lyle White said he saw. Big Jim wasn't walking along the tracks. He was stretched out across them—out cold."

Bert, the trainman, nodded. "Dead drunk. Had to be."

"I don't believe it!" Johnnie shot back.

"Then how do *you* explain it?" Copely demanded.

Johnnie stared at him. She couldn't.

6:30 A.M.

Dawn had just begun to lighten the sky to the east, toward Anvil Mountain, when Carl Rieger, chairman of the Tenoclock Board of County Commissioners, coaxed his sputtering old green pickup truck into the driveway of Tenoclock's mayor, J. Maxwell Copely. The rusty squeal of the pickup's brakes set Rieger's teeth on edge. Before he could get the rackety engine shut off, he spotted lights going on in the upstairs windows of two large, white stucco houses just to the west of the Copely place. Rieger wondered how many more of the neighbors had been jarred awake by his howling brakes in this, Tenoclock's most fashionable old-town neighborhood.

Rieger hated the old truck. He hated driving it. But there were enough old-time ranchers remaining in the far reaches of the county to make driving a rusty old junker good politics; let some of them see their county commissioner driving around too often in his candy-red Mercedes, and they would rebel, figure he was tapping the taxpayer till, and vote him out of office.

Carl Rieger lived in constant fear of being voted out of office. He was willing to do just about anything to stay a county commissioner, and sometimes had.

This morning he was mightily upset.

Managing to button the front of his single-breasted dark suit coat over his ample belly, he walked swiftly around his truck, shiny little black leather shoes mincing from stepping-stone to stepping-stone in the wet, vivid green grass. Chillier this morning, and a touch of snow at the highest elevations. Clear now, however, and from the sprawling front porch of the mayor's big house Rieger could look out over the adjacent yards and trees of the nearby city park to the slightly lower elevation—center of Tenoclock Valley—where downtown had not yet begun to come awake. Streetlights still twinkled gold down there, and darkness lay over the rows and humps of old-fashioned wood shingle roofing.

They had made a break with the past and taken advantage of the new highway, and now with the excellent airstrip in place they had everything going their way, Rieger thought. But Jim Way's death could create a terrible scandal and hurt everyone.

The front door swung open. The mayor, wearing a red flannel shirt and jeans a bit too tight around his middle, motioned Rieger inside. He looked like he hadn't slept much. "Come in, Carl. We'll go to the kitchen. Keep your voice down. The old lady is still asleep upstairs."

Rieger followed his political colleague back through the big house, passing living room, parlor, game room, and dining room, all stuffed with heavy, dark, expensive furniture. Who would have thought a ski lift and a few miles of rebuilt narrow-gauge railroad would make a man wealthy? But Copely was one of Tenoclock's richest permanent citizens now, although like Rieger he worked hard at concealing it for political and business reasons.

Carl figured he and Copely both deserved all they now had, or could still get. Both had been willing to gamble their political futures by setting up the self-liquidating bonds that had started the airport and the first lift. They had jammed through the county-wide zoning rules that kept Tenoclock's downtown looking like something out of the last century. They had both risked everything they had in personal assets, too—Rieger in acquiring the land and then bankrolling the development of both Sky Estates and the new golf course, Copely by going in hock up to his eyebrows in order to build the first champion-quality ski slope as well as rebuilding the old narrow-gauge railroad line.

As Carl Rieger saw it, people like himself and Copely had *made Tenoclock happen.* They deserved their prizes. They had every right to do anything necessary to keep the dream growing.

Big Jim Way's death, if it became a scandal, was a threat to the dream.

The Copely kitchen was the only room in the house that hadn't been redone within the past year or two. Old wooden cabinets, peeling yellow enamel, looked down onto faded amber linoleum and a large, white-enamel wood table and chairs. But the coffee smelled good.

"Sit down, Carl, sit yourself down. I'll pour."

Rieger watched the rotund mayor pour coffee into two dainty china cups. "What are we going to do?"

Copely replaced the coffeepot on the heater. "It was a mysterious accident, a real tragedy. But life goes on. The less said, the better."

"I talked to Niles Pennington again."

"What's he going to print?"

"Not what we all think must have happened."

"Thank God for that! But what?"

"The *Frontiersman* story will say Jim must have been investigating something, fell, and knocked himself out."

"Good! Good!"

Rieger sipped coffee. "Gadfrey! I wish we all could have known Jim had this drinking problem before we decided to get him elected."

Copely looked vague. "Drinking problem? What drinking problem?"

Rieger hung up on that a moment, then understood. "Right. Exactly."

"The funeral," Copely added, "needs to be that of a hero."

"Yes! I see! Make it a civic occasion!"

"The only problem I see at all," Copely added, "is this thing with the state investigators coming in."

Rieger's eyes widened. "What investigators?"

"Good lord, man, do you mean that girl deputy called for them on her own, without even getting the county commissioners' approval?"

Rieger's chair scraped as he leaned forward. "I don't know what you're talking about!"

"That girl! Johnnie what's-her-name. Chief Mayfield told me she used our fax machine about three o'clock this morning to send a letter to Denver, asking for the state boys to come in and investigate Big Jim's death."

"Investigate?" Rieger echoed, eyes wide with surprise. "What's to investigate? And who told her she had the authority to do anything?"

"All I know, Carl, is what the chief told me. They're sending down a couple of men later today."

Rieger's fist banged on the table. "This is terrible! Who *told* her she could do that? That's all we need—a bunch of reporters and TV people following some state probers around, speculating there was something funny about the way Jim died!"

"Well, of course, the worst they could find out was that he was drunk, but still . . ."

"Still, it makes us look like idiots for supporting his election! And it makes the whole county look bad!" Rieger's eyes went metallic. "I'll have her by the ass for this."

"Or," Copely said, "maybe not."

"What? What? What do you mean, 'maybe not'?"

"I haven't gotten much sleep, Carl, and I've thought a lot about this. My first thought was that you ought to fire the young woman, too. But then what would we all get? Just more publicity, more speculation—the Good Lord only knows what-all."

"Is there an alternative?" Rieger shot back heatedly.

"There might be. It's a cornball proposition, but it might just actually turn this whole thing to our advantage, and take the spotlight off big Jim's death altogether."

Rieger's face tightened with skeptical interest. "Tell me about it, Mister Mayor. And then maybe after you convince me on this one, you'll go out back and walk across your swimming pool for me."

6:50 A.M.

THE SUN HAD just put in a blinding crimson appearance over the south slope of Anvil Mountain when a sound roused Dave Dickensen from fitful sleep. Fully clothed, he climbed out of his big chair beside the cabin fireplace and moved to the draped window facing his road. A dark green Buick Regal appeared through the trees: his guard Hinson's car.

Flames still danced in Dickensen's fireplace. He had fed it regularly through a night of prowling his cabin, wrestling with the decision last night's debacle had forced upon him. It had been 5:00 A.M. when he finally decided.

Hinson, pasty and shaky, pulled his car up close to the cabin and stepped out as Dickensen opened the cabin's front door. An overnight stubble beard darkened the small, wiry man's narrow face, and his eyes had the look in them of a pursued animal.

Dickensen gestured for him to come inside. Hinson obeyed anxiously, moving with quick, nervous strides.

"What's happened?" Hinson demanded. His face shone with a sick film of sweat. "Did you find the other one?"

"Not yet," Dickensen said. "We will. In the meantime, you know what you have to do."

Hinson's eyes darted. "I know. I'm cool. I'm outta here."

Dickensen reached into his hip pocket and pulled out a very thick envelope. He slapped it into Hinson's hand. "You weren't there and you aren't coming back."

"Right. Right."

"You goddamn stupid bastard," Dickensen said with great precision and bitterness. "If you hadn't been asleep in the guard shack and missed all those blinking lights for the perimeter alarms, maybe none of this would have happened."

"Yessir." Fear made Hinson's eyes dart again.

"If you ever show your face around here again . . ."

"I won't! I'm gone!"

Dickensen turned his back on him. There was a sound of scuffling footsteps, and the door closed. Moments later, the Buick's engine started and the crunch of tires on gravel faded into the morning stillness.

Dickensen put another log on the fire, insurance against the deep dawn chill. His insides twitched.

There was a good chance, he thought, that it would all blow over. He simply must not allow himself to keep thinking about it.

The only thing he had to think about, he told himself, was keeping up normal appearances and at the same time finding out who had been in that car that almost collided with him in the driveway last night. All he knew so far was that it had been a girl. She was the one weak link, totally unpredictable. She could destroy him. He had to find her.

7:30 A.M.

HEADING BACK TOWARD town after a frustrating dawn return to the scene of Jim Way's death, Johnnie picked up the microphone of her two-way radio. "Sheriff's unit two to base."

There was no response. Gritting her teeth, she banged the flat of her hand on the instrument panel and repeated the call. Again she got only silence. The old intermittent had reared its head again, just when she didn't need any more problems.

Banging the microphone back on its clip, she turned on the Jeep's ordinary AM radio. It worked, anyway. The final bars of Glenn Miller's "In the Mood" came from the dashboard speaker, and then the voice of the morning DJ: "A sunny good morning, everybody. This is your morning host, Charles Ducharme, speaking from the studios of your Tenoclock station for the good old music, radio KTCK. The temperature at this hour is forty-eight degrees, with nary a cloud in the sky or on the horizon, another perfect day here in the Tenoclock Valley. For our next selection we'll hear another wonderful old standard from the incomparable Jo Stafford, this one from the year 1952, and it's called 'You Belong to Me.' " Ducharme sighed audibly into the mike. "Ah, doesn't this one bring back the memories? Listen."

Johnnie reached down and turned the radio back off with an irritated twist of her wrist. What a phony, she thought. She had met Ducharme, and despite his mellifluous voice he was about twenty-two; maybe his father could have remembered a song popular in 1952, but he certainly couldn't.

She realized that getting irritated by such a petty thing showed how frayed her nerves were this morning.

Her return to the death site near Jumbo Mountain hadn't helped. She had found Dean Epperly dozing peacefully in the front seat of his old Oldsmobile up on the side of the road, and two carloads of gawkers down on the trackage, taking pictures over her yellow crime scene tape. The morning sun made the bloodstains on the white rock fill stand out sharply.

After chasing them away, Johnnie had reexamined the scene herself. The residual mess made her feel sick all over again. She didn't find anything new. A call to the police station—her radio had worked that time—had obtained the loan of a city officer to guard the scene until the crime experts arrived from Denver. But the need to borrow help had only made her more sharply aware of how thin her resources were.

Who, she wondered, would they name acting sheriff? Butt Peabody was the only logical candidate, but the same political enemies who had gotten him voted out of office were still in control and not likely to put him back, even temporarily. That left . . . who? None of us can handle it.

Thoughts of Butt Peabody tugged at something else she had been trying to avoid for several hours now. As long and as well as she had known him, as much as she admired and cared for him, the little suspicion curling in her mind made her feel guilty. But Butt had been defeated by Jim Way in a bitterly fought election, and Butt had left office a very angry man. Johnnie had seen him out late last night, alone, which was not characteristic of him. She hated the very idea of it. But she had to check it out.

Reaching town now, she turned onto Gunnison Avenue, driving past a long row of clothing and souvenir shops on the north side and city park on the south. Despite the early hour, a handful of tourist children played under the pines, and a few adults strolled the board sidewalks, gawking at the ordinance-mandated wood shop signs, all hand painted. At the corner entrance of the park ahead, a man was taking a picture of his wife standing in front of the stacked elk antlers that formed a portal over the sidewalk. On the other side of the intersection, in the chamber of commerce parking lot, two of the old gents paid by the chamber "to add local color" were adjusting the saddles on the old nags they would walk up and down Main Street most of the day. In leather chaps and vests, with soaring cowboy hats, the old-timers looked their parts. It was not widely known that, while one was from Wyoming and came by the job honestly, the taller and more authentic-looking of the two was from New Jersey, where he had only recently quit the seminary.

Up over the wood-shingle roofs of the town, the sun had already turned the aspen to blazing color at the higher elevations. The wind that rushed into the open door-flaps of Johnnie's Jeep had an autumn bite. Before long the snow would come, and even more of the rich and famous would flock in to ski and gossip and be seen. Already enough of them had arrived for the aspen to make Tenoclock's traffic heavy with celebrity seekers.

Feeling the start of a headache, Johnnie turned onto Court Street and drove down the alley to the back parking lot of the courthouse.

Finding a spot, she parked and hurried to the pale, rotting wood roof that covered the rear basement entrance to the building, and went inside. The familiar odors of dust, cigars, mildew, and sweat enveloped her as she went across the dirty, cracked tiles of the back landing, then descended the scabby steel staircase to the bare pavement floor of the basement. One old-fashioned door had JAIL printed on it in peeling black letters. The other said SHERIFF. Swinging that door open, she entered the familiar sprawling office space.

She found three people at work, which was two more than she had anticipated.

Office clerk Hesther Gretsch, lanky, graying, perpetually glum, sat at her desk near the back of the room, hammering away at the keyboard of the office computer, possibly the only Intertec Superbrain (CPM, 64K of RAM) still operating in the Western Hemisphere.

Billy Higginbotham stood with his back to Johnnie, talking on a telephone; he was in uniform, which meant he expected to meet the public today, serving summonses from the county court here or the district court in Gunnison.

At the front reception counter, Jason Ramsey was on another telephone, talking to someone else. He had changed clothes at some point, and his jailer's badge, which looked just like a deputy's, gleamed gold on the front of his dark wool shirt. Johnnie had never seen him wear his badge before.

She walked toward the counter. Ramsey spied her and lifted a hand in greeting. He looked bright and alert, none of the shufflin' Mose act in evidence. He was filling out an incident report with a ballpoint as he listened on the telephone, and Johnnie saw that he was almost to the bottom of the page.

"Thank you, Mr. Hunt," Ramsey said in a brisk, official-sounding voice as Johnnie reached the desk. "We'll have this report sent to all units immediately. Yes, sir. Thank you, sir. Good day."

The old man hung up the phone and wheeled half-around in the swivel chair Johnnie so often occupied. "Morning."

"Morning, Mr. Ramsey. What's up?"

"Butt Peabody called, said he'd heard about the sheriff, and didn't want to add to our trouble, but he was out night-fishing on Lake Luma last night, and somebody swiped some tools out of his pickup while he was away from it. He'd like a report made for insurance purposes."

So that was it, Johnnie thought with sharp relief. But then she immediately realized that she wouldn't have accepted such a story from any other possible suspect without checking it out. *Damn.* "You got all the information, Mr. Ramsey?"

Ramsey nodded. "Want me to write it up?"

"Sure. Anything else?"

"Orville Hunt, out on Route 4, says there's an apparently abandoned car up on the North Mountain road. He says it's on a curve, and the back end is sticking out just a little, might get hit if somebody came around there too fast and didn't see it in time to slow down and go wide."

Johnnie nodded. "Up toward Sky Estates?"

"Pretty close, he said."

"Okay, let's send the wrecker out there and haul it in."

Ramsey reached for the telephone. "Impound it?"

"Right. I suppose we'll have an irate camper on our hands later today, but we can't leave it sitting out there if it's a hazard. By the way, Mr. Ramsey, what are you doing here on the day shift?"

The old man shrugged. "Day jailer is here. Thought maybe I could help out a little. So I went home long enough to shower and change—try to make myself presentable in case I was needed."

"God, you're needed, all right. But when are you going to sleep?"

"Oh, I got a pretty good night's sleep back in the jail office. Usually do."

"Well, it's sure a great idea as far as I'm concerned. Of course, the new acting sheriff, when the commissioners name somebody, may have a different opinion."

Ramsey grinned. "You figure you ain't going to be it?"

"*Me?*"

The grin broadened. "Sure 'nuff. Who else they gonna ask?"

Nonplussed, she stared at him. The other two deputies were order-takers, and she didn't think either of them would take the job and the added pressure if asked. Did that leave only her? The poor county! she thought.

She walked over to Billy Higginbotham's desk. He looked up expectantly.

"Morning, Billy. Busy?"

Higginbotham sighed and rubbed the back of his hand over his eyes. "Swamped! Lots of calls. Lots of warrants and subpoenas."

"Billy, I think you should drive out to Jumbo and take over from the city officer out there. The state boys will be here sometime today, but until then I want it watched, and nobody messing up anything we might have missed."

Higginbotham grimaced. "I've got all this stuff to do already, Johnnie. The county already owes me four days off."

"Maybe we'd better forget the normal shifts for a while."

"But I'm *tired*, Johnnie! I need the rest!"

"Dammit, Billy, I guess I can't make you do it, but I'm asking."

Her voice sounded far sharper than she had intended, and Higginbotham flinched. "I guess you're taking over for now, huh?"

"*Somebody* has to, Billy. Do you want to?"

Higginbotham's eyes widened with alarm. "Me? God, no!"

"Well, will you go out to Jumbo, or not?"

He heaved a great sigh. "Do I have time to type this report first?"

"What is it?"

"Missing person. Runaway kid. Teenager, I guess. I got all the info. Lady said she had called several times before. She was real pis—real irate."

"Just leave your notes and I'll ask Hesther to type it."

Higginbotham nodded, pushed himself up from the desk, and headed for the back door. He met Carl Rieger coming in.

"Morning, Johnnie," Rieger puffed, a little out of breath. "What's this I heard about asking the state to send in a crime investigator or something?"

"I just want to be sure we know everything we can about Jim Way's death, Carl."

Rieger frowned. "Might not be a good idea, Johnnie, having the state come in. Makes it look like it wasn't just an unfortunate accident."

"On the other hand, having a report from them will ensure there aren't any rumors floating around later."

Rieger's eyebrows went up. "Hadn't thought of that. We just need to make sure there isn't a lot of talk about Jim's drinking. We don't need that kind of PR. Respect for the dead, that's the ticket." Abruptly he glanced up at the wall clock. "Like you to come up to the commissioners' meeting room, Johnnie."

"Now?"

"Please."

Rieger led the way out of the office and up the musty stairs to a corridor on the second floor, which led to broad double-glass doors at the far end with a COMMISSIONERS sign over it. Entering with Rieger, Johnnie saw the other commissioners waiting.

Seated at one end, wizened old Earle Fisch, seventy-four, blinked at Johnnie through his granny glasses as if he didn't remember ever seeing her before. He looked like a stack of bones inside a faded seersucker suit that should have already gone into the garment bag for another year.

Standing behind his chair at the other end of the table, Madison Blithe had his back turned, but Johnnie recognized him by his expensive dark suit and the portable cellular telephone held to his ear, as usual. At thirty-six, Blithe was one of the youngest men ever elected to high office in Tenoclock County. His real estate business had also made him one of the wealthiest.

Rieger strode to the front. Blithe concluded his telephone call and turned to give Johnnie a conspiratorial wink, which she didn't understand. Rieger sat down and rapped on the table with his gavel, making old Earle Fisch jump with alarm.

"Johnnie," Rieger said with great solemnity, "the commissioners have just held a brief executive session to discuss last night's tragedy and its implications for the county." He rapped the gavel again. "The board is now in open session." He looked right and left at his colleagues. "The chair will entertain a motion."

"Move," Blithe said instantly, "that Tenoclock County name Johnnie Baker as acting sheriff effective immediately."

Johnnie's insides flip-flopped. Maybe it made sense to name her, but she felt about as competent as a high schooler.

"Do I hear a second to the motion?" Rieger asked. "Earle?"

Earle Fisch jumped again. "Second."

"All in favor?" Rieger asked. "Opposed? It's unanimous." He leaned over the table, extending a hand. "Congratulations, Johnnie. The judge is standing by to swear you in at once. Oh, and needless to say, your salary will be raised ten dollars a week. I'm sure you don't expect the county to pay you quite as much as an elected sheriff would receive."

Johnnie had begun to catch up. "But I can hire another deputy to keep the force the same size?"

Rieger glanced at Blithe and got a small nod. "Of course, of course. Just try to find someone with the right qualifications, right?"

"Yes. Of course."

"We know you'll do a grand job, Johnnie."

The side door of the meeting room swung open. In swept County Judge Fred Otterman, six feet, five inches tall, handsome head of white hair impeccably brushed, long judicial robes swirling with each long stride. Someone had told Otterman once that he resembled actor Joseph Cotton, and he had never stopped trying to sharpen the resemblance. His smile was cool and thin-lipped, and over the years his hair had mysteriously become curlier. The voters adored him. Johnnie knew him as a judge who bucked all the hard cases on up to Gunnison, yet still had one of the state's highest records for reversals.

"Johnnie," Otterman said, making his voice deep and melodious as he reached out with both hands to clasp one of hers. "This is a sad day, but a good one, too. I know you will do a splendid job!"

From somewhere he produced a small Bible. Johnnie stumbled through the words of the oath. A kid from the newspaper office appeared and popped his strobe light several times. After that there was a confused minute of handshakes and even a hug from Earle Fisch. Leaving the commissioners' room, Johnnie felt her eyes get slightly wet. She paused to dig a hankie out of her back pocket. They had made her *sheriff*. She felt so proud she could hardly stand it.

Beyond the closed doors of the meeting room, a sudden burst of male laughter startled her. She leaned closer to listen.

"Great public relations!" Blithe's voice echoed. "A pretty lady sheriff."

Rieger's voice: "This will completely take the news play away from Jim's drunken escapade."

"You know the only thing that would make her more perfect?" Blithe asked.

"What?"

"Tighter jeans."

Laughter.

Johnnie beat a retreat toward the basement.

8:30 A.M.

THE FIRST GUNSHOTS boomed deafeningly across Frontier Street, out on the board sidewalk in front of the ornate green and red Mountain Man Theater. Then the half-dozen rough-clad "cowboys" who had just happened to be sauntering up the street chose sides, everybody grabbing a six-shooter, and the fusillade of gunshots racketed back and forth between wood-front buildings. A flock of pigeons took startled flight from the maples and aspen in the park. Gunsmoke wafted across the pavement. Only one of the cowboy actors remained standing. He walked to one of his fallen assailants, looked down at him for a moment, and turned to stroll away.

The thin crowd of tourists on hand for the first gunfight of the day applauded and stowed cameras.

Inside the Pick & Shovel Cafe two blocks away, the noises were scarcely heard over the rumble of morning breakfast conversation. The crowd consisted mainly of old townies who wouldn't have been impressed anyway.

Mabel rushed back toward the kitchen after delivering plates of flapjacks and sausage to one booth. Her best waitress, a middle-aged woman named Anne Yosac, waved at her from the wall telephone.

"I can't talk now!" Mabel fumed, starting on into the steamy kitchen.

"It's Donna," Anne said.

Mabel swerved back. "That little floozie is thirty minutes late already. Am I going to give her a piece of my mind!" Taking the telephone from her waitress, she barked into the mouthpiece: "Hello! Donna? Why aren't you here?"

There was so much conversation going on in the cafe that she almost couldn't hear the tiny voice that answered: "Miz Murnan, I'm awful sorry, but I've really come down sick."

"So what time will you be here?"

"I don't know. Maybe by ten."

Mabel slammed the receiver on the hook and bustled into the kitchen. Sometimes she could not believe her bad luck in hiring. She had thought at first that Donna might be a good one. But this was the third time in less than a month that she had called in sick. What made it worse was the fact that the newer girl, Barbara, hadn't shown up either, and hadn't even bothered to call.

Chippies, Mabel thought, hefting heavy platters of steak and eggs. That's what both of them were, if you asked her opinion. Babble all the time about the stars, and when Paul Simon walked down the street three days ago, you would have thought from their reactions that it was the Good Lord Almighty his own self. All they thought about was meeting the stars. As if it would ever do them any good.

She should have been doubly warned about Barbara, Mabel thought. The child was precocious in her physical development, no question about that. But if she was eighteen, as she put down on her job application, then Mabel would eat your galoshes. But there had been the hope that if the child was underage, maybe she would work hard to prevent being fired and forced by hunger to go back home.

Well, fat chance. It seemed like the younger they were, the less responsible they were. What was the world coming to?

There was a sudden change in the nature of the commotion out front. Carrying her armloads of laden platters, Mabel brushed backward through the swinging kitchen door and went out to see what was going on.

Several of the townies were gawking, and a few away from the street windows actually had gotten to their feet to see better. Outside, in the gathering chill gray of the morning, a Lincoln the size of a Greyhound bus had drawn up in front. A driver who looked like he should have been in a monster movie hurried around the car and opened the passenger door near the curb. There was a stirring inside, and then out stepped a plump, middle-aged man, his long, thinning dark hair riffled by the cold breeze, wearing a long black cloak with a crimson lining, dark trousers and dark turtleneck beneath. He looked around haughtily, peering down the long, aristocratic slope of his nose at the beginnings of a crowd already forming on the sidewalk. He said something to his giant chauffeur, then with a dramatic sweep of his arm tossed his cloak back over one shoulder and made for the door of Mabel's cafe.

Holy shit, Mabel thought, it was the one celebrity you never saw in town—the man who hadn't made a movie in several years but was still considered the best of them all—Brandon Warner himself.

Even Mabel, who considered herself too jaded to be thrilled by anything, felt the goose bumps form. *Brandon Warner!* The man who had made Captain Ahab leap to life for film audiences the world over. The actor whose Hamlet, on the legitimate stage, had been hailed as the finest performance of the century. The man whose eccentric portrayal of Fletcher Christian had simultaneously enraged and enthralled the critics. Subject of rumors of the wildest kind, yet seldom seen in public.

But here he was—my God!—opening the front door of the Pick & Shovel and *coming straight at Mabel,* who stood transfixed behind the end of the counter in front of the one vacant stool in the joint.

Warner slid onto the stool. His bright black eyes bored into Mabel in a way that made her shaky. His small smile flickered. "Good morning. I've been told your breakfasts are the best in Tenoclock."

Mabel found her voice. "Best in the world."

Warner chuckled. "And the best of your best is . . . ?"

"Uh . . . the frontier omelet. I—"

"Then that's what I shall have. And orange juice in a very clean glass, with chipped ice, and a mug of your finest coffee."

"Right," Mabel croaked, turning away and bumping into Suzie, her counter girl.

Suzie followed Mabel back into the kitchen. "He's mine!" Suzie hissed. "I always wait the counter folks!"

"Back off," Mabel grated. "You even refill his coffee mug, and you die."

She hurried back to the counter with a glass of ice water and a mug of steaming black coffee. Brandon Warner kept his back to the room, appearing oblivious of the stares.

A teenage girl, possibly fifteen, got up from a far table and hurried nervously toward the counter, a sheet of tablet paper and ballpoint in hand. "Mister Warner—"

"No, no," Warner said irritably, waving her away. "I never sign autographs. It can be never ending." Then he stopped and looked at the girl for the first time. His smile, cruel and arrogant, returned. "But for you, my child, I shall make an exception." Taking the paper, he scrawled his signature hugely across its width.

A woman at a nearer table started to get to her feet.

"No more!" Warner snapped. The woman sat down, deflated.

Mabel put his coffee, a napkin, and a spoon on the counter in front of him.

"Ah," he murmured, reaching for the sugar.

"Is he coming in?" Mabel blurted.

Warner frowned. "Who?"

"The big guy. Your driver."

"Boris? No. He will await me in the car. I assume it's all right for the car to remain parked in front?"

It blocked four parking places, but so what? "Why, hell yes," Mabel said.

"Tell me, my good woman, which establishment in our

fair city would you recommend that I visit in search of fine leather boots?"

Mabel almost didn't hear what he said, his voice was so hypnotic. She swallowed with difficulty. "Well, the Leatherworks is good. . . ."

"Thank you. I've seen the sign. I shall try there."

Mabel felt her breath catch in her throat. His face was heavily lined, proof of his legendary dissipation, and his eyes at close range were bloodshot and tired. Oh, and he was too heavy now, yes, and the forehead really was very high. He was getting old. But none of that mattered. He was still Brandon Warner.

Just wait, she thought, until the absent Donna and Barbara heard about *this*. They would have puppies.

Scurrying back into the kitchen, she almost collided with Anne Yosac, carrying out several plates of flapjacks. Yosac's faded eyes darted worriedly past Mabel. "Is he coming in?"

"Who?" Mabel demanded.

"The big stoop—Boris!"

"No."

"Thank the Good Lord!"

Mabel was puzzled. "Why? What's wrong with him?"

"Let me take this stuff to table eight, and I'll come back and tell you."

Mabel went on into the kitchen and grabbed another order of her own. When she had taken that out to the booth, Anne was back, too, and they huddled a moment in the narrow corridor outside the kitchen.

"There's something funny about this Boris guy?" Mabel whispered.

"He's just crazy, that's all!"

"Well, now, how do you know something like that?"

"Listen, I've read about him. He was a college wrestler a long time ago—back at Oklahoma, back in the days when college wrestling was a big sport in that part of the country and Oklahoma was great at it. He got drafted—Korea—before he graduated. He went over there and got a Bronze Star or something. When he came back, he brought a wife he had gotten over there, half Chinese or Korean, half black. I saw her picture in a magazine once; she was gorgeous."

"What's any of this got to do with—"

"I'm getting to it, I'm getting to it. Well. The way I read the story, when Boris came back, he couldn't get much of a job anywhere. He played a bit role in some movie of Warner's and they were sort of odd couple pals for a short time, but then he couldn't get any more acting work and ended up selling cars. About that time, somebody got the bright idea of making him a pro wrestler—a villain.

"It worked real good. Boris was a convincing villain, and he was making big bucks.

"Then, though, he had a match down south someplace, Columbus, Mississippi, I think, and he took his wife along. Well, I guess some of the local boys took his villain act in the ring too seriously, and they didn't like the idea of somebody like Boris—or maybe any white man, for that matter—openly living with a black woman.

"So when Boris and his wife were driving out of town one fine night in October, the good old boys flagged down the limo. They dragged Boris and his wife out of the car. He hurt a couple of them, but there were too many of them and they got him tied up. Then they made him watch while they gang raped his wife and beat her up. Then they worked Boris over with baseball bats. And castrated him."

One of the cooks called "Number seven, pick up!" but Mabel ignored the call. "And?" she prodded her waitress. "And?"

"His wife died," Yosac told her. Boris was in a coma a long time. The story got out in the papers and Brandon Warner, remembering him, flew to Mississippi or wherever it was and paid for everything and bullied the local county attorney into dropping some bullshit charge of disturbing the peace, or something like that, that they had filed against Boris.

"Well, Boris got better slowly, but he's not right. Brandon Warner keeps him on as sort of a bodyguard. They say Boris talked to mirrors a lot in those days, and had spells where he passed out.

"Boris has never left Warner's side since then. More than thirty-five years, they've been together. Boris's whole life is dedicated to Warner for what Warner did for him. Boris would do anything for him. *Anything.* He would die for him. The way I happened to read all this stuff, he had beat the living hell out of five or six guys who heckled Mr. Warner somewhere, and there were some charges that eventually got dismissed . . . or paid off, more likely."

Mabel studied her waitress's somber expression and shuddered. "Brr! I see why it's better he stayed outside. We don't need somebody wrecking the joint."

"He might," Yosac said. "He's crazy. He might do anything if somebody acted wrong toward Mr. Warner."

The other cook yelled, "Counter four!"

Brandon Warner's order. Mabel hurried to get it. As she placed it in front of the famous, fading actor, she felt thoughtful and puzzled and a little sad. Who would have guessed it? Why did this man keep a kook at his side—even let him be his chauffeur? The world was full of surprises. Nothing was ever quite what you thought it was.

9:00 A.M.

BACK IN CONTROL of her emotions after a few minutes' routine work, Johnnie hiked up the back stairs of the courthouse again and found County Judge Fred Otterman in his office, boots on the desk.

"Come in, Madam Sheriff, come in! What can I do you for?"

"Judge," Johnnie told him, "I thought you ought to know. I'm going to ask Max Shoemaker, as the assistant DA for Tenoclock County, to request a court order for a full autopsy and forensic examination on Jim Way's body."

Otterman's boots hit the floor. "What would you want to

request that for? There's already been the usual coroner's report. They did that first thing at the funeral home, and it's already been filed with the court."

"Fred, you know as well as I do that exams like that are quick and dirty unless there's reason to suspect foul play. I want a *real* post."

Pale beads of sweat appeared on Otterman's forehead. "Johnnie—Madam Sheriff—I don't see how I could see my way clear to issue an order like that. It would be tantamount to suggesting foul play in this case! It would set tongues wagging . . . make everyone look bad!"

"You mean," Johnnie said in dismay, "you won't issue the order even if Max requests it in a formal pleading?"

"Max won't do that! Look, Johnnie! We get along here. All of us get along. You don't get along by causing trouble. I'm sure no one would benefit from a full-fledged autopsy. I'm sure Mrs. Way wouldn't want it—only drag things out and make them more painful." Otterman whipped out a linen handkerchief and mopped his face. "No. No! Out of the question!"

Returning to the high-ceilinged central corridor of the courthouse upstairs, Johnnie headed for Max Shoemaker's office. She had expected opposition but not outright refusal from Otterman. This was all getting a lot harder than she had expected even an hour ago.

9:45 A.M.

Tenoclock Police Chief Chubby Mayfield strolled into the courthouse basement with a seven-inch black cigar sticking out of his habitual jolly grin. "Johnnie!" he bawled across the empty expanse of unused desks. "I just heard the great news! Congratulations!"

Johnnie got up from the swivel chair behind Jim Way's desk. Her search through his desk "files" had startled and dismayed her, and she hadn't gotten anywhere with Max Shoemaker on so much as asking for a real autopsy. Feeling grim, she tried to hide it from Mayfield. "Morning, Chief. And hey, thanks for lending us that man this morning."

"Nothing to it, nothing to it," Mayfield drawled, swaggering across the big room. "Like I always say, what are friends for? Right? Right!"

Few people knew the chief's real first name, Johnnie concluded. He had earned his nickname the old-fashioned way, by eating his way up to it. At forty, he had to have been a very busy eater all his life; standing just five feet seven, he weighed somewhere in the vicinity of 230 pounds. The big silver belt buckle of his cowboy-style jeans was almost entirely buried under the thick roll of fat that threatened to burst every button on his red and blue checked lumberjack shirt. His yellow bola tie had a heavy oval glass clasp with a huge scorpion embedded in it. His pale gray Stetson was the old high-hat type, with an immaculate five-inch brim all around and a single-pleated peak that made him look top-heavy. Big silver rings gleamed on most of his thick fingers, and a silver and turquoise bracelet held his multiple-dialed wrist chronometer in place. Pink, wide-eared, and always grinning his gap-toothed grin, Chubby Mayfield was one of Tenoclock's best-known civic oddities. He spent most of every day clomping around the board sidewalks in his high-heeled cowboy boots, glad-handing everyone and singing the praises of the city. On weekends he wore his chief's uniform, dark blue with gold braid on the sleeves and gold stripes down the sides of the pants, and little gold brushes on the shoulders. A complete moron, apparently, and totally inept, except that a year earlier when two men staged an armed robbery at a convenience store on the west edge of Tenoclock, it had been Mayfield on the scene first, coolly killing one of the men and shooting the legs out from under the other as they fired on him from ambush.

Reaching the desk, he stuck out a paw. "Is there anything else that Tenoclock's finest can do to help you, *Sheriff?*"

Johnnie gave him her hand, and then remembered almost too late how proud he was of his man-sized grip. She snatched her fingers back just before they were permanently deformed. "I was just going through some of Jim's records, Chubby, and I've found quite a few reports that apparently never got any farther than his top drawer."

Mayfield chuckled. "Poor old Jim, God bless him! A man after my own heart. I know your department is understaffed just like the city police force, darn it, but good old Jim knew how to live with realities, right? Right! Sometimes you've just got to shitcan some reports if you're to maintain your sanity, if you'll pardon my French."

Johnnie hesitated before replying. Everyone knew that Tenoclock's town board was just as stingy on law enforcement as the county was. The entire Tenoclock police force, counting Mayfield and two female office typists, stood at ten. On the good days, Mayfield got four cars on the streets. At night there was seldom more than one. The town, like the county, was plowing all its newfound tax dollars right back into projects designed to bring in even more tourist dollars: a new park, a city swimming pool, total renovation of the old city golf course, extension of sewer and water services miles into what remained, so far, brushy boondocks.

She decided finally that she had to ask, at least: "Did you by any chance get any of these, too?" She held up the sheaf of missing person reports.

Mayfield took them out of her hand and glanced at them with a frown. "Some are pretty old. . . ."

"The oldest I can find dates back six weeks. It looks like the parents started calling regularly. The last two calls were just last weekend."

Frowning, Mayfield scanned the form generated by Hesther on the old Intertec. "Gregg . . . Gregg . . . Barbara Gregg . . . Now why does that ring a bell? Say! I bet we got a call or two over at headquarters, too!"

"Has she been found?"

"I don't recollect that she has." Mayfield brightened

again. "But that's one thing you'll learn in this job, Johnnie, my girl. You can't let the little details get you down. You get too involved in the details, the worry can kill you. That's what ruined Jimmy Carter, wasn't it?"

"Chief, I wish we had done more on this case. The parents sound desperately worried in these reports, and I can't tell that we turned a tap."

"Well, then, Johnnie, I guess you can give it some priority."

"Right now," Johnnie admitted, "I'm waiting for the crime investigators to get here from Denver."

"Oh, heavens, they've been here already. Been here and gone."

Johnnie's insides lurched again. "What?"

"Got here bright and early, over an hour ago. Went out to the scene, looked 'er over. Came back to the police station. Of course, I already did an incident report on the whole thing about Jim's death, leaving out the idle speculation about drinking, of course. So we visited a bit and I explained the situation and burned them a copy of my report, and they were satisfied, and headed back to Denver a few minutes ago." Mayfield squinted his eyes. "Say, do you feel all right? You look real pale!"

Johnnie swallowed hard. "Tired, I guess. Chief, I'd better get to work. Thanks for stopping by."

"Don't mention it!" Mayfield said, waving his cigar. "It's nothing."

10:00 A.M.

DAVE DICKENSEN, ALMOST dozing at his desk in the small private office at the rear of DD Security Systems, jerked awake when he heard the unmistakable voice of Brandon Warner up front. What the *hell?*

Dickensen hurried to his office door. The famous actor stood at the front desk, speaking to Kit Niles, the DD receptionist. Beside him loomed the giant figure of Boris O'Neal.

Dickensen started toward the front. Warner spied him and raised an arm in a stage gesture. "Just the man I'm looking for. Dave! What can you tell me about automobile alarm systems?"

Dickensen needed a moment to react. He was amazed that Warner was in shape to go anywhere this morning, and appearing in town was unusual for him under any circumstances. "Well, um . . ."

"We've taken a short drive to look at the aspen and stop by town for breakfast and a bit of shopping," Warner said, coming around the counter. "I thought it would give me a good opportunity to speak to you in person about car alarms. You remember we spoke briefly about it months ago."

Dickensen continued to be confused. They had never discussed the matter. "Oh, right. Of course. Do you, uh, want to come into my office?"

Warner tossed his cape over his shoulder. "Capital! Come, Boris."

Once in the office, Dickensen closed the door, sat at his desk, and punched the intercom. "No calls, Kit." Folding his hands, he looked at Warner, who had taken one of the chairs facing the desk. Boris remained standing just inside the door, eyes dark and watchful under the massive shelf of bone overhanging them.

"What is it?" Dickensen asked. "Has something happened?"

"No, no," Warner said smoothly, fitting a cigarette into a pale metal holder. "Under the circumstances, I thought it well to be seen today, so everyone would know everything is perfectly normal with me."

"It isn't normal for you to come to town!"

"Nonsense. I come occasionally. You know that."

"But why did you come *here*, of all places? Christ, for us to be seen together after what happened . . ."

Warner made his expressive face register surprise. "Did

something happen? I don't recall anything happening."

"Right, right," Dickensen grated. "I get it. Did you have anything you really needed to talk about this morning?"

"The other girl. Have you located her yet?"

"No."

"Are you trying?"

"I've looked around, but all I know about her is that she drives an old compact car! I can hardly start asking anybody questions!"

"She's a waitress. Doesn't that help?"

"There are over a hundred eating places in Tenoclock. If I start making the rounds, all I'll do is call attention to myself. And I don't have anything to go on—any description, anyway!"

Warner raised the cigarette holder to his lips. Boris moved—quick, ponderous, frightening fluidity—to produce a small lighter, which flamed in his huge fist to provide a light. Warner puffed. "Her name is Donna."

"Yes, and she's blond. But Christ, that's nothing to go on!"

"All right, Dave, all right. Calm down."

Dickensen's teeth grated painfully. "You haven't come up with any memory about that girl who brought this Donna out that first time?"

"I'm afraid not. But my recollection is that she's gone back to Albuquerque or whatever miserable place she lives in during the school year anyway."

"And you still can't remember her name, either?"

"Of course. It was Jennifer."

"Jennifer *what*?"

"How should I know, man? Names are unimportant. They come and go. They're all alike." Warner leaned forward, showing for the first time a tightening of facial muscles that betrayed worry. "You have to find this Donna girl. When she realizes her friend is missing, there's no telling what she might say or do . . . or to whom."

Dickensen's nerves unraveled. "Mr. Warner, I can lose everything, too."

"I realize that, Dave. You got rid of the guard?"

"He's gone."

"Then the girl is our only worry. Find her!"

Dickensen's frustration brought him half out of his chair. "I should have never listened to you in the first place, you—!"

Boris made a low guttural sound, almost a growl, and moved fractionally away from the wall.

"It's all right, Boris," Warner said quickly. He turned back to Dickensen. "Calm down, man. Just *find* the child. A generous cash settlement will keep her quiet permanently. But she must be located before we can deal with her."

"What if she won't take money?"

Warner looked genuinely shocked. "Of course she'll take the money! Everyone has a price."

Dickensen almost shouted his frustration. Fighting for self-control, he raised his eyes to the ceiling. In one corner, a spider had begun to spin a web. Dickensen felt like he was in a web, too, the sticky strands of the lie enmeshing him, crushing him, making it impossible to breathe.

10:15 A.M.

"WELL, YOU CERTAINLY picked a fine time to report to work!" Mabel Murnan said sarcastically.

"I felt awful this morning," Donna said. Her insides trembled. Maybe it was a mistake to come in at all. I feel like I'm flying to pieces.

"Get to work," Mabel said disgustedly. "Bus those tables and then start setting out the salad bar. And you can work late tonight to make up for this morning, or you can start looking for another job."

The words were dragged from Donna's mouth. "Mrs. Murnan?"

Mabel looked back with a scowl. "Yes? What now, Miss Priss?"

"Is Barb working today?"

"No, and she'll never work here again. At least you called in sick. She hasn't even bothered to call in yet. As far as I'm concerned, she can be dead and buried; she's no employee of mine anymore!"

Donna hurried into the back hall, past the kitchen doors, to the closet where the waitress aprons and little white caps were stored. Her hands shook so badly she had trouble opening the closet door.

Another of the waitresses, Phyllis Shaw, came out of the kitchen and walked over to her as she tied on the apron. Phyllis was twenty, a year older than Donna, a dropout from Ohio State. Mabel had a rule that said her waitresses could wear only minimum makeup, but that didn't detract from Phyllis's striking, dark-eyed good looks. She had befriended Donna the first day she had come to work at the Pick & Shovel; behind her beautiful eyes had been an amused sophistication that Donna instantly recognized and yearned for.

"Hey, honey," Phyllis said with a knowing smile. "You look beat! You must have had some kind of fun last night."

"Have you heard from Barb?" Donna asked nervously.

"No." Phyllis frowned. "Why? Is something wrong?"

"I don't know. Look, I can't talk now. Mabel will kill me. But I've got to talk to *someone.*"

"Geez, you look really scared, honey! How about after the lunch rush?"

"Yes. That will be great. Maybe I'm just letting my imagination get the best of me, but . . ."

Mabel's sarcastic voice sounded behind her. "Are you going to get busy, Miss Priss, or does it take all day to tie on an apron?"

"I'm hurrying," Donna said, startled. "I'm sorry."

That surprised Mabel. She had never heard Donna Smith sound so meek or apologize for anything before. She wondered what was wrong with the child.

10:50 A.M.

DRIVING OUT KILLDEER Road into the mountains south
of Tenoclock, Johnnie Baker knew she was asking for
trouble. She tried to calm her nerves by paying attention to
the scenery.

Her Jeep chugged happily up the steep grade, and she had
the narrow paved road all to herself. A fine, fat brown
marmot sat up on the side of the road and watched her pass.
A hawk turned slowly over the seventy-foot firs, wings black
against the bright blue sky. Out her left window Johnnie
spied three deer grazing in a sun-flooded opening in the
forest. The cool wind felt good and so did the forest smells
around her.

She had been getting ready to leave the courthouse for this
mission when Jim Way's widow, Myldred, had appeared in
the office. Johnnie had walked over to her, intent on offering
her sympathies, when the tearful older woman lashed out
at her, saying all these attempts to smear her dead husband's
name had to stop. Stunned, Johnnie had said she was only
trying to make sure how the sheriff had died. Mrs. Way had
said everyone knew Jim drank, and to drag out a useless
investigation or try to postpone the planned Saturday funeral for something horrible like a full-scale autopsy in
Gunnison or Grand Junction would only make matters
worse. Let the dead sleep in peace, she had sobbed, and stop
trying to make a name for yourself by doing all these stupid
things that no one wanted.

Thrown for a loss, Johnnie had tried to remonstrate. But
the grief-stricken woman had turned and rushed out of the
office before she could get in a word.

Myldred Way had it all wrong, Johnnie thought now.
Somebody had called her and made it sound like the requests
for a fuller investigation were self-promoting on Johnnie's
part. No one wanted further investigation; they would go to
any lengths to let Jim Way's death go into history as quietly

as possible. Public relations: town and county image; don't dig or you might just find something, and a bizarre accident was more quickly forgotten than any other explanation for his death.

And maybe they were right, Johnnie thought despairingly. Maybe he had just gotten drunk and done something that stupid. Far easier to let it go the way they all wanted.

But how could she do that when everything she knew about the dead man—and every nagging instinct inside her—said something was terribly wrong here?

For some reason, memory of her father leaped into her mind. He was still a touchstone. What would he have done?

He had been the most stubborn man she, or anyone else in Tenoclock, had ever known. Life had been simple for him. Even if he had been able to see the future, Johnnie thought— even if he could have known his driven, obsessive work ethic would kill him—he wouldn't have changed an iota. "You can tell the character of a man by three things," she could still hear him saying. "By how he pays his debts, by how well he provides for his family, and by how hard he's willing to work."

Johnnie did not think her father would have given up. He would have urged her to press on. But would he have expected her to do so? Had he ever—really—been satisfied with anything she had done? He had not wanted her to go to New York, had thought it a doomed, quixotic notion. But if he had been alive when she finally saw the truth about her own talent and came back to the Tenoclock Valley, he would have thought she was a quitter. He would never have said so, but she would have known. It was a fact of her life that she might never get over. Unless she someday did something really right—really well, all the way through, no matter what—she was never going to feel good about herself.

"Are you going to quit again on this one, too?" he would have asked now.

No! But I'm scared! I'm not sure I can do the job!

Turning off the highway not far past the crest of Killdeer,

she took a dirt and gravel road. A half mile farther on, she had to go to four-wheel drive. The pathway—it certainly couldn't be called a road even by Colorado mountain standards—twisted down through a sloping stand of mixed firs, pines, and spruce to a small, narrow valley. Aspen scattered on the valley floor had not begun to turn yet, but it was chilly in the late-morning shade of the mountain. Johnnie drove alongside the nameless creek where she had caught trout in years past, and after a while she smelled the wood smoke and saw Butt Peabody's cabin in the clearing up ahead.

Peabody was more than sheriff when he hired her. She could not remember a time when he was not in her life. He and her father were the closest friends despite the difference in their ages. He watched after everything for Johnnie's mother after she became a widow. He was a very special man.

Movement near Peabody's weather-blackened log cabin caught her eye as she drove out of the trees. Out on the sunny east side she spotted Butt himself, tall and thickset in dark sweats and a wool cap, chopping firewood. He had an enormous stack already done, and a dismayingly large pile of rough-cut logs yet to trim and split for stacking. The ax swung in a smooth powerful arc, and another log split with a shower of chips. You could see his breath as he put another log on the splitting block.

As Johnnie pulled up, he straightened with a grin, buried the head of the ax in a stump, and walked toward her with the perpetual slight limp that a horse had given him years ago. She was struck by the realization of what a wonderful-looking man he was: sinewy, easy-moving, shaggy graying hair showing below the cuff of his wool cap, a stubble beard, and wide-set gray eyes lighting a face beaten and weathered by the outdoors. Johnnie felt good just being here. She always had.

"Hey," he said, his voice weather-roughened, too. "Don't tell me you already got yourself fired and need to chop some firewood to work your mad off."

"You heard about that already?"

"Sure. Long ago. Didn't you hear it when the rumors went

supersonic a couple of hours ago?" Peabody paused and fished in the flap of his sweat jacket for cigarettes. "Besides. It's all been on KTCK already."

"You know about Jim then, too, of course."

He cracked a wood match with his thumb and lighted a cigarette. He puffed a big cloud of smoke. "Heard what they've reported. Then Reg Sweeney was by a while ago, said everybody is saying Jim was drunk out of his mind." He inhaled again. "The Good Lord knows I was no big fan of Jim Way, after they rigged that election. But it sure seems a poor way to die."

"Yeah," Johnnie said, trying to figure the least awkward way to get to the first subject she had on her mind.

Peabody, smiling warmly, helped her out. "So what brings you clear out here, anyway?"

"I saw the report about your stolen fishing gear. I thought I'd check it out."

Peabody's smile died and his face went granitic. "Zat so?" He pointed toward his pickup beside the cabin. "You might want to look at the damage they did, breaking in."

Feeling like a fool and a fraud, Johnnie marched over to the truck. The lid of the steel toolbox astraddle the back bed just behind the cab stood bent and open. Gouges made by a crowbar or similar tool had ruined the box as well as its hinged cover.

Going on tiptoe, Johnnie peered over the side to see that only a few old and rusty hand tools were left at the bottom of the broken-open box.

Peabody's voice, quiet but close behind her, startled her: "Of course, if a man went out late at night to murder Jim Way, and then needed an alibi, he could get a prybar and tear his toolbox up himself, and throw the tools in the lake."

Johnnie turned, her insides going to ice.

Peabody's face was white with rage, and she had never seen his eyes like they were now. "Then," he added in the same steely tone, "he could call in a theft report to further cover his ass."

"I didn't—" Johnnie began.

"Don't bullshit me, Johnnie Baker," Peabody cut in sharply, his voice burry on the edges with controlled anger. "The minute I heard about Jim this morning, the first thought that entered my mind was that somebody must have seen me driving around late last night. I figured anybody would remember the hard feelings left over from the campaign, start putting two and two together, and come up with me as a suspect."

The big man paused and his chest heaved with powerful emotion. Shockingly, his eyes suddenly glistened. "Anybody would do that, I thought. Except you."

"Butt," Johnnie groaned. "I didn't think for a minute—"

"But here you are, checking me out!"

"I never thought you might have done it, but I had to *check!* If you think about it a minute, wouldn't you check *me* if our positions were reversed?"

Peabody turned his back on her and walked back toward the woodpile, his tall frame stiff with resentment. Johnnie ran after him and grabbed his arm. "Dammit, Butt Peabody! Don't treat me like this!"

He looked down at her. His face worked with emotions she couldn't read.

"You're my best friend in the whole world!" Johnnie cried. "We love each other! You've done everything for me, always! But if I didn't at least come take a look, wouldn't I be going against everything you tried to show me and teach me after you took me on as a deputy?"

The anger drained out of Peabody's strong, craggy face. With a sharp gesture he rubbed the back of his hand across his eyes, and sniffled. "Damn fool busybody," he muttered. His chest heaved again. "All right! Yes! I would have checked you out, too, but—"

Johnnie threw herself against him in an impulsive hug. "I knew you didn't do anything bad, you big turd!"

He laughed and hugged her back for an instant, and then pushed her away. "All right, then. So are you satisfied?"

"I'm satisfied, yes."

He cocked a stern eyebrow. "You shouldn't be."

"I shouldn't?"

"No, you goofus. You should ask if I've got an alibi witness."

Johnnie stared into his handsome eyes, unable to bring herself to ask and risk his wrath again.

"Which," Peabody told her gently, "I do. Mort Cunningham was out at the lake with me the whole time."

"God! Why didn't you say that in the first place!"

"I meant to, but when you marched over here and started playing Sam Spade, it just ticked me off so bad I lost my temper." He slowly shook his head. "We go back a ways, Johnnie, you and me. Maybe I expected you to be more up front about it."

Johnnie continued to look into his eyes, feeling the bond between them. If all friendships could be like this, she thought.

"So you like it right up front, do you?"

"That's the way I am. You know it."

"Okay, then . . . Butt, I need help."

His keen eyes raked her. "You sure do, if you're going to work for that bunch of hyenas."

"They said I could name a deputy, going in on my old pay line."

"Hope you can find somebody good." He started on toward the woodpile.

"Butt, I want you. Will you help me?"

He stopped in midstride, shoulders tightening as he turned to stare at her. There was absolutely no way to read his expression. "You've got to be kidding."

"No."

"Johnnie, you've got enough trouble already, with the scandal about Jim's way of dying, plus a couple of deputies that between 'em couldn't fill a teacup with brain cells. Those county commissioners do not consider me one of their favorite people, you know that. Why cause trouble?"

"There won't be any trouble," Johnnie snapped. "They said I could name whoever I wanted, and I want to name you."

Peabody took a last puff and ground his cigarette out under his boot.

He had been sheriff of Tenoclock County for three terms up to the last election. But he had made the mistake of speaking out openly and often about the failure of both the city and the county to enlarge law enforcement staffs to keep up with the wildfire population growth. The mayor, the city council majority, and the county commissioners hadn't liked having a gadfly make them look bad for plowing all the new tax revenue into further schemes to promote Tenoclock's celebrity and tourist boom. It hadn't been a great surprise when Jim Way announced his candidacy, but the potency of his expensive campaign had been a shocker. Peabody had run the old-fashioned way—the only way he could afford: a few posters, a few small spots in the newspaper. Way's campaign had blanketed the valley and was boosted by endorsements from just about everybody else holding local public office. When the votes were counted, Peabody had lost by fifty-two votes out of almost four thousand cast.

Johnnie added, "I know you ought to tell me to stick it in my ear."

"Yes, I should."

The wind, soft in the trees, was the only sound. Peabody reached for another cigarette.

"Well?" Johnnie prodded when she couldn't stand it any longer.

Peabody looked at her. Lord, she was beautiful! He thought he had had a crush on her ever since she was a little girl and he was a pimply teenager. She had been pretty then and prettier as a college girl. But now, with the first tiny lines around her eyes, and that wisp of what might be premature gray in her flaxen hair, she was just . . . well, he didn't have the vocabulary to cover it.

He felt a lump in his throat. He wondered how long he had loved her. But she would never know it, because he was a decade too old for her, and all stove up from that horse fall twenty-five years ago, and she had her potter friend in town anyway.

Still he didn't speak.

Johnnie put her hands on her hips. "Aren't you going to say anything?"

He tried to act like he hadn't been paying attention. "Might snow."

"Butt!"

"You got Dean and Billy. They're good old boys. Ramsey can help out."

"I'm also convinced Jim Way didn't wander onto the railroad tracks and kill himself. I've also got a missing person report that nobody has even looked at yet, much less checked out, and an abandoned car to trace down, and Ellis Newton called in a while ago to say two of his horses have been stolen out of his pasture."

"Ellis Newton," Peabody snapped, "is too cheap to put up decent fence. He's been yelling horse thief for as long as I can remember. Those horses just wander off through holes in the fence because they can't stand being so close to a jackass like Ellis Newton."

"Butt," Johnnie said, "please."

Peabody had to clear his throat. "Hiring me will just cause trouble, and you know it."

"But I *need* you!"

"You really play dirty, Johnnie Baker."

A small, hopeful smile began to dawn on her face. "Then I can count on you?"

Shit. "I'll be in after lunch."

Johnnie yelped gleefully and rushed over to hug him again.

He held her at arm's length and scowled down at her. "You say you're not buying the idea Jim got drunk and ran off the road by himself?"

"No."

"Why?"

"For one thing, he didn't drink that heavily and he was

never stupid enough to wander down and collapse on the tracks. For another thing, they found whiskey all over his clothing, and a fifth of Maker's Mark in the Bronco."

The ghost of a smile quirked Peabody's lips. "Jim would never have spilled expensive whiskey. I know that much."

"He didn't drink expensive whiskey!"

Peabody thought about it.

"You're right," he said finally. "I'll be in as soon as I can change clothes."

2:00 P.M.

A BLUSTERY NORTH wind had obscured the sun by early afternoon, taking the thermometer on the bank building down ten degrees. It was getting chilly. The worsening weather had not, however, thinned the crowds of shoppers and gawkers on Tenoclock's famous Packer's Alley.

Spanning a single block between Silver Street and Gunnison Avenue, the alley had been entirely rebuilt in the past three years. Most of Tenoclock's new, frightfully expensive shops had located on it, along with four posh restaurants catering exclusively to the glamour crowd who could afford a menu with prices worthy of a Pentagon shopping list. A number of tourists stood by wide-eyed as Butt Peabody, wearing his deputy's badge, clomped along the board sidewalk, but they weren't wide-eyed over him. Sweeping up the far side of the street were four tall, beautiful women in spike heels and ankle-length fur coats, accompanied by four bulked-up, wavy-haired young men in furs that were, if anything, fancier. Peabody had no idea who they were, but obviously they were *somebody*. All wore dramatic dark sunglasses, the disguise worn by all the stars to (a) be anonymous and (b) make sure everyone noticed them.

A teenage girl with one of the tourist groups squealed, evidently recognizing one of them, and hurried ahead of her group with an autograph book in hand. The celebrities ducked into the little Saks store, leaving her to stop and stand forlorn on the boardwalk, all alone.

Peabody sighed and climbed into his pickup. On the short drive back to the courthouse he saw a small clot of people crowded around the front window of the TCBY frozen yogurt shop. He slowed, rolled down his window, and motioned to a boy of about fourteen standing curbside.

"What's going on?" Peabody asked.

"Merv Griffin is in there!" the boy said excitedly.

"Wow," Peabody said. "Groovy."

He had been on the job for well over an hour now, his first piece of work being to start checking on a handful of untouched missing person reports Johnnie had found in Jim Way's desk. The reports had all been about the same person, a seventeen-year-old runaway named Barbara Gregg whose parents had located as being somewhere near Tenoclock by a postcard sent by the girl to a Texas friend. Peabody didn't think there was much chance of turning anything up, but the postcard—according to one of the reports—had mentioned working in a restaurant. So he had started the laborious process of checking out some of the most likely employers.

So far, his results lived up to his expectations.

Peabody was proud of Johnnie Baker. He hadn't been in the courthouse ten minutes this afternoon when Carl Rieger appeared on the scene, white faced with anger, to tell Johnnie that she couldn't add Peabody to the department staff. Her face tight with anger of her own, Johnnie had informed Rieger that Peabody stayed or they both went. When she began to point out how bad *that* could make the county look, Rieger had backed down with bad grace and slammed out of the office.

Now, Peabody thought, if he could just be of some real help.

In the courthouse basement, he found Jason Ramsey still at the front desk, Hesther Gretsch pounding away at the keyboard of the Intertec, Dean Epperly at a corner desk with a telephone stuck to his ear, and Johnnie coming out of her chair to meet him partway down the length of the room. The chill in the air had caused the county to start the furnaces, and Johnnie had a number of tiny flecks of pipe soot stuck to her forehead. She looked smashing anyhow, he thought. Tight, but neat despite that.

"Any news?" she asked.

Peabody pulled off his coat and started rolling up his sleeves. It was too hot in here now. "I checked all the fancy places, even the budget-busters on Packer. Our missing girl never worked in any of them. Of course, that only leaves about ninety or a hundred cheaper places to try. Don't know why I thought I might get lucky right off. You want I should keep on with that, or what?"

Johnnie inclined her head toward Epperly, who had completed one call and was just punching in another, reading from one of the Yellow Pages. "I've got Dean running the telephone book, top to bottom." Her eyebrows tightened in a frown. "I think it's a lot more important now than it seemed a while ago to find that girl, Butt."

"How come? What's happened?"

"Did I tell you about the car we had towed in from up on the North Mountain road this morning?"

"Don't think so. Why?"

"Well, the driver still hasn't shown up to claim it, which is odd. I had Mr. Ramsey trace the plates. He found it's a rental out of Dallas. He called down there and got the name and other data on the man who rented that car in Richardson—that's a north Dallas suburb—last Tuesday." Johnnie paused and put a warm hand on Peabody's bare forearm. "The man who rented that car was named Gregg—Henderson Gregg."

"Same name as our missing girl? Hell! Wait a minute, let me guess. This Henderson Gregg is her daddy, right? Or her brother, maybe?"

"Daddy," Johnnie said. "Right the first time. I called the

home telephone he gave the rental agency down there. I got Mrs. Gregg. She was all over me like a wet hen—where's her daughter, have I spoken today with her husband, because he didn't call her last night as he was supposed to."

"Uh-oh," Peabody muttered. "I'm beginning to not like this a lot."

Johnnie's frown deepened. "Mom confirmed the stuff we already had in all those memos Jim had never worked on. She says Mr. Gregg finally decided to drive up here himself and try to track daughter Barbara down. He must have arrived the day before yesterday, Wednesday."

"Well, then, where is he now?"

"Butt, that's my question."

Peabody fished for a cigarette. "This is getting a little weird."

"Tell me about it."

"What do you want me to do?"

"I think we'd better stay on the missing girl angle. How about if you split the telephone directory with Dean and we really try to find where she was working."

"Got it," Peabody said.

Johnnie's eyebrows knit with worry. "Do you agree with me that this doesn't feel quite right—first the daughter, now the father?"

Peabody thought about it. "It's just possible that he found her, grabbed her, and is on the way back home with her."

"Is that what you think, Butt?"

"No."

"What *do* you think, then?"

"I don't have the slightest idea."

2:30 P.M.

IT TOOK SEVERAL tries before Johnnie got through to Dave Dickensen's cellular telephone. He said he was just driving back into town from security-checking some of the cabins in Elk Canyon, and could come right over.

Ten minutes later he walked into the office. Wearing one of his familiar, pearl gray gabardine suits, cut western style, he looked every bit the cool, competent, successful security man he always proclaimed himself to be. Johnnie thought he might also look tired and strung-out.

"Thanks for coming by, Dave. I didn't want to talk about this on the radio phone. Too many people with scanners."

Dickensen sat down opposite her, crossed his right knee over the left, and slid his fingertips down the razor crease. "What's up?"

"We've got a missing girl, and now her father evidently is missing here, too."

"Really? I wouldn't know anything about that. Why talk to me about anything like that?"

"Hey, my gosh, take it easy! I'm just looking for some help in gathering information. I want to find out if anyone up around Sky Estates has seen him."

Dickensen's face went stiff. "Not likely. A mouse couldn't get past the Sky Estates security system."

"I'm not suggesting that Mr. Gregg got inside the grounds," Johnnie explained. "But his car was abandoned near the wall, and I just thought that maybe your man at the gate might have seen something."

"We were shorthanded last night and I was on the gate myself. I didn't see or hear anything."

"Damn. It's a long shot, but do you think anybody inside the wall could have seen anything?"

"Brandon Warner was the only resident home last night. I saw him earlier today. He didn't mention anything."

"Well, Dave, would you mind calling him just to make sure?"

"Jesus, Johnnie, I hate to bother him. You know how he is."

"Just a quick call," Johnnie insisted gently. "Just so I can cross him off my list of people who might somehow know something."

"Okay." Dickensen's change of expression was as much grimace as grin. "I'll do it this afternoon. Anything else?"

"Thanks, Dave, I appreciate it!"

It didn't have to mean anything, Dickensen thought, driving back to his own office. But now that they were searching for both the man and the girl, things were more complicated. Warner needed to know.

Dickensen didn't take the extra time to drive to the lot behind DD Security Systems. He angle-parked in front and entered through the customer doors.

"Calls for you," Kit Niles said, waving memo sheets as he hurried past her desk.

Dickensen took the pink slips and carried them back to his office. Oh, great, oh, wonderful. Susan Sarandon's secretary had called, and Miss Sarandon and her party would be landing Sunday afternoon, so please have the house opened and ready for them, with security on site. Mr. Jackson and his party had arrived. Senator Glenn and his party had arrived. Miss Dey's secretary had called to say the estate intercom system had to be repaired today, before the other guests arrived at six. Please call Barry Switzer in Oklahoma City. Please call Clive Cussler in Golden.

It was starting with the climax of the aspen color, Dickensen thought. Then the snowfall would begin, the snow machines would start spewing, the snowpack would build whether nature intended it or not, and *everybody* would be here. As if half of them weren't here already, along with two thousand winter tourists intent on doing precisely what Dickensen's firm was hired to prevent: getting close to the celebrities.

All of that, however, had to wait.

He used his secure personal line to dial Brandon Warner's unlisted number. It rang three times before a deep bass voice answered.

"Hullo?"

"Boris?"

"Yus?"

"Dave Dickensen. Please let me speak to Mr. Warner."

Back came another cavernous monosyllable: "Why?"

Dammit! "It's important, Boris!"

The telephone clattered on a table at the Warner house. Wincing, Dickensen rubbed his ear.

A new voice came on the line: "Halloo?" High pitched, with a thick Slavic accent, it was one of several eccentric disguises Warner used when forced to pick up his telephone. Sometimes he answered in this absurd fake-female voice, other times gutturally, with a thick Italian accent.

"It's me," Dickensen said.

Instantly Warner's normal voice took over. "What is it?"

"We have to talk. In person."

"You've located her?"

"What? Oh. No. Something else. You need to be filled in."

"Dave, I've decided to have some people in this evening as a further demonstration of how everything is hunky-dory around here. Are you sure we have to meet?"

"It will take five minutes. I don't want to talk about it on the phone."

"You're sure this is necessary?"

"Dammit, yes!"

"Four-thirty, then," Warner said, and hung up.

Dickensen stared at all the telephone memos. Sweat dripped off the tip of his nose, wetting the top one.

He carried the slips back to the front desk and handed them back to Kit Niles. "Call Harrington in. And Swiker. Put them on these arrangements. I'll be back later. I've got something I've got to do."

Kit Niles reached for the telephone. Dickensen went back out to his truck. It was colder.

Under a leaden sky, he began cruising Tenoclock's streets, looking for an old compact car, dark green, with a young blonde behind the wheel. What were his chances? One in a million? No matter. He had to try. He didn't know what else to do right now. He hoped his special resource was on the job; inside information was vital at the best of times. Now . . .

4:00 P.M.

Aᴆᴛᴇʀ ᴍᴀᴋɪɴɢ ꜰɪꜰᴛʏ fruitless telephone calls, Butt Peabody decided he needed a break. His left leg slightly gimpy from sitting so long in the same position at his desk, he limped over to Jason Ramsey at the counter.

"I need some coffee that doesn't taste like battery acid," he said. "If Johnnie gets back from Gunnison before I come back, tell her I walked over to the Pick & Shovel for a piece of pie and some real java."

"Might bring me a nice, fat chunk of Mabel's apple crumb if she's got any left," Ramsey replied, reaching for his wallet.

"Pay me if I come back with it." Peabody left.

The clock on the bank corner was just striking four when he reached Mabel's establishment. Except for four local construction workers sitting at the counter, the cafe was devoid of customers at this hour. Peabody bellied up at the far end, and Mabel walked over from her usual station just inside the kitchen doorway.

"Hey, Butt," she said with a crooked grin. "I heard you're among the employed again."

"Hell of a way to get a job," Peabody told her. "How about some coffee, and is that lemon or banana cream under all that meringue over there?"

"Lemon."

"Guess I'll try it. And a piece of apple crumb to take back for Jason Ramsey, if you have any left."

"Are you kidding? That was all gone at twelve-thirty."

"Poor Ramsey."

Mabel poured the coffee, provided a glass of water, and went to the back of the counter area to get the pie. "So what does Johnnie have you doing so far, besides manufacturing cigarette butts?"

"Making phone calls, trying to track down a girl," Butt said.

"Yeah?" Mabel put the pie in front of him.

Peabody dug in. "Yeah. Might as well ask you while I'm here. Save one call. Girl's name is Barbara Gregg. Supposed to be working in a hash joint somewhere in these parts. If you haven't seen or heard of her, maybe her daddy was in here, asking about her, too."

"I don't know anything about her daddy, but you just missed her by one day."

Peabody carefully put down his fork. Sometimes, he thought, you had to step in it before you found it. "She works here? Amazing."

"*Worked* here," Mabel corrected him.

"When did she quit?"

"Didn't quit. I fired her little ass."

"When?"

"This morning."

"She was here this morning?"

"No. That's just the point. For the second straight day, Miss Priss chose to stay home in bed, or do whatever she did all the days she was supposed to be in here for the early shift. So I fired her little buns *in absentia.*"

"Shit. Pardon me. Where does she live?"

"Over on Orchard Avenue. Say, is she wanted for something?"

"Just trying to locate her, Mabel, that's all. Have you got an address on Orchard?"

"No, but Donna lives over at the same rooming house. You want to talk to her?"

"Who's Donna?" Peabody asked, feeling his hopes rise again.

Mabel turned toward the kitchen door. "Hey, Donna! Get in here, please."

A slender, short-haired young woman, probably not yet

twenty, hurried in. She glanced at Peabody, her eyes going to his badge, and went decidedly pale. He found that interesting.

Mabel gestured for her to come over. "Man here is looking for your friend Barbara. Butt Peabody, Donna Smith. Donna, this is Butt. Sit down by the man, Donna. Butt, you've got five minutes of her time. After that she goes off my time clock and onto yours until you give her back to me."

"I'll try to hurry," Peabody promised, forking in some pie to conceal his pleased excitement.

4:40 P.M.

JOHNNIE GOT BACK from Gunnison with a roaring headache. She figured she had just failed in one last attempt to clarify the circumstances surrounding Jim Way's death.

Red Plechton, the longtime district attorney for the Gunnison district, had been sympathetic but unmoved. He knew all about the case, he said. He was satisfied with the examination performed by Tenoclock mortician John Lemptke. "We're overloaded, Johnnie. We don't need any goose chases. Lemptke is satisfied the death was accidental, and that's that. Sorry."

Descending to the basement of the Tenoclock County Court House, she found Butt Peabody waiting to pounce on her. He looked pleased with himself.

"You've found the Gregg girl," Johnnie guessed.

"Well, no. But by brilliant detective work I found where she was working until this morning, when she got fired for not showing up. And I also found a friend of hers."

"Great! Where is she now?"

"Don't know. Don't look at me like that, dammit. We're making progress."

Watching his cigarette smoke curl between them, Johnnie wished she hadn't quit. "Like?"

"Her friend is named Donna Smith. Nice enough little gal. Pretty. I checked her driver's license. She's not a minor like Barbara Gregg was; she's nineteen."

"And she told you . . . ?"

"She's been here awhile, plans to stay permanent. She and Barbara Gregg became pals when Barbara came here this summer. They both live in the same rooming house."

"Could she say where Barbara is now?"

"No. Said she hadn't seen her since sometime yesterday. Said she had been thinking that maybe Barbara had bugged out, gone back home."

"Why," Johnnie asked, "would she get that idea?"

One of Peabody's eyebrows tilted. "Seems like Barbara had told Donna that she was afraid her daddy would come haul her home by the hair of her head if she didn't go back voluntarily. Donna had the impression Barbara expected Daddy to show up around here."

"Have you checked Barbara Gregg's room at the boarding-house yet?"

"Nope, no time yet."

Johnnie thought about it. "I think we ought to go check that out. Is there anything else you learned?"

Peabody frowned, worried. "Just that the Smith girl is holding something back."

"What?"

"I have no idea. But she was lying part of the time. I can tell when someone is lying, and she was. And she's scared, too."

Johnnie looked around the office. "Let's find the rooming house."

"One other thing before you go," Peabody added.

"Yes?"

He walked to the nearest desk and picked up a copy of the *Frontiersman*. "You seen today's special issue? It just came out an hour or so ago."

Johnnie picked it up.

Two stories and three pictures made up the tabloid front page. Under a one-column mug shot of Jim Way was a story about his "accidental death." A larger picture, two columns wide, very murky and dark, showed workers at the death scene; the headline under that one read, "Reporter Barred from Death Scene." The type below had an inserted line keying to an editorial, "People's Right to Know," inside.

The worst was halfway down the page, a wide, shallow photo of Johnnie that she remembered reluctantly posing for almost ten years earlier when she was trying out for the role of a club songstress in a Lorimar production. The swimsuit photo showed her reclining on a pier railing, making goo-goos at the camera; the swimsuit left little to the imagination.

Niles Pennington had gotten a good print job on this one. Under it, his headline read, "Former Pinup Girl Named Sheriff."

Johnnie sank onto the desk chair.

"Nice likeness," Peabody said quietly.

4:55 P.M.

BORIS O'NEAL, STANDING guard outside the living room where Brandon Warner and Dave Dickensen had just started talking, was startled when the hall telephone rang. It seldom rang.

Boris moved ponderously across the hall and picked up the ornate white and gold instrument. "Hullo?"

"I have to speak to Mr. Warner right away, please," a feminine voice said.

"Busy," Boris said, and started to hang up.

The woman's voice shrilled, catching his attention just as the receiver was near the hook. "Boris? Is that you, Boris? I have to talk to him!"

Boris brought the receiver back to his ear. "Who is this?"

"It's Donna. I was there last night. You let us in, remember?"

"Yus," Boris said, fully intent now.

"Boris, nobody knows where Barbara is! Now the sheriff is looking for her! A deputy was at the cafe, asking me questions. I lied, but he said he would want to talk to me again. I don't know what's going on! I have to talk to Mr. Warner!"

"Yus," Boris said. Often he felt confused, but at this moment he saw exactly the nature of the threat and exactly what should be done. "He wants to talk to you, too. Only not now. Not here."

"Why? Why? What do you mean?"

The last pieces of the scheme clicked into place. Boris said slowly, "You know the other North Mountain road? Around the east side?"

"The dirt road? Sure. But—"

"You can't be seen here. He can't come to town. I can drive him out the back road." Boris looked at his Seiko. "Six?"

"Why can't I just talk to him now? Why do we have to meet?"

"He's been worried about you," Boris said. "He . . . wants to give you money."

"Money?" It was only one word, but Donna's voice changed from anxiety to sudden surprise, followed by a quick, crafty greed: "You mean . . . to make sure I keep quiet?"

"Yus. Maybe take nice trip."

"Oh, God. Wow. Yeah . . . I see. Uh . . . but what about Barb? I have to know about Barb!"

"No problem. We can bring her along."

"Jesus, you mean she's still out there?"

"Yus." Boris almost chuckled, something very rare for him. He was being very, very clever, he thought. "Six. Back road. Where the logging road angles off. Nice place. Six. Okay?"

"Okay—yes, I can get there by then. Oh, Boris, I'm so relieved about Barb! Tell her I said hi. And tell Mr. Warner thanks, and I'll see you guys at six, right?"

"Right," Boris rumbled. "Goodbye." He hung up.

Standing at the telephone, he considered what he had told the girl, and what needed to be done to protect Mr. Warner. He knew he had done well, and his plan was the best thing.

He walked to the closed doorway leading to the living room. He could hear the voices of Warner and Dickensen, still in conversation within. Turning, he crossed the hall again to the staircase and went upstairs with silent agility surprising in such a big man.

In his bedroom, he unlocked the steel case hidden inside the desk drawer and took out his .357 Magnum. It was a beautiful weapon, he thought. He liked it. It did good work. He made sure the chambers were fully loaded, and then laid it on the bed while he put on the shoulder holster, slipped his bulky cardigan back on, and holstered the weapon.

He would say he needed to road-test the Jeep, he thought. That was brilliant, too. He was having a very good day.

5:30 P.M.

"SHERIFF," DEPUTY DEAN Epperly called across the room from the front counter, "it's for you."

Just back from a search of Barbara Gregg's deserted room, Johnnie half expected more bad news. She and Butt had not found anything helpful in their search. Barbara Gregg had lived a Spartan, if messy, existence, one of the wanderers who could put everything they owned in one small bag and be gone from anywhere within minutes. The room looked like she had planned to return to it. But she hadn't.

She picked up the telephone. "This is Johnnie Baker."

"Sheriff Baker?" a deep, resonant voice intoned. "Permit me this introduction by telephone. This is Brandon Warner speaking."

Surprised, Johnnie recognized the voice now. "What can I do for you, Mr. Warner?"

"Mr. Dickensen from the security firm called to say you thought I might have seen or heard something that would provide a lead on some missing person—a man who abandoned a car, I believe?"

"That's right," Johnnie said, amazed that he would call back personally. "I know it's a long shot," she added, "but we try to check everything."

"Most commendable, I'm sure. Unfortunately, I can be of no help whatsoever. I was alone here last night, except for my associate Mr. O'Neal, who retired early. The household staff left immediately after an early dinner. I stayed up until almost midnight, studying some script proposals. After that I had a brandy—a solitary nightcap—and also retired for the night. I saw and heard nothing."

Johnnie wasn't surprised. "Well, as I said, it was a long shot."

"Sheriff, will you permit me a suggestion? As you know, many of my friends from both coasts have arrived in the past few days. I've invited a few of them in for drinks this evening about eight. It's conceivable that one of them might have seen or heard something—many of them live in this general area. Why don't you come to the party, too? I'm sure everyone would like to meet Tenoclock County's new sheriff, and you can ask questions."

Johnnie hesitated. Going to a party tonight was the last thing her tired body needed. But it was worth a try. "Thanks. I'd like that."

"Excellent! We'll expect you, then. Good day!" The connection broke.

Johnnie thought about it for a minute or two, then punched in another number.

"Gallery," Luke Cobb's voice answered.

"Would you like to take a lady to a party for an hour or so this evening?"

6:25 P.M.

TIRED BUT EXCITED, Donna Smith drove carefully up the twisting dirt road around the east side of North Mountain. The sky overhead had turned to solid lead, and a few bitter snowflakes dusted the windshield of her car.

Boris had not been telling her the whole truth, she thought. *Something* had happened last night. Something bad.

But Barbara was all right, she thought. That was great news. Brandon Warner had probably already paid her off to keep quiet about whatever had taken place, and now it was Donna's turn. She loved it! Her greedy little heart sang. No more slinging hash at places like the Pick & Shovel after tonight. She had finally scored!

As the narrow dirt roadway made its final outside curve before the logging road cutoff, the wooded slopes on Donna's left fell off more sharply, providing a fifty-mile view out over the farthest northeast reaches of the Tenoclock Valley and the Alvina Mountain Range far beyond. The Alvinas were almost invisible through the snowy clouds, but she knew it probably wasn't snowing a flake at the lower elevation of the valley floor.

Donna felt a surge of something almost like nostalgia for the pretty valley.

Oh, she had heard the old folks complain about the traffic, all the strangers, the hustle and bustle, how it would never again be like it had been only a few years ago, before the new highway opened the area, and the town and county got together on what some diehards still griped were illegal self-liquidating bonds for the airport and the first big ski lift. Those were all technicalities as far as Donna was concerned, and she didn't care about technicalities. The reality for her was that Tenoclock now was *rich*, really rich. She loved the crowds, the big tips, seeing some of the famous stars sometimes as they breezed through town. Why, even Kevin

Costner had come to visit, and everyone knew how committed he was to his ranch near Jackson Hole. Donna herself had seen a lot of other stars, too. She had even been close enough to former President Ford last winter that she could have almost reached out and touched his arm as he went by.

It was beautiful country. Tenoclock, with its frontier-architecture ordinances, had been blasted by someone in *Time* as being "about as authentic as an old Gene Autry movie—and less appealing." But Donna thought it was cute. As far as she was concerned, there hadn't been a serious mistake made about Tenoclock since its naming.

There were three stories about how it got its funny name, and none of them sounded quite true. But the one most people tended to believe was that, in the very early days before the silver rush, a party of prospectors had arrived near the present townsite—there was a brass historical marker to indicate the alleged exact spot—but when the prospectors arrived, they found two other silver seekers camped out ahead of them.

"Who are you men?" the leader of the newly arrived band is supposed to have said.

"Mining for silver," said the older of the two already on the scene. For he was almost totally deaf.

"What's the name of this place?" the new prospector asked.

Misunderstanding again, the older man pulled out a pocket watched, popped open its cover, and said, "Ten o'clock."

Donna thought that story was cute, too, accurate or not.

She drove slowly up the logging road, being careful to avoid the worst mudholes, some of which looked bottomless. Heavier snow dusted her windshield. She worried that she might break something in her car, or the weak battery might fail or something. But then the happy thought came that after this meeting she would have money—lots and lots of money, if her guesswork was right—and she could buy a new car, right after she went by the Pick & Shovel and told Mabel

Murnan where she could cram her crummy job.

The closer she got to the meeting place, the more excited Donna became, thinking about the money. It had scared her for just a second there at first, having to meet way up here. But then she had realized that people like Brandon Warner couldn't just meet her in some public place. Meeting out here seemed a little strange, but you paid your money and you took your choice, and she already was well aware, God knew, of how strange Mr. Brandon Warner could be.

It was just like Phyllis had told her this afternoon, when she was so shook up. Maybe something weird had happened last night, but it was probably more embarrassing than anything else. Nothing *really* bad could have happened, or someone would have known about it by now.

Phyllis was so smart. Donna just loved her. But even Phyllis would never know about this trip. Nobody was going to share in this good luck, ever. Donna would wait awhile, and then just say an old aunt had left her a pile of money. Who would ever know otherwise?

The logging road got worse, pitching the car up and down as Donna inched along. Despite the down-sifting snow, she noticed that the aspen up here were really gorgeous. Maybe in a day or two she would come back, if the cold didn't turn them too fast. In her new car. With a great camera, and take pictures. Maybe some of them would turn out good enough to frame and hang in the new house she was going to buy. Of course, she would wait awhile for the house, so as to not make herself and her new wealth conspicuous.

The meeting place was just ahead now. Donna could make out the tracks Mr. Warner's vehicle had made in the newly fallen light snow. She was so anxious to get there. She hoped Barb had decided to come.

Donna's fears had vanished. She hummed to herself, happy, and up ahead, standing beneath the snowy golden trees, Boris waited.

8:25 P.M.

Bone-tired, Johnnie drove up to the floodlit gates of Sky Estates. A man of about forty, wearing the blue-gray uniform of DD Security Systems, came smartly out of the guard shack and through a narrow personnel opening in the fencing.

Clipboard in hand, he peered in through the side window of the Jeep. "Yes, ma'am?"

"Johnnie Baker, for Brandon Warner's house."

The guard glanced down a list of names on the top page of the clipboard. "Yes, ma'am. One moment, please." He turned and went back into the shack. The heavy iron gates started to open.

Beside Johnnie, Luke Cobb made a clucking sound. "Wait till I get this rich."

Johnnie pulled through the gate opening. "Will you move out here?"

"Sure. And lock you inside, and never let you out of my sight again."

Beyond the floodlight glare, the Jeep's headlights shone on a narrow gravel roadway curving through aspen and ponderosa pines. The ground was dusted lightly by the earlier brief snow. The Jeep's tires chuttered on the gravel through two sharp bends. A large redwood home, well lighted, could be seen briefly off to the left. Another's lights shone distantly through the trees to the right. The brightest lights came into view directly ahead. Past another curve in the roadway, the wide, soaring wings of Brandon Warner's house came into view. Seven or eight other cars were parked around the circular driveway.

"I don't know what we're doing this for," Luke muttered.

Johnnie slowed the Jeep, looking for the best place to park. "Maybe somebody will know something."

"Why can't you believe that this man Gregg had car trouble and just wandered off on his own, and is probably still lost out in the woods someplace?"

"All I know is that our mechanics say that car is in perfect running order. It wasn't abandoned because of a breakdown." Johnnie found a spot halfway around the big paved circle, nosed the Jeep into it, and turned off the headlights. She reached for the microphone clipped to the instrument panel. "Hang on a minute." She pressed the red button. "Sheriff's unit one to base."

The radio was silent.

Johnnie repeated, "Sheriff's unit one." Again: only silence.

Johnnie backed off the squelch control. The radio refused to hiss at her, as it should. It was dead again.

"You need to get that fixed."

"It's intermittent, and just like a bad tooth, it never messes up when I take it into the shop. I guess what I'll do, first chance I get, is just have them yank the unit out of Jim's Bronco and change it over into mine. Damn, everything is a problem."

"For a lady about to go mix with the rich and famous, and even wearing that cute leather skirt, you're sure cranky."

"Lack of sleep does that to me. Then I was supposed to go see that girl Butt located, Donna Smith. She stood me up. It hasn't been my best day."

The door chimes were answered promptly by a giant of a man wearing a rumpled black suit, white shirt, and dark blue tie. Johnnie had seen him before, of course, but the suit only made Boris look more bizarre and menacing, somehow. She thought momentarily of the character with the metal teeth in one of the 007 films.

They went inside. Music—Mozart—issued from a powerful stereo system somewhere, softly filling the immense entryway. Mixed cedar and stone, it soared to a skylight three stories above. Several doorways opened off the area, and bright contemporary artworks brightened the walls. A glass table-cabinet, internally lighted, stood at the left. It contained a surprising collection of simple pieces: Hummels, Lladros, crystal glassware. Dominating everything, a curving

contemporary staircase, glass and white tiles, led to a
second-floor balcony.

Boris took their coats. He raised a thick arm to point
toward the wide double doorways to their right. "There." He
added, "Please."

"Just what I like," Luke muttered. "A nice little fishing
cabin in the Rockies."

"Behave yourself." Johnnie started toward the double
doorway.

Brandon Warner, thin dark hair wetly glued back, a drink
and holder-fitted cigarette clutched in one hand, met them
as they reached the doors. In his maroon smoking jacket he
reminded Johnnie of a role he had played in one of the
remakes of *The Great Gatsby*. He was older now, thick
around the waist, with thinning hair and fatty lines that
made his facial muscles sag.

He seemed genuinely pleased to see them. "And who could
this be but our new sheriff!" He bent to brush his lips over
her fingers. "Let me say I was mortified to see that cheap-
shot photo in today's newspaper, Johnnie." He looked at
Luke. "And you would be . . . ?"

Johnnie made introductions. "Of course!" Warner cried,
pumping Luke's hand. "This is an honor, sir. I have several
of your pieces here. Over there—you see the urn on the
mantel? And I have several more at my home in California,
of course. Come in! Come in, both of you!"

The next few minutes were total confusion for Johnnie,
and she felt dumb for feeling a slight rush of excitement. The
first person she and Luke met was Richard Crenna, who
seemed very nice, and while still talking to him and his lady,
Johnnie recognized Bruce Willis on the far side of the room.
Nearby, listening politely to Mayor Copely, were a handsome
man Johnnie didn't recognize and a woman she definitely
did: Mel Harris. Madison Blithe came over to say a few words
and introduce his latest wife, a striking redhead who seemed
a bit awed by it all. Dave Dickensen, looking drawn and
tired, came over to say hello. Janis Varner, a television actress

Johnnie had worked with once, waved and hurried over to hug and kiss and make eyes at Luke. Novelist Jackie Collins smiled and didn't recognize Johnnie after the several intervening years.

"Good God," Johnnie murmured to Luke. "Are all his parties like this?"

"I don't think he has many, and *I* damn sure have never been to one before."

A handful of additional guests arrived. Two waiters circulated with trays of champagne. Another pair of young men served behind a bar at the back of the room. Luke went off to get a scotch, and was waylaid by the mayor. Jackie Collins appeared at Johnnie's side and apologized for forgetting her earlier.

"Isn't this place beautiful?" she asked Johnnie. "I've wanted to see it for ages."

"It's your first visit, too?"

"I imagine it's a first for virtually everyone here, dear. I doubt that few, otherwise, would have accepted such a last-minute invitation."

Johnnie mentally filed the remark. It suddenly struck her as odd: Brandon Warner had come to Tenoclock this morning, a highly uncharacteristic act. Now this equally uncharacteristic party, set up on short notice. She wondered if that meant anything, but immediately her self-critical irony created short circuits. That's it, try to be like Miss Marple, you jerk.

A half hour passed. Luke was looking twitchy, and Johnnie's legs were about gone. She edged out of the main room, looking for the bathroom.

The entry foyer lay deserted, not even a sign of the hulking Boris. Seeing no rest room door, Johnnie went up the staircase without giving it a second thought.

Reaching the balcony, she realized she must have made a mistake. The balcony led into a wide hallway that seemed to extend all the way to the back of the house. Lights along the art-studded walls were dim. This was obviously a private area, unintended for inspection by guests.

Well, there still might be a handy bathroom. Heels silenced by the thick gray carpeting, she walked to the first closed doorway on the right. Testing the knob, she found it locked. The second door was the same, and the third, on the other side, likewise.

At the far end of the hall she tested another door and found it ajar. Looking inside, she saw that the bedroom beyond was brightly lighted. Long and wide, with a high-beamed ceiling, it had heavy dark furniture and an oversized canopy bed at the far end. Brandon Warner's room.

Johnnie stepped inside. To her right was a wall of mirrors. It had a door in it. You've gone this far; you might as well be totally nosy. She tried the door. It swung open onto a long, very narrow closetlike room. Inside, facing the glass wall, were three video cameras on tripods, along with other recording gear on shelves. Slender cables snaked along the floor.

Amazed, Johnnie examined the glass wall between the equipment and the bedroom. It was one-way glass.

The sound of a burst of laughter from downstairs brought her back to the moment. Hurrying out of the bedroom, she fled down the hallway to the staircase and down the stairs. As she crossed the foyer, she spied another female guest coming out of the area behind the stairs, went in that direction, and found the bathroom at last. She felt breathless and tense—and thoroughly fascinated. It was going to take a while to sort out the things she had just learned about Mr. Brandon Warner.

$\triangledown$

Friday, September 28

THE EARLY-MORNING breakfast crowd, mostly construction workers and truck drivers, filled the Pick & Shovel Cafe
when Johnnie walked in on Friday. She went to the end of
the counter by the doors to the kitchen and waited for Mabel
to show up; less than thirty seconds later she did, hustling
out grimly with one of her magic tricks: five platters of steak
and eggs at one time, no tray.

"Mabel?"

"Hi, Johnnie. Hold on."

Johnnie waited. Mabel delivered the breakfasts to a large
booth of truckers, then hustled back, frowning.

"I need to talk to—" Johnnie began.

"One sec." Mabel grabbed a fresh pot of coffee and hurried
around the room, doling out refills. When she came back,
the glass container was almost empty again. Juggling pots
and containers, she started a fresh brew. Maybe I ought to
have a job like hers, Johnnie thought suddenly. God, it would
be so neat not to feel like you had to be a lot smarter—like
everybody expected you to be a dumb, complacent decora-
tion, and if you didn't fool them all by doing something right
for a change, missing people would never get found and
mystery deaths would never get straightened out . . . and you
would never stop wondering if you could cut the mustard at
anything.

Mabel finally finished with the coffeemakers and came to
the end of the counter. "What's up, Johnnie?"

"Donna stood me up last night. I want to talk to her."
Mabel screwed up her face. "Not here, you won't."
"What do you mean?"
"She hasn't shown up for work. Again! Hasn't even called in yet with one of her flimsy excuses! I've had it with her. She's outta here."
"She didn't call in sick or anything?"
"Hell no!"
Johnnie slid off the stool. "Thanks, Mabel. I'll go try to find her."
"If you do, tell her to come and pick up her last check!"
Outside, Johnnie sat in her Jeep for a few seconds, thinking. The sun was up over the slope of the mountains, and today's sky was cloudless and sharply colder. The chill air smelled crisp and fresh. The brief cold snap would fade later today, according to the good time boy on KTCK, and the temperature would near sixty by late afternoon. A good day to get the radio switched in the Jeep, Johnnie thought. But first things first: Donna Smith.
The manager didn't seem surprised to see her again. He walked with her up the stairs to the Smith room, where loud rapping on the door brought no response. A master key unlocked the door.
Inside, fully opened draperies let sunlight into a drab room that was a carbon copy of Barbara Gregg's just down the hall. The bed was neatly made, and a clean ashtray gleamed on the nightstand.
"She sure wasn't here last night, Johnnie."
"Couldn't she have gotten out early?"
"Are you kidding me? The maid service comes in on Thursday. They're instructed to leave the drapes open like that. Fresh towels and linen, and cleanup. Donna never made a bed in her life. She was a slob, and she smoked like a furnace. Made-up bed, clean ashtray, open drapes. Nope. She didn't sleep here last night."
Johnnie walked farther into the room, taking a quick look in all directions. A small desk stood against the outside wall

beside the window. On a corner of it, a framed snapshot showed a middle-aged couple standing in front of a mountain vista. Parents, almost surely. A handful of letters and a couple of unopened bills lay on the writing surface, and beside the telephone was a cheap plastic telephone number index device.

The room had a gaunt, unlived-in ambience about it. Johnnie was struck by how chill and impersonal it was, just like Barbara Gregg's room had been when she and Butt checked it. People like this came and moved into a place but put no mark on it, as if giving a room any personal touch might tie them down. Drifters.

Johnnie noticed a small, flip-open telephone booklet on the dresser. She edged closer to it. "What kind of car does Donna drive?"

The manager thought a moment. "Old dark green Mustang. Burns oil like mad. Every time she pulls in the lot, it smells like a diesel just went by."

"Is that her car I can see there out the window?"

Frowning, he moved to the window and peered out. Johnnie took the opportunity to pick up the small telephone directory and slip it into her hip pocket.

"I don't see the car you mean."

"I must have been mistaken. A green Mustang, you said? I'll keep an eye out for it. When Donna comes back, please tell her to get in touch with me immediately. And give me a call to let me know she's back, okay?"

Back in the parking lot, Johnnie looked for an old, dark green Mustang. There wasn't one.

Slipping the cheap metal telephone directory out of her pocket, she riffled through the tabbed pages. It contained precious few numbers, and even fewer with Tenoclock prefixes. Johnnie started the Jeep and backed out. She would call all of the local numbers. She hoped she was not being melodramatic, but her intuition about Donna Smith—now also suddenly among the missing—did not make her feel good at all.

* * *

Returning to the courthouse, she went down to the basement offices. Jason Ramsey was all alone at the front counter.

"Morning, Mr. Ramsey. No sign of Butt yet?"

"He called on the radio a minute ago, said he's on the way in."

"Okay, good. Any important messages?"

Ramsey's dark face showed nothing. "Well, Commissioner Blithe was in early, more than an hour ago. He said he was leaving you a list of how the big funeral will be handled tomorrow."

"Okay." Johnnie studied his face. "Why are you looking at me like that?"

"Did you know they want all the sheriff's units in the procession from the church to the cemetery? Everybody in uniform, with black armbands? He left the armbands."

"Goddammit," Johnnie exploded, "they're going to make a Roman circus out of poor Jim's funeral!"

"Guess so." Ramsey still showed nothing. "I hear the police are going to have all the side streets blocked, and the high school band is going to march in front of the coffin from the funeral home to the church."

"What are they going to play? " 'Dixie'? Damn! This town's got all the class of a . . . of a . . ."

"Miz Gretsch called in to say she'd be a little late. Overslept."

Sometimes Johnnie wondered why Hesther kept the job. She made no secret of the fact that she hated it. She was an expert at being glum and dissatisfied. "What else?"

"Memo here from Deputy Epperly, might make you feel better."

Johnnie took the report form. Making calls to local motels in an attempt to trace the missing Henderson Gregg, Epperly had scored. Joe Roczini, the manager of the Days Inn on 16 North, said a man named Gregg had registered late Tuesday, saying he would stay two nights, but hadn't slept in the bed since that night. Roczini asked if Mr. Gregg had had an accident or something.

"Or something," Johnnie said grimly. "Mr. Ramsey, get Butt on the radio. Ask him to stop at the Days Inn on the way here and check out the room this man Gregg slept in one night."

Ramsey nodded and turned to the microphone.

"I'm going out and getting that stupid radio switched in the Jeep," Johnnie added. "I'll be right back."

Ramsey nodded and leaned over the desk microphone. "Sheriff's unit four, this is headquarters."

Johnnie headed for the door and went out back. In the rear garage area she found Jack Kalman, the county's vehicle maintenance supervisor, scratching his head over the engine of one of the big county road trucks.

"Jack, can I get the radio out of Jim's Bronco into my Jeep?"

Kalman spat disgustedly. "Can't right now, Johnnie. We have to get this son of a—this gravel truck cooled off and back on the road, if we can. We might be able to do it in an hour or two."

"No problem," Johnnie said resignedly, and strolled back out to where her Jeep and the Bronco, as yet unclaimed by Mrs. Way, sat side by side.

Walking around the dead sheriff's truck, she noticed for the first time how filthy muddy it was. She wondered where in the world he had been to pick up so much mud. The Bronco had been Jim Way's best-loved toy; she could recall countless afternoons when he had been found out in the lot washing it, when he should have been working on cases. She remembered, too, that it had been spotless as late as noon Wednesday. It wasn't like Jim to drive places that would get it this nasty, unless he absolutely had to.

Nasty mud, she thought, walking around it again. Silvery gray gumbo around the wheel wells and in the tire treads and wire wheel covers. She seldom paid attention to such things, but even she could see how Jim would have thought this was a little gross.

Then she realized how uncharacteristic of Tenoclock County this kind of mud was.

She stopped dead in her tracks, skin tingling, suddenly seeing what she had earlier missed. How could she have been so stupid?

Walking fast to her Jeep, she jumped in, started it, and backed out. Pulling into traffic on Court Street, she grabbed the microphone. "Sheriff's unit one to base."

Nothing happened.

Well, to hell with it. It wouldn't take long to drive out there and see what she could see, if anything. She wasn't about to waste time going around the block. Too much time had been wasted already.

8:40 A.M.

BUTT PEABODY HAD to slow his pickup at the corner of Stinson and Orchard because some celebrity couple had just left their rented Lexus and were being mobbed by a crowd large enough to spill into the street. The pair—dark sunglasses, fur coats, identical blond hairdos—seemed to be signing autographs. One of Tenoclock's finest could be seen hustling up Stinson from his squad car, intent on liberating them.

Peabody sighed. He hated being one of the dinosaurs who couldn't shake the feeling that Tenoclock would never again be as nice as it had been when the population starting about now every year shrank below three hundred. But facts were facts, and he yearned for the old days. Incidents like Wednesday night would never have happened then.

Don't get morbid, he lectured himself. Get with the program instead.

Spying the Days Inn sign ahead on the left, he reviewed

what little was known about the missing Mr. Henderson Gregg. It wasn't much, and certainly didn't give any hint about where Gregg might have vanished to. Maybe the Tenoclock High Climbers, along with some people from REACT and part of a local Boy Scout troop, would find something when they started walking the area at nine o'clock. If they found Gregg out there, it was not likely to be a pretty scene. The temperature had gone below freezing the past two nights. A city-type man out in the elements over that period was not likely to be found alive.

Peabody thought of Johnnie, and hoped fervently that *something* would break for her soon. He would be glad, he thought, when Jim Way was safely in the ground and she didn't worry about that anymore. Maybe things would calm down, and there wouldn't be any more cheap shots like the old pinup picture in the current issue of the paper.

Peabody felt the dull ache in his chest whenever he thought about Johnnie Baker. He wondered when he had stopped loving her as a child and started secretly loving her in the way a man loves a woman. He didn't think she had ever given him a second thought, but that didn't help dampen his feelings any. All he wanted to do was shelter her, take care of her, yet give her all the freedom she needed, the way you would any splendid wild thing.

It didn't seem like much to want. But he knew it would never be. She had Luke Cobb, and Luke was a younger, handsomer, more glamorous gent. Peabody's job right now, emotionally, was to accept that, because a man's primary obligation to a woman he loved was to see to her happiness, whatever that took.

He knew that was kind of dumb, old-fashioned, and probably chauvinistic thinking, but he was a hopelessly old-fashioned person: He believed in men looking after their women, worrying about their well-being, wanting to take care of them, protecting them from as many bumps as possible, and above all else respecting them and the things they held dear. He also believed in hard work, paying your bills on time, keeping your property in good condition, setting aside a little time each day for some fun, keeping promises, honesty, the flag, cleaning up your tools after a day's work, and if you ever borrowed a tool or something of that nature, returning it promptly in at least as good condition as when it had been borrowed.

Peabody also believed in not talking about most of these things because you sounded like some kind of weirdo when you did. He was somewhat relieved to pull into the Days Inn lot so he could stop thinking about the whole business.

Inside, Joe Roczini, the manager, was waiting behind the desk.

"He in trouble, Butt?" Roczini asked, showing the signed registration card.

"Dunno." The card provided no new information. "He might be—might be lost out in the woods someplace."

"Oh, hell! I suppose you'd like to look at his room and stuff?"

"I don't have a warrant."

"Oh, fuck that. I know you can get one in fifteen minutes." Roczini produced a heavy bronze key with a room number on it. "Around the side, with a view toward Red Mountain. You want me to go with you?"

"No need. Come if you want."

Roczini didn't want. Peabody went back outside and walked around the north side of the complex to reach the designated room. Climbing the steel stairs to the second level of the building, he walked along the back railing until he came to 218. From old habit learned the hard way, he knocked loudly, waited a full thirty seconds, and then knocked a second time before using the key. Once, years ago up in Montrose, he had eager-beavered through a locked door without making sure no one was home, and he still had some chunks of the bullet in his shoulder and chest. The bullet had hit something in there and shattered into many pieces, not all of them easy or necessary, the doctors thought, to dig out. Every once in a while, a tiny fragment still worked its way to the surface of Peabody's skin and began to hurt, and then he could gently squeeze the spot, almost like a blackhead, and out would pop another tiny, gritty-gray reminder of his youthful exuberance.

The motel room swung open now on a dark room. Peabody snaked a hand around the corner and found the light switch before entering.

The overhead room light showed your classic medium-class motel room: big bed with a dark red cover on it, a dresser, a couple of cheap plastic chairs flanking a cheap plastic table, a color TV bolted down so you couldn't carry it to your car next morning and drive off with it by mistake, an alcove with a mirror and wash counter and basin, and a door into the toilet and tub. Peabody moved into the room, shot the drapery cord full open, then crossed quickly to check out the john.

Okay, he was alone in here. So look around.

There was little to look at, beyond the grand view through the opened drapes. The cold snap had turned the aspen golden another thousand feet down the slopes, and today's sun made them blaze and seem to move with a transparency of vivid color no one had ever truly captured on film. But inside the room it was decidedly less interesting.

Gregg had left a few toilet articles in his leather kit beside the sink: razor, toothbrush, toothpaste, dental floss, etc. That settled any lingering thought that Gregg might have planned to stay out overnight or longer. Men who carried and used dental floss did not go off overnight without it, without even their toothbrush. Also, Gregg was a meticulous man, careful about personal hygiene and his appearance, at least under ordinary circumstances. You could begin to put together this kind of picture of a man and his habits by looking at his shaving kit, what he carried, how it was arranged. Neat, meticulous, almost picky.

No clothes hung in the open closet area. Peabody went to the suitcase, resting with its lid loosely closed on the suitcase holder beside the bolted-down TV. He raised the soft cover and looked carefully through the contents.

Except for telling him that Mr. Gregg hid spare cash—in this case, $450 in the lining of his bag where presumably no thief would ever look but where in fact every thief looked either first or second—examination of the bag told Peabody little. Gregg was a man of slight to medium build: 14½ collar on a dress shirt; pants with thirty-three-inch waist and what looked like about a thirty-one-inch inseam; nylon windbreaker, medium; extra shoes, 8-C. He liked to save a buck when he could, witness the jar of instant coffee, plastic bag of sweetener, and plug-in, one-mug heating coil. And Gregg had not come here for fun—no sign of camera, tourist brochures, film, or even a town map.

Beginning to feel disappointed, Peabody walked over to the dresser where the telephone sat. The motel brochures and other advertising had been neatly arranged by the maid. On top of the thin stack was a motel notepad with a motel ballpoint beside it. The first two or three pages of the pad had doodles and telephone numbers, and a couple of names, block printed all over them, some crosshatched, some encircled repeatedly, some windowpaned. Some had been run over and over so often, and with such ferocity, that the ballpoint had cut through to the sheet below. Angry doodles, the work of an angry, frustrated man.

Peabody studied the names and numbers. This, he thought, was extremely interesting.

Putting the entire motel notepad into his inside coat pocket, he closed the draperies again, turned out the lights, locked up, and returned the key to the front desk.

"Any luck?" Joe Roczini asked, arching dark eyebrows.

"Nope," Peabody lied. "No sweat, though. He'll probably turn up. Just routine, you know how it is."

"Take care, Butt! Glad to see you back in the saddle!"

"Hi-o Silver," Peabody muttered, and walked out, careful to slouch and go slow so no one could guess that he might have just found something extremely important.

9:15 A.M.

JOHNNIE DROVE CAREFULLY on the crumbling curves of the backcountry mining road off old Colorado 16. Jim Way had often returned to town via this route after "showing the flag" and having his nightly, solitary tipple, but she had never understood why. The road was downright treacherous.

It was not far now, however, to the abandoned Interocean mine property.

What she had finally realized, walking around Jim Way's Bronco, was that the silvery clay mud all over its lower sections could have come only from near the old mine.

Way's Bronco could not have picked up so much of the stuff on the highway, bad as it was. The pale clay all over his vehicle was old mining fill, not found on the roadway, having been gouged out of the mine decades ago and simply allowed to pile up where it was dumped or be washed away in the river, as tortured Mother Nature saw fit. The lower working level of the mine property near river level was covered with the stuff. That was where Big Jim had to have driven to pick up so much of it.

Even old-timers around Tenoclock might not have realized this. The color of the clay would have meant nothing to them. But Johnnie's ranch—site of her childhood home— was less than five miles northeast of here. She had gotten her bottom tanned once for hiking down to the old mine site, climbing through the security fence and having the delicious thrill of forbidden exploration of the grounds. When she had gotten home late that afternoon, the telltale clay on her shoes had given away her secret to her father. "That stuff exists nowhere else in the county!" Dad had said, whacking her with a thin yardstick that hurt her pride far more than her bottom. She had never forgotten. After that, on other clandestine explorations at the site, she had cleaned her shoes very carefully before venturing home.

But why had Jim left the road and driven down to river

level at the mine site? Had he pulled down the claybank entrance drive to have a last nightly nip before going on home? Or could he have been checking something down there, or meeting someone?

Johnnie didn't know. Maybe this was another trip to disappointment. But she intended to find out, and if she was being silly, playing Miss Marple again, no one knew she was coming out here and she didn't have to mention it to a soul when she got back to the courthouse.

The road ran alongside and slightly above the rushing Rock River now, pale foam bursting over boulders in the stream's hurry to join the Sacramento a few miles farther down. Firs and aspen dominated the hillsides, with a few gray-bearded old ponderosas hanging on as the last survivors of the big forest fire of 1951. Johnnie's father had talked often about that one, of helping fight it. Her mother had spoken of it, too, but in a far different tone; her younger brother had died when a flashover trapped and killed the small crew of which he had been a part.

Johnnie did not think she would ever completely get over the nagging feeling that she had come back to Tenoclock a failure and something of a fool for having tried, for having actually thought she was good enough to make it in the big-time entertainment business.

The commissioners had named her interim sheriff as a publicity stunt, a bad joke, thinking she would be decorative and not make waves. Unless she could find these missing people and also satisfy herself about Jim's death, that was always going to eat at her, too.

The old mine property lay just ahead and to her left, along a broader, erosion-wrecked section of the Rock River. First the miners had dredged it, using steam equipment in a search for gold. That had left the river widened, filled with great boulder-strewn piles of dug earth and sediment. Then, with the silver strike, they had simply brought out the ore-bearing rock from far beneath the surface and dumped it and the telltale white clay everywhere. That had been a century or more ago. But the mine property and the ground all around it still looked raped and dead, barren except for clutters of weeds and small brush that could somehow find sustenance in the litter of pebbles and sterile subsurface dirt.

It had all been abandoned for a long time now. The engine building, the conveyor structure, the separator sheds, the big crusher building, and other smaller frame buildings had long since lost the last of their paint, if they had ever had any. Wooden structures leaned this way and that, gray from the weather, missing planks letting sunlight through. Everything looked like it might tumble down at any moment. High, well-maintained steel mesh fencing surrounded the area, and signs flashed past Johnnie's window like the old Burma Shave signs as she slowed for the driveway ahead. All of them said it was private property, very dangerous, keep out, violators would be prosecuted. The owners were doing their best to avoid possible lawsuits that would inevitably follow if someone wandered in and got badly hurt, or worse, as had happened several times in years past. The stout fence and all the signs seemed to have done the trick, however: There hadn't been a party of would-be spelunkers lost for several years now.

Johnnie reached the sharply downsloping clay and gravel driveway that led into the property, and turned in. She saw that the double chain gate was up across the entry halfway down. She coasted slowly that far, then set the parking brake and hopped out.

The big padlocks on both heavy chains hung open. Their rusty sides showed multiple bright dents where somebody had hammered on them—or shot them—to break them open.

Frowning, Johnnie looked at the roadway down below the chains. She could make out several recent sets of tire tracks.

Her curiosity intensifying, she lifted the broken padlocks out of their hasps, letting the chains that barred the entrance fall to the ground. Walking back to the Jeep, she noticed that it had already begun to pick up the unique grayish clay on its tires. She had some on her boots, too, as she got back inside the vehicle, released the parking brake, and coasted downhill. At the bottom she pulled around to the far side of one of the old equipment sheds to let the sun warm the Jeep while she was away from it.

The bubbling roar of the river filled her hearing as she stepped out again, this time into wetter, slipperier clay. Examining the ground, she picked up the tire tracks again: at least two sets, one a double diamond tread pattern and the other a more conventional stud tread like Jim Way had on his Bronco. There were footprints all over the place, too, two or three different sets.

Widening the circle of her examination, she saw that the footprints *didn't go anywhere*. She stopped, surprised. People had milled around this immediate area, then just gotten back into their trucks and gone away? That didn't make much sense. Bending at the waist, she moved around the circle of footprints in a widening arc, carefully examining the ground. Then she saw the regular, minute series of thin lines in the moist clay. They looked a lot like a concrete sidewalk looked after it was partly hardened, then given a final broom brushing to give the surface a slightly textured finish for better foot traction.

Johnnie knelt on one knee, feeling the cold wet instantly go through to the skin. The tiny, multiple brush marks had also been made with a broom, or something resembling one. Somebody had quite carefully obliterated tracks. The area had been swept—literally.

She walked a wider circle, approaching the rotten board tunnel that extended out of the hillside from the mine entrance itself. A big black and white sign adorned the heavy planks nailed across the entrance, warning of unsafe supports and dropholes inside the abandoned mine. The owners had used 2 x 8s for the latest boarding up several years earlier, after some college kids out for adventure had decided to explore the shaft and ended up almost dying before rescuers could locate them three days later.

Johnnie examined the planks sealing off the shaft. The wood had darkened with age, but still appeared stout. Weather had roughened the wood surfaces so that they were splintered and soggy from constant drip of rain or snow.

She was about to turn away when she noticed the brighter look of some of the splintered areas along the left and right edges of the tunnel opening. Here and there, the dark-weathered boards showed fresh wood chunks, where splinters had been broken loose very recently. Stooping closer, Johnnie realized that the splinters had been broken out around the heads of the spikes used to fasten them in place.

Somebody had pried some of the thick old boards loose very, very recently.

Johnnie took hold of one of the slanted cross members and tugged at it. It gave a fraction of an inch, but stuck.

She thought about it.

Then she turned and hurried back to the Jeep, where she had a prybar under the seat.

9:30 A.M.

DAVE DICKENSEN LOOKED worried coming out of his office at DD Security Systems to meet him at the front desk, Butt Peabody thought.

"Morning, Dave! Beautiful morning, isn't it?"

Dickensen looked puffy eyed, like a man who was losing too much sleep. "What do you want?"

"Dave, old pal, what can you tell me about a young lady named Donna Smith?"

Dickensen's expression went totally blank. "Who?"

Well, that torpedo hadn't hit the mark. Peabody reached for his cigarettes. "Lady named Donna Smith. Friend of our missing young woman, Barbara Gregg. Seems they worked together and were good pals."

You could see Dickensen's mind working fast. Unless he

was a consummate actor, Donna Smith's name was new to him. "What kind of car does she drive?" he asked.

"Now, Dave, that's a real odd question. Why do you ask?"

"I don't know. I don't know why I asked that. Just a random question." Dickensen had gone slightly pale. "Is there more? Do you want to go back to my office?"

"Yeah, there's a little more. Let's go."

Peabody followed the taller man back through a maze of cheap metal desks, each with a name sign on it, none presently occupied. Dickensen led the way into his office, took his seat behind the desk, and gestured for Peabody to sit down facing him.

"I just thought," he said slowly, "that maybe I had seen this woman driving around town or something. Sometimes I remember cars better than names." His face contorted into a ghastly, lying grin. "You know what a car nut I am, Butt."

Peabody didn't, but he let that pass. "I understand she has an old green Mustang."

Something changed behind Dickensen's eyes. "I'll keep an eye out. Maybe I can help find her."

"Did I say she was missing, Dave?"

"I . . . guess I just assumed."

"Well, it was a good guess. She's missing, all right. We talked to her yesterday, and then she dropped from sight."

Dickensen's eyes darted around the surface of his desk. The torpedo had hit after all; the fuse had just been delayed. "I'll . . . keep an eye out." He grabbed a convulsive breath. "Anything else?"

Fire two. "Matter of fact, yes. What can you tell me about Barbara Gregg's daddy, Henderson Gregg?"

"Nothing! What the hell makes you think I might?"

Peabody had begun to feel a lot better about coming here without waiting for Johnnie to get back from wherever she had gotten off to.

"Henderson Gregg," he said sleepily, "is the man that left his rental car up there next to the wall that goes around Sky Estates."

"I know that," Dickensen said testily. "I heard the REACT boys and the climbers chatting on the CB a while ago; I know they're up there combing the mountainside. I don't know anything else."

"Who was on duty as the Warner gate guard Wednesday night?"

"I think I already told you or Johnnie that. I was."

"But you don't know anything about Gregg, right? Never heard of him?"

"Not before you started asking, no."

"Hmm. Very strange." Peabody put his unlit cigarette behind his ear and pulled the motel memo pad out of his shirt pocket. "Seems our man Gregg was staying at Days Inn. I went over there. No sign of him, of course. In his room he had this notepad. Your name and phone number all over it. Brandon Warner's name written down, too. Looks to me like he must have called you several times that afternoon. But you don't remember him at all, huh?"

A sweat sheen appeared on Dickensen's forehead. "I get a million calls every day. He might have called. I don't know."

"Motel charges fifty cents a local call. Their records show he called your number eight times."

Dickensen's eyes darted again. "He must have gotten our recording. Or talked to Kit."

"And never got through to you even once. Now isn't that strange! Some of these scribbles look like he was writing down stuff you or somebody spoke to him. Let's see here . . ." Peabody flipped memo pages. "Here's one: 'company protects privacy.' Here's another one: 'I have guards everywhere.'" Peabody looked up innocently. "Who else would say stuff like that, Dave?"

Dickensen rubbed his hands over his face. "Maybe I do remember talking to him once. Yes. I remember him now. He was a pest. He wanted Mr. Warner's autograph and seemed to think *I* could help him. Imagine!"

"Hard to," Peabody said. "The man was looking for his little girl, not autographs. He's thirty-seven years old. Works as an electronics engineer for Texas Instruments in Richardson. Not the kind of guy you would expect to be out hunting movie star autographs. Not even much of a moviegoer, from what the wife tells us."

Dickensen threw up his hands. "Then find some other theory! All I know is that he called a couple times, was a pest, and after the second time—if I did talk to him more than twice—I hung up on him."

"Don't guess," Peabody said, watching carefully, "he ever got through to Brandon Warner?"

"Of course not!"

"Or, um, managed to get inside the Sky Estates grounds?"

"Nobody gets through that alarm system!"

"I'm real confused, Dave," Peabody said with a sigh. "First the Gregg girl seems to vanish, then her daddy. Now, maybe, a friend of hers, this Donna Smith. I was hoping you could give me something to help us."

"How the hell can I help you? I don't know anything about any of it!"

Peabody heaved himself out of the chair and put the memo pad back in his shirt pocket. "Thanks, Dave. Wish you had known more. But if you think of anything else, you call us, ten-four?"

Without waiting for an answer, Peabody walked out of the office.

Dickensen sat unmoving, numb, at his desk. He heard the front door chime sound, indicating Peabody had left the building.

Donna Smith. Donna Smith. That had to be the name of the girl in the old compact car Wednesday night.

And now she was missing.

Nerves jangling, Dickensen dialed a number on his secure line.

"Yus?"

"Boris, this is Dickensen. I have to speak to him, please."

The telephone clattered to the tabletop at the other end. Dickensen waited in a near-frenzy of worry.

"Yes? Who is it, please?" This time the voice sounded like a German or Austrian maid, high pitched, with a thick accent.

"Dickensen here. I have to come out. We have to talk."

Brandon Warner's real voice came on. He sounded petulant. "Is it really necessary?"

"It is." Dickensen hung up.

It was the stuff of nightmares, he thought. It was worse than that. Maybe everything he had done had been wrong. But now he could never turn back. What was done was done.

Now Peabody had him linked to Gregg. Jesus, what would they come up with next? Something about the girl? Her father? Something that Dickensen himself didn't know—and didn't want to know—about the death of Jim Way? And where the hell was this girl Donna Smith?

Dickensen hoped his guess was not right. Fear tightened his throat.

9:50 A.M.

JOHNNIE LUNGED BACK against the prybar, putting all her weight into it. The third heavy oak timber groaned and broke loose at one end. Shoving the 2 x 8 up a few inches, she saw that she now had opened a hole large enough to crawl through.

It had been hot work, even here in the river coolness, and had taken longer than she had anticipated. She was sweaty and muscle trembly from the effort. It occurred to her to drive partway back to town and call in her whereabouts, but a quick look-see inside should take only another few minutes now.

But she knew the job would have been impossible if someone else hadn't pried open a large section of the shaft-blocking boards very recently, then done a hasty job of respiking them.

Sheriff Jim Way had been here, she thought, catching her breath, and so had someone else. She didn't think Jim would have had anything to do with breaking open the barricade to the mine shaft. But he could have seen somebody down here, messing around, come down to investigate, and somehow gotten into trouble. Maybe he had been hit on the head, then tried to drive back to town in a daze, which might explain how he had come to run off the road and stagger down to the railroad track.

If any part of her theory was correct, Johnnie thought, maybe there was something close inside the mouth of the mine shaft that would tell her a great deal more. Maybe Jim had caught someone hiding something in there. Whoever had taken the time to pry the boards loose, then respike them, hadn't gone to all the trouble for no reason.

She knew the inside of the mine well enough from memory to take a quick look. She had helped Butt Peabody, then sheriff, with the search for the college boys who got themselves lost a few years back. Butt had put her in charge of working the old charts on the outside, giving radio information to the searchers probing into the mountainside.

There were at least three levels in the old Interocean. Early miners had cut vertical shafts here and there to go deeper, and in one place higher, inside the mountain in their search for a new vein. Some of their upper and lower shafts extended almost a mile. But in addition, the old-timers had discovered that parts of the mountain and surrounding terrain had been carved apart by once-underground legs of the Rock River; in addition to being riddled by mine shafts, the mountain's interior was pocked with naturally formed granite caverns, some (people said) as large as a ballroom, others smaller than a linen closet, much of it connected by horizontal and vertical cracks and stress fractures in the rock of the mountain itself.

It would take weeks to explore all of it, Johnnie thought

now. But if something illicit had been going on here, and Jim had stumbled onto it on the night of his death, that "something" couldn't be very deep inside the mountain.

Going back to her vehicle, she stowed the prybar and tried the radio one more time. It was still dead. Giving up, she pulled her big, four-cell plastic flashlight off its steering column bracket. She hurried back to the mine opening, ducked her head, and scrambled through. Chill stale air engulfed her immediately. She had forgotten how dead and stale it always was inside an old mine.

She sprayed the flashlight beam around. The first part of the shaft was in reasonably good shape. Some small chunks of rock, fallen from the timbered roof, littered the rusty ore cart tracks, but the side support timbers still looked solid.

She moved cautiously, with the creepy feeling that a stumble or loud noise could bring the whole mountain down on her. Water seeped from rock, glistening in the flashlight beam. Something—probably a rat or a mouse—scurried ahead, making a scrabbling noise in the rock debris and causing her heart rate to accelerate. I'm not going much farther.

It was hard to gauge distances in the tunnel. Looking back, she saw that she had come only forty or fifty feet. The brightness of sunlight beyond the splintered opening boards looked like heaven, and she almost turned back right then and there.

But this was ridiculous, she scolded herself. She imagined what her father would have said. "Afraid of the dark?"

No, Dad, she wasn't . . . not much, anyway. But she knew she wasn't going much farther alone on her own. She paused to think about the old charts.

Not far ahead, as she remembered it, the main shaft divided, one leg running back into the mountain at a slightly rising angle, the other leg digging deeper toward the rock underlayment of the river. It was at this junction point that the miners had sunk a vertical shaft about twenty feet, then dug out in several new directions at the deeper level, hoping to find the main vein again. Some caverns and natural shafts connected to some of those deeper tunnels, she remembered. It was down there someplace that the college kids had finally been found.

She decided to go on at least as far as the fork in the tunnel. If she hadn't found anything by then, she would return to town for help.

Moving forward with her light trained ahead, she found herself bending over as she walked. The tunnel had narrowed, and the roof slanted lower. Another critter scuttered around the rock debris ahead someplace.

After another minute or two, the strong beam of her waterproof flashlight picked up the dark double maw of the tunnel dividing point. She saw that heavy planks had been laid over the mouth of the vertical shaft that went down to the lower level. She edged up to the boards and shone her light on them at close range. They looked waterlogged and none too sturdy.

Okay, she thought, far enough. She shone the flashlight beam down the tunnel on the left, seeing evidence of a partial cave-in perhaps thirty yards down that way, nothing more. Swinging the light to the right branch, she sprayed it into the dark.

Down that branch of the tunnel, almost out of the flashlight's reach, something gleamed. She went past it with the bright spot, then returned and found it again. It looked like black plastic. Fresh, not even dusty.

Wanting to get down there to have a look, she again shone the light on the planks at her feet. There was plenty of pale dust here, and she saw what she had missed before: bootprints—a man's bootprints, judging by their size—and long furrows where something had been dragged over the planks covering the hole. Moving the flashlight beam, she made out more tracks on the far side, heading back toward where she had spotted the shiny black plastic.

That decided her. Flattening herself against the wet stone of the tunnel wall, she edged out onto the boards over the hole, making sure to stay on the periphery where her weight would not be multiplied by a levering effect. She moved quickly. The planks shook and groaned, but held as she hurried across to the far side.

Breathing hard, she hurried down the shaft toward the place where she had seen the black plastic. Before she reached the spot, the odor imprinted itself on her. She went on with a sinking sensation of horror.

She reached the place and shone the flashlight beam down. Two long black plastic tarps, the kind campers used under their tents sometimes, lay side by side. Each was bulky, tied with heavy twine at each end.

Johnnie knelt and tried to brace herself mentally as she fished out her small Buck pocketknife and used it to cut a slit in one of the crudely made bags. The plastic parted and she looked.

"Oh, God," she groaned.

Scrambling to her feet, she started back the way she had come. Her stomach was about to revolt, and she couldn't get out of here fast enough. Breaking into a run, she had the flashlight beam far ahead when she reached the plank flooring at the tunnel junction.

The instant her left foot hit the middle of one of the planks, she realized her mistake. Her momentum carried her forward. The sound of cracking wood sounded like a gunshot. She tried to throw her weight to the side, toward the better-braced planks near the wall, but it was too late. Everything gave way beneath her and she plunged through the shattered old timbers into the blackness below.

10:10 A.M.

"YOU MEAN YOU have no idea where she is?" Butt Peabody demanded.

Jason Ramsey spread his hands. "I told you! She went out to the back lot, and that's the last I saw of her."

"Darn her," Peabody said without rancor. "I can't wait. I've got something going here, I think, and I need to move on it right now or it will be too late."

"I'll tell her to call you on the radio the minute she gets back."

"Okay, you do that. Also, Jason, you might get on the CB and give those searchers up on North Mountain a shout. If they've found anything, yell at me on our frequency."

"I'll do it, massah."

"Cut that shit. I'm outta here."

10:11 A.M.

THE FALL WAS quick and sickening. Johnnie's hands and arms bashed against rock and support timbers as she flailed to catch on to something, but before she could cushion her fall in any way, she hit the bottom. Instead of the stunning solid impact she tried to brace for, she hit with a shock into the coldest, blackest water she had ever imagined.

The icy impact made her gasp, choking in some of the brackish fluid. She was under—upside down and about to drown. Desperation took over. She flailed upward and got her head into the air again, gagging and coughing. The bright blip of her flashlight bobbed in the water beside her, throwing crazy patterns of brightness on a bare rock ledge. She grabbed the flashlight and lunged for the edge, catching it with one hand. Her breath whistled in her lungs as she shook herself, trying to see more clearly.

Beginning to get control of her breathing spasms, she tossed the flashlight up on the pool shelf, then got both elbows up over the rocks and heaved herself convulsively up and out.

Bits of dirt and rock tumbled down, peppering her with the aftermath of her plunge. Amazingly, she didn't seem to have any broken bones. A violent spasm bent her double, and she retched up some of the oily water she had swallowed. She couldn't seem to stop shaking. She sprayed the flashlight beam around, first looking up, the way she had fallen.

It looked like a long way up there, more than the twenty feet she remembered from the charts. The walls were mostly rock, chiseled out very smoothly, with only a half-dozen vertical timbers still in place from whatever bracing the miners had built when they dug to this lower level so long ago. At the top, she could see the shattered ends of the timbers that had given way under her weight.

There was no way she could climb up: no handholds, no niches she could dig her toes into, and it was too wide to try any kind of body-wedge tactic like the rock climbers did on the sheer face of Red Mountain. She was stuck down here. She had been stupid.

She mentally shook herself. No matter how dumb she had been to forget to watch her step, it was done and she was in this mess and what now?

Her arms and legs had taken a beating, hitting against rock and wood as she fell. Her head still had a ringing sound in it. Using the flashlight to examine herself, she saw numerous bright cuts and scratches, but nothing that seemed too serious.

She hugged herself, but couldn't stop the shivering. It was much colder at this lower level. Panic pounded on the door of her mind, wanting to take over.

Just try to be calm and rational, she told herself, and think.

All right: She couldn't climb out from here. She was stuck, but good. Should she look for another escape route, or sit tight in hopes someone would find her before dehydration or exposure took her out permanently?

No one knew where she was, which was her own fault. But wouldn't they start looking for her in another hour or two, and spot her Jeep from the road?

With a new sinking sensation, she knew the answer to that. She had parked beyond the maintenance sheds in order to let the sun shine through the windshield and keep the vehicle warm while she was away from it. But when it was parked behind the sheds, it was invisible from the road above.

Panic knocked again. Remembering what she had discovered on the upper level, she shuddered. I have got to get out of here and report this.

How was she going to do that?

She couldn't climb out. How, then?

Fighting to stay calm, she thought back to the old charts. There had been some ventilation shafts marked on them. Could a person climb out through one of them?

This level extended more than a mile in both directions, she remembered. It was intersected here and there by natural fissures, cracks, and caverns. She remembered someone saying that some of those natural fault lines reached the surface, too.

So what was she to do? Bumble back into the bowels of the mountain, hoping for a lucky break?

It wasn't quite that bad, she told herself. This was level two. She knew there was a level three, and at that point she remembered the chart showing another vertical shaft. She also remembered that level three had been started only a few hundred yards to the south.

Which way was south? She shone the flashlight left and right, into the tunnels extending in both directions off the seepage pool into which she had plunged. To her left, the flashlight beam stopped less than twenty feet away, shining on rubble that filled the tunnel in that direction. Swinging her beam to the other end of the shaft, she saw an uneven carpet of fallen rock splinters and some support timbers leaning at spooky angles. But the tunnel in that direction appeared to be intact.

So she didn't have to strain her brain trying to figure out which way to go, she thought with dismay. There was only one direction open to her.

The little girl part of her started to yammer and bawl. I don't wanna go, I'm too scared!

She gasped for air, fighting to regain control of her feelings. How long could she last down here in this cold darkness? Long enough to be found alive? Could she sit tight and *count on that!* She thought of Luke—momentarily yearned for him. But then her mind conjured another image: Butt Peabody. Would Luke know what to do? She doubted it. Would Butt? Yes. Somehow Butt would know.

But Butt wasn't here. If she was going to get out of this mess anytime soon, she had to do it on her own. And something told her she couldn't just sit and wait.

Getting shakily to her feet, she eased her way around the black seepage pool that had cushioned her fall and scared her half-witted at the same time. Beyond it, her flashlight lit up the first few yards of blackness that filled the only mine shaft open to her. She limped into it.

10:40 A.M.

BRANDON WARNER, WEARING royal blue velvet sweats that bulged with every overweight fold of his torso, strode back and forth in his living room, Reeboks leaving pale indentations in the thick carpet. "What is it that's so damned crucial you couldn't talk over the telephone?"

Dave Dickensen wiped his forehead with a linen handkerchief already moist with nervous sweat. "The sheriff's office found a record of the telephone calls the girl's father placed to my office."

Warner stopped pacing, his beefy face slack. "That's not good. Not good at all. But it doesn't necessarily mean anything, either, does it?"

"Butt Peabody seems to think so. Apparently the father had written your name all over the same memo pad at the motel. So he came asking me about it."

Warner's face tightened. "What did you say to that?"

"I played dumb, of course. I don't think he's through with

it. I think he'll be contacting you next. You needed to be warned."

Warner resumed pacing, then stopped again. "You think your phone is tapped?"

"Christ, I don't think so! My tap detector hasn't blipped. But they keep coming up with all this new technology; how do I know?"

Warner paced again. "Some random scribbling doesn't prove anything. If asked, I stonewall it."

"Yes," Dickensen agreed miserably. "But what if they're more suspicious than Butt let on?"

"What do you mean?"

"What if they come here with a search warrant?"

Warner stopped dead, his beefy face going slack. "A search warrant? For *my* house? They wouldn't dare!"

"You don't know Johnnie Baker. She might do anything. Have you erased the tapes?"

"Yes . . . yes. And the carpet has been cleaned."

"The gun. What about the gun?"

"Both guns have been deep-sixed, Dave. I told you that."

"What else?" Dickensen asked nervously. "Have you overlooked anything?"

Warner obviously tried to get hold of himself. He seemed to succeed: His lower lip curled in his famous sneer. "Aren't you overreacting just a bit, Dave?"

"You don't know it all yet."

The sneer vanished. "There's more?"

"The other girl. Donna Smith?"

"I believe that *was* her name, yes! Wonderful! You've located her at last?"

"No. They did."

"They!"

"That part is all right. Guess she didn't tell them anything. But now she's vanished."

"Donna is missing? But how could that be?" Warner rubbed pudgy hands over his face like a man emerging from a plunge into the pool. "Do you suppose the child panicked and ran away? That would serve our purposes in the short term, perhaps, but—"

"No. It wasn't like that. She went back to work once, it appears, and then she dropped out of sight. Peabody wouldn't be looking for her if she had just quit the job, or taken her clothes with her when she left."

Warner's face twisted in a puzzled frown. "But what could have happened to her?" He paced again, chin in hand, thinking about it. Then he stopped like a man who had hit a brick wall. Face darkening, he rushed to the door that led to the foyer. He jerked the door open. "Boris!"

Footsteps scuffed heavily on the tile outside the door, and Boris O'Neal hove into view. In black cotton trousers and a black pullover sweater, he looked the aging former athlete he was. His forehead wrinkled worriedly at the sharp tone in Warner's voice.

"Boris," Warner said, "the other girl who was here Wednesday night? Donna, I believe her name was?"

Boris blinked. "Yus?"

"The girl is missing. Do you know anything about it?"

Boris licked liverish lips, and seemed to take a long time formulating the thought. "I took care of her."

Dickensen's stomach lurched. "What do you mean, you 'took care of her'?"

Boris's eyes rolled his way.

"I took care of her."

"What do you mean?" Warner yelled. "What did you *do?*" Reaching up, he grabbed both fists full of Boris's sweater and shook him violently. "Aren't we in enough trouble already? You did something without asking me first? What did you do to her, you goddamn moron? Answer me!"

"She was going to talk," Boris said slowly. "She called. I met her. You don't worry, Boss. I had plenty of time this time. Nobody will ever find her."

Warner stared. His eyes bulged. His throat worked. Then he threw up his hands and turned away, raving. "You creep! You imbecile! Weren't we already in enough trouble here without this? Jesus Christ! Who told you to take things into your own hands? Who told *you* to think!"

Boris stared back, mute shock making his Neanderthal features slack.

Warner had walked halfway across the room. He turned back, hesitated, and then tore across the carpet at his hulking bodyguard. His hammy fists pounded Boris's chest. "I ought to fire you for this! You have the brains of a hoe handle. You had no right! You had no right! Everything you do gets us in trouble! Goddamn you, this is the last straw! I think I will fire you—get you out of my sight once and for all."

He got no further. Boris, facial muscles twitching, reached out with one huge hand and caught both Warner's wrists. He squeezed. Dickensen, watching in horror, saw all the color go out of Warner's face and his knees begin to buckle.

Boris held Warner frozen by the shuddering strength of one hand around his wrists. Looking down, Boris bared his teeth in a sudden, terrifying show of emotion. "You. Not. Send. Boris. Away."

"All right," Warner moaned, going limp. "All right, all right! I understand! I shouldn't have spoken to you that way, Boris! I won't send you away."

Boris released him. He slumped to his knees. Boris swayed like a great tree in a high wind. "You don't fire me."

"No," Warner choked. "No."

"I did ... . good. Right?"

Warner cowered. "Yes. Right. Whatever you say."

Boris's eyes swiveled around to Dickensen for an instant. There was craziness in there, Dickensen thought. *Worse* than craziness. Dickensen didn't say anything, or so much as move a finger.

Boris exhaled explosively, turned, and shambled out of the room.

The door closed quietly behind him.

Profound silence fell. Rubbing his wrists, Warner climbed to his feet. He shot Dickensen a ghastly smile. "He gets excited now and then."

"What are we going to *do?*" Dickensen whispered hotly.

"Nothing. It will be all right."

"Christ, he's going to just keep getting us in deeper and deeper."

"No, no, no," Warner said, motioning to hush. "It's a terrible thing, Dave, but perhaps . . . after all . . . it's for the best. Now there are no loose ends."

Dickensen worded the question that had simmered in his mind for two nights now. "Did Boris have anything to do with Jim Way's death?"

"Of course not," Warner snapped. He said it too quickly, too easily.

"Oh, Jesus," Dickensen groaned.

Warner came to him and put a hand on his shoulder. "We'll be all right. Make sure your records are clean. The next few days may be difficult, but they don't have a thing; we can ride it out."

Dickensen let himself be escorted out of the room, through the foyer, to the front door. Warner kept talking soothingly, but Dickensen didn't hear a word that was said.

Getting into his truck, he pulled away from the house. He did not look back.

It was all right for Warner, Dickensen thought. Maybe, with all his money, all his prestige and power, he could beat almost any charge. But Dickensen knew his own situation was different. *He* was the one they could—and would—pursue and prosecute all the way. He was an accessory to everything now.

He slowed at the front gates, waiting for his man Hennigan to open them for him. He had the sudden feeling that he was being watched, the short hairs on the back of his neck standing up. He had to get hold of himself, he thought.

Approximately three miles away, high on the slope of Baldy Mountain, Butt Peabody stepped back from the eyepiece of his tripod-mounted 30 x 25 scope. Dave Dickensen had reacted exactly as Peabody had thought he might.

Peabody felt a distant satisfaction. He knew now he was on the right track; he just didn't know where the track was leading him.

Hiking back about two hundred yards to his truck, Peabody fired it up and reached for his microphone. "Sheriff's base, this is special four, over."

Jason Ramsey's voice came back at once: "Go ahead, four."

"Heading back in."

"Okay on that."

"Sheriff back?"

"Negative, four."

"Anything on that list we gave you?"

"Affirmative. I found one of the people."

Peabody smiled. Better and better. Locating someone on Donna Smith's telephone list offered at least some hope of learning where the girl had gone off to.

Now if he just knew where Johnnie had gone off to.

11:45 A.M.

"GODDAMMIT, BUTT," MABEL Murnan snapped, "we're just starting the noon rush."

"It won't take five minutes," Peabody said, amiably winking at the pretty, dark-haired young waitress standing beside her boss at the counter. She looked scared already, he thought.

Mabel turned to the girl. "Are you in some kind of trouble, Phyllis? Because if you are—"

"She isn't in trouble," Peabody cut in. "Can I use your office to visit with her a minute?"

"Sure," Mabel snarled. "You want to borrow a pencil and paper, too?"

"We'll manage." Peabody put his hand on Phyllis Shaw's shoulder. "Come on."

Shaw, the only name in Donna Smith's telephone list that they had located so far, walked stiffly ahead of him past the doors to the steamy kitchen, then down a narrow hallway to the small cubicle Mabel used for an office. A small metal desk, a filing cabinet, a Radio Shack computer, and two folding metal chairs nearly filled the cramped space.

Peabody closed the door and gestured to one of the metal chairs. "I really appreciate your talking to me, Miss Shaw, I surely do."

Phyllis Shaw sat on the edge of one of the chairs. "What do you want, Mr. Peabody?"

He was surprised she had picked up his name so fast, as nervous as she appeared. But then he remembered the name tag on the lapel of his jacket. "You can just call me Butt, if you want. No sense being formal, this is no big deal."

She gave him a slight, tentative smile. She was scared out of her mind.

Peabody sat on the other metal chair, facing her. "I just need to ask a couple of routine questions."

"About what?"

"Your friend Donna Smith."

The scare flitted past the back of her eyes again, and she folded her arms over her chest. "Gosh, we're hardly real *friends*. We know each other. We both worked here . . . before she got fired for missing work again."

"Yeah, I heard about that. Where is she?"

"Probably home, sleeping in."

"Nope. Checked there."

Worry tugged wrinkles between the waitress's eyebrows. She didn't say anything.

Peabody crossed his legs and leaned back, looking relaxed. "I need to talk to Donna one more time, you see, and I'd really like to track her down. It's about her friend, Barbara Gregg."

Phyllis's eyes changed, but she said nothing.

"You know her, too, right?" Peabody said gently.

"Oh, sure. I mean, she worked here, too, for a while. You know how you know people at work. I mean, it's not like we were close or anything. But I knew her when I saw her, that's all."

"Barbara's listed officially as a missing person. You know that?"

Chill bumps appeared on Shaw's bare arms. She hugged herself more tightly. "No."

She was lying—had gotten enough control of herself to keep right on lying. Peabody saw he wasn't going to get anywhere. She was too scared. His impulse was to take her to the courthouse and try to scare her a lot more. He realized that might be going too far unless he got Johnnie's okay first.

He got up and reached for his hat. "Well, I thank you kindly."

Outside, he scarcely noticed that it had become a beautiful, sun-bathed day. He tried to figure out what Phyllis Shaw might know and why she had lied to him. He was getting really tired of being lied to by pretty young women.

He was starting to get tired of worrying about Johnnie, too. He headed back for the courthouse, hoping she had shown up.

12:50 P.M.

SHIVERING, JOHNNIE BEAMED her flashlight ahead for a moment, seeing more of the tunnel, poorly shored-up rock walls, sagging timbers overhead, the narrow rusty track of the old mine carts turning slightly to the left and going out of sight. She quickly flicked the flashlight back off again, trying to conserve the batteries. With her left hand groping along the jagged rock wall of the shaft, she moved slowly forward again, shuffling on numbed wet feet.

She had no idea how long she had been down here now. A few minutes—hours?—ago, she had inadvertently smashed her wristwatch as she groped along in the dark. She knew it couldn't be as long as it felt.

Just stay calm, she kept telling herself. You'll get out of this.

Why was she having such a hard time believing it?

The tunnel had remained level for what seemed a very long time as she moved ahead, searching for another vertical shaft where she might climb out. Then the floor had begun to rise at a very gentle angle, following what must have been a workable vein long ago. Twice she had come to side tunnels, branches off the main one, but had kept going in what she hoped was a straight line.

The fact that the floor seemed to be edging slightly uphill told her that she was moving deeper into the mountain. The air did not smell as dank and stale here as it had an hour—two hours?—ago, which told her that maybe she could yet find a natural vertical vent that was letting in fresh air.

Abruptly the wall on her left veered to the left. She stopped at once and used the precious batteries again. The weakening beam showed that the miners had split the tunnel here, making two branches that went off at about forty-five degrees from each other. The two looked equally high, equally wide, equally poorly braced. She couldn't remember this branching on the charts, so all she could do was guess. She went to the right.

Moving along in the same way, shining the flashlight ahead to see sixty or eighty feet, then groping that far in the dark, she stumbled along for several minutes. Her head throbbed and she was hungry. It seemed amazing that her body could want food at a time like this. Worse, however, was the thirst. There was water seepage everywhere, making the walls glisten, forming black puddles on the gravel floor here and there. She had tried catching a few drops off one of the walls and touched her wet fingers to her mouth. She spat it out at once, and could still taste the rank gypsum in her mouth. Water, water everywhere . . .

She had to get out of here. The idea of being stuck and slowly dying made the panic dance in the corners of her mind. She reminded herself again to stay calm. But the thought of climbing out of this damned black, wet hole and feeling fresh air and sunlight on her face again . . .

She had to stop thinking about that all the time. You could go mad in a situation like this.

She paused again and turned on her flashlight to look ahead. What she saw made her spirits sag further. Another twenty or thirty feet ahead, the tunnel simply stopped. A chalky rock wall with pick marks still engraved in it . . . and nothing.

Forgetting to turn off the flashlight, she limped on forward to make sure the shaft didn't make a right-angle turn. It didn't. This branch simply stopped. The miners had lost the vein, or orders had come down to work somewhere else more promising, or the company had folded. However it had happened, here the digging had come to an end.

Which meant she had to backtrack and go the other way. She felt like screaming. Juststaycalmjuststaycalmjuststaycalm. She turned around and stumbled back the way she had come.

Reaching the fork once more, she sat down on a two-hundred-pound chunk of granite that had fallen out of the roof. Muscles in her legs spasmed. Five minutes later she started up the other shaft.

After she had proceeded perhaps two hundred yards, the tunnel's width and height both reduced considerably. It was such a low bridge now that she had to walk half bent, cracking her skull a couple of times in the dark when she forgot and raised up an inch or two too much. There was no longer any cart trackage underfoot, and she didn't like to think about what that might mean—another dead end. Her wet boots crunched on fallen shale and pebbles as she limped along, bent over, flashing the light ahead, then groping in the dark again.

When she stopped some time later and shone the light ahead, the shock of what she saw almost pushed her over the brink into mindless panic. The ceiling lowered drastically at this point, and up ahead she could not see any more timbers. There were a few pick scratches, but not many.

This tunnel, like the other one, had been abandoned. She had reached another dead end.

Tears tried to come. Grow up, dammit. You're not whipped yet. She inched forward to the farthest end of the shaft and shone the light on all sides.

The roof was no more than four feet from the floor here, the shaft perhaps five feet wide. The flashlight batteries were fading, but the amber glare in such tight quarters bounced off the white and gray rocks, making everything so bright that her eyes ached.

She saw that the miners here had encountered some kind of natural break in the rock. Near the top of the shaft, ancient forces had cracked the mountain's guts and made different layers slide over one another, resulting in a broad black open vein in the stone. The slash in the mountain extended past the limits of the tunnel, she saw, and when she shone the flashlight into the crevice, all she could see was the same horizontal opening, possibly as much as three feet high, as far as the flashlight could penetrate.

She turned the flashlight off and sank to her haunches. This time the tears did come, silent and hot, making her madder at herself.

She had to go back, she thought. But how could she go that far back? She had encountered the last branching-off point, prior to the latest one, hundreds of yards back. The support timbers in that branch had looked so rotten and unsafe that her decision to come this direction had been made almost automatically. She couldn't go all the way back there. But what choice did she have?

Despite the cold, she was sweating from exertion and fright. She pulled her man-size handkerchief out of her hip pocket and, hunkering down, wiped her face. The slight stirring of fresher air felt good.

It wasn't until she had this thought that she sat up so straight and fast that she cracked her skull sharply on a rock protruding from the low ceiling.

The fresh air was coming out of the horizontal fissure.

Maybe the miners had gotten this far and abandoned their efforts because they saw they had angled upward so sharply that they were virtually on the surface of the mountainside, she thought. Or maybe the fractures in the mountain simply made proceeding seem too dangerous, even for those hardy old-timers. But that didn't matter; none of that mattered.

What mattered was the soft, continuous wafting of fresher air coming out of the horizontal crevice.

She knew then what she had to do. Didn't want to do it—*hated* the thought of doing it. No choice. She had to climb up into the low crack in the solid rock and crawl ahead, looking for the blessed source of the fresh air.

Reaching up, she put the flashlight on the shelf of the crevice and got her elbows up on the chill rock. She pulled herself up and into the crack. Instantly, claustrophobia tried to take over.

It would be all right, she told herself. These rocks had been like this for ages. They wouldn't move. They wouldn't stir, and crush her to pulp. She would not get stuck. All she had to do was be careful. It couldn't be far now.

Flat on her belly in the mouth of the fissure, she shone her flashlight around. The crack seemed to extend in all directions. But the ceiling seemed highest straight ahead. She started to crawl in that direction. In the pitch blackness she worked to concentrate on the feeling of warmer fresh air in her face.

1:20 P.M.

"Y OU MEAN *NOBODY* has any idea where she is?" Luke Cobb demanded incredulously.

"Well, I'm sure she's all right," Butt Peabody growled.

"That's easy enough for you to say!" Cobb cried. "But how can you know for sure? I've never liked her having this job! I demand that you start a search for her right away. I've got a right! She and I have a special relationship!"

Peabody clung to his temper. "Well, now," he said quietly, "I'm sure I don't need to be reminded about your relationship, Luke. She's probably out checking something, and her damn radio has gone out on her again. You just cool it, ten-four?"

Before Cobb could answer, the radio blatted on the front counter: "This is sheriff's unit three to base."

Peabody walked over. He had sent Dean Epperly out to scout around, see if he could pick up any trace of Johnnie.

Jason Ramsey keyed the base station mike: "Go ahead, three."

The radio crackled back at once with Epperly's voice: "Is Butt around there handy?"

Peabody reached over Ramsey and keyed the mike. "This is Butt. Go ahead."

"Butt, I haven't found any sign of, uh, you know. But I found out something else real interesting. I just left Pratt Texaco, and I think this is a good lead on another deal."

Peabody frowned. Too many people had scanners. He didn't like discussing anything important on the radio.

He pressed the transmit button. "Dean, give us a landline on this, whatever it is, ten-four?"

"Negative," Epperly's voice came back. "I'm already a couple miles up the road, so here it is. You know that abandoned car deal? Gregg?"

Goddammit, Peabody thought, jamming the mike button, "Dean, give us a landline!"

When he released the button, Epperly was in the middle of a sentence. They had doubled transmissions and the deputy hadn't heard a word. ". . . so I asked Billy about that, too, since I was there, and he said a man in a car that matches the one we got out in our unclaimed lot stopped at his station the other night and asked for directions. I described Gregg, from what we know, and he said that sounded like the guy. Listen to this, Butt. Billy said Gregg asked for directions on how to get to the Warner property, over!"

Peabody's teeth clashed with his frustration. Of all the things to put out on the airwaves! Godamighty! "Continue on your other assignment, three. No more about this on this frequency, is that a roger?"

"Roger that." Dean Epperly sounded both puzzled and hurt. "I thought it was kind of an interesting thing."

"Base out," Peabody snapped, and slammed the microphone back onto the counter in front of Jason Ramsey.

Ramsey raised an eyebrow. "Sounds like a dandy clue."

"Yeah," Peabody retorted, his gut suddenly starting to hurt. "And now everybody in the county knows just as much about it as we do. Probably including Brandon Warner." He started for the back door, hurrying.

"Where are you going?" Luke yelled after him. "Aren't you going to start looking for Johnnie?"

Peabody didn't answer. He was beginning to want to start searching for Johnnie, very badly. But first he had to go back to the Pick & Shovel one more time. Whatever was going on here, Phyllis Shaw held a piece of the puzzle. He wanted to get back to her before she had a chance to disappear like everyone else.

2:10 P.M.

JOHNNIE CRAWLED AHEAD in the pitch black. The knees and elbows of her clothing had been worn through as she dragged herself deeper into the rock fissure, and every time she pulled or kneed herself forward another dozen inches, the rock tore new abrasions in places already raw and bleeding. Her hands had gotten so bad that it was hard to hang on to the big flashlight.

It must be night by now, she thought. Even so, they must be looking for her. Wouldn't someone have thought by now to check the abandoned mine property even if her car was hidden from view by the shack she had parked against?

She knew, and kept reminding herself, that panic would kill her faster than anything else. She had to keep herself under control. But every passing minute made control harder to maintain. Her thirst, combined with dust she stirred as she crawled along through the cleft in the mountain rock, made her tongue feel like sandpaper, swollen in her mouth. It was hard to swallow, and when she did so, it seemed like there wasn't any saliva left, and the swallowing was only a spasm in her throat that made it feel worse. Her eyes itched, and the panic kept yammering to be let free.

She had no idea how far she had crawled; it seemed a very long way. She could still feel occasional wafts of drier, cleaner air—fresh air from somewhere ahead. Was it less of a draft than it had been at first? Surely not. Surely not.

Abruptly she bumped the top of her head on the low-hanging rock ceiling. She stopped, heart pounding, and closed her eyes to the blackness while catching her breath. She might be under a thousand feet of solid rock, she thought. She might be crawling deeper into the mountain. The crevice was only about two feet high now. She felt more trapped, and wanted to jump up and claw her way out. If she let go of her self-control for an instant now, she might go mad.

Her memory leapt to a story she had read once about the graves of people who had been buried in earlier times; when some of the graves had been opened decades later, scientists had found claw marks all over the insides of the wood coffins, and signs that the person buried so deep had not been dead at all—had awakened from a coma later to realize they had been buried alive—had screamed and clawed and—no, no, stop that. You have to stop that.

She maneuvered her arms around to point the flashlight ahead. The fissure had become so shallow now that even this simple movement made her shoulders and elbows brush the solid rock encasing her. She turned on the flashlight. All she could see was pale rock, layers of it forming a slice ahead that seemed to go on endlessly into darkness. A trick of the light made it look like the vertical space became even smaller ahead, the overhead stone and the floor almost meeting in a vee. But that couldn't be; it had to be an optical illusion.

The flashlight beam was dark amber now, definitely fainter; the batteries were going. How long had it been since she had changed the batteries? She couldn't remember. If they failed entirely, and she had no way to see at all . . .

By sheer force of will, she shut off that line of thought, too. Turning off the flashlight again, she resumed crawling. Slide your arms forward, dig in with hands and elbows, raise one knee as high as you could before your backside crunched against the rock above. Pull and push, slide.

Maybe it had been a mistake to come this way at all, she thought. But it was too late to turn back now. She could never find her way back. No one was going to find her in here soon enough to save her life. She had to keep going, get herself out of this alone, just as she had literally fallen into it alone.

Reaching forward again, she raised her right leg this time and pushed and pulled, sliding. How bad could something *hurt?* She rotated her trunk and brought up the other knee this time, pushing again. Push, pull, slide. It was mechanical. It was insane, unending.

She reached ahead and managed to get her knee partly bent beside herself, and pushed and tugged again. The rock above and below seemed to merge, pressing down on her head, shoulders, and back. The panic almost got out. She lunged forward, angry with herself for being so weak.

As she lunged, her head cracked the solid rock above. Her left shoulder jammed. She stopped, gasping for air. She felt wedged in—stuck.

Managing to get the flashlight halfway up to her side, she thumbed it on. What she saw made her moan.

The fissure had tightened. Ahead, it became a pencil-thin seam. She couldn't go on.

To her right and left it was the same. She had crawled into a constantly tightening crevice until now she lay flat on her belly in a slit not much more than eighteen inches high.

She turned the flashlight off again and rested her forehead on the dusty stone under her face. Her nerves began to go. Suddenly it seemed there was no air. She gasped. The heaving of her chest made her back press tight against the rock overhead. No, no, no, no, I can't stand it. She heaved herself up against the rock crushing down on her, and possibly screamed.

Did scream. The shocking loudness of the sound in this tight space snapped her back out of the momentary panic.

Heart racketing, she considered what to do next. She had to go back now; there was no choice. But she was so wedged in now that there was no way to turn around.

So. Crawl backward. Have to do it entirely with hands and elbows pushing back until she could reach a place where the fissure was not so tight.

Maybe she couldn't do it. Someday maybe they would find her like those corpses in the coffins, her hair torn out . . .

She had to stop thinking about that. And she had to try, dammit. Wasn't that what Dad had always said? At least *try?*

She pushed herself a few inches backward with her hands and elbows. She couldn't tell exactly where she was going.

Biting her tongue, she pushed herself backward another ten inches. Just get back to where you started into this crack, she thought. Get back that far, be able to stand up and stretch and not be crushed this way. Then you can think. Just don't think now. Just push yourself back, an inch at a time.

2:15 P.M.

Butt Peabody drove up to the front of the Pick & Shovel Cafe and parked across three angle spaces. His patience was gone and he had no time to fool around with niceties.

Entering the cafe, he saw a handful of locals having coffee. He headed straight for the door to the kitchen-office area.

Mabel, coming up from the back, intercepted him in the doorway. *"You* again?" She canted her hands on her hips. "Don't you have a home, Butt Peabody?"

"Where's Phyllis?"

"In the kitchen, waiting for an order to come up. You don't mean you want to talk to that girl again! Aren't you taking advantage of my good nature just a little?"

Ordinarily that would have called for a joke, but there was no time, and good humor didn't fit his planned tactics here anyway. He pushed brusquely past her. "Sorry, Mabel."

In the kitchen, two male cooks in white paper hats worked at the flat black grill. Hamburgers and bacon and eggs. Phyllis Shaw, with another young waitress, stood waiting. Her eyes changed when she spied Peabody bearing down on her.

"You're back—? Gosh, I feel popular today! I—" Her nervous smile vanished when she saw the nickel-plated handcuffs. *"What?"*

Peabody caught her left wrist and clamped a cuff on it. Then, turning her more roughly than he had to, or really wanted to, he twisted her right arm behind her back along with the left and slapped the other cuff on her.

"Holy shit!" the other waitress gasped. "What's happening?"

"I didn't do anything!" Shaw protested in a scared tone.

Mabel hustled in, her face slack with surprise. "What the hell are you doing?"

"Shut up, Mabel." Peabody nudged Shaw in the back. "Out through the front. Move it. Now."

The slender brunette stumbled ahead of him, out of the kitchen hall and through the main part of the restaurant. Everybody in the place gawked. Peabody felt bad about putting her through this, but it was necessary.

Outside, he shoved her into the passenger side of the pickup. "Don't move." Slamming the door, he went around the front to his side and got in. Phyllis Shaw looked like she was going into shock, just as he intended.

"I haven't done anything!"

Peabody started the truck and jerked it away from the board sidewalk. He turned hard right at the first corner and looked for a parking place in the chamber of commerce side lot. Seeing one, he pulled in fast, braking roughly, to shake her up some more.

Cutting the engine, he turned on her. "You lied to me before about some things. If you lie to me now, you're going in the can."

Tears suddenly streamed down Shaw's face. "What do you want to know? I don't know what you're talking about."

"You know what I'm talking about."

"What? *What?*"

"Donna Smith. She was scared. She talked to you about it. You're best friends. She told you a lot more than you told me. You'd better tell me now."

She shook her head, making her dark hair fall over her tear-filled eyes. "I'll tell you! I will!"

"Talk, then."

"A lot of it didn't make sense. She said she was in the other room, asleep. She was stoned, there had been a lot of pot smoking earlier, and she didn't know what was going on. She never did find out. She just heard the yelling and the awful noises, and got out of there. She ran straight downstairs to her car and drove straight home. She was afraid that—"

"Hold it! You're not making sense! Where was she when this stuff happened?"

"At *his* house!"

"Whose?"

"Brandon Warner's."

Another bit of the puzzle clicked into place. Peabody kept glaring at her. "What else?"

"She didn't know what happened to Barb. It was her first time out there, and Donna took her, but she didn't know what happened. She was scared something terrible had happened to Barb, and if she said a word to anybody, something terrible would happen to her, too, for telling. But she hated it, the way she panicked and ran, and just left

Barb there. But then she thought probably nothing had happened."

"You say she was in another room, asleep?" Peabody cut in.

"Yes."

"She heard yelling and noises?"

"Yes. Yes."

"What kind of noises?"

"She wasn't sure. She was so stoned. But she thought it sounded like guns."

"Guns?"

"Guns. Guns being shot. Going off."

Good God. "What else?"

"That's all. That's all she told me. She was just so worried about Barb and everything. And felt so bad about bugging out on her."

"Who else was there that night?"

"I don't know."

"You're lying again."

"No! I don't know! I really don't! Anytime I've been out there, it was me alone, or with one other girl."

Peabody stared at her tear-streaked face. He almost felt guilty about treating her so roughly. He almost felt sorry for her. But he saw that this was the truth he was hearing now. And it all added up.

He started the truck again.

"Where are you taking me?" Phyllis Shaw asked sharply.

"Jail."

"I didn't do anything!"

Peabody backed into the street and started east, turning at the first corner to head back toward the courthouse. He had a lot to think about now. He thought he could begin to see how things had happened. But Shaw's testimony was all hearsay. Johnnie's continued absence complicated everything tenfold.

"You can't just put an innocent person in jail!"

"Watch me," Peabody said.

"What are you going to charge me with?"

"I'll think of something."

"This is crazy! I want to call a lawyer."

"Lady," Peabody said wearily, "you'll get to exercise every one of your constitutional rights. Tomorrow."

"You mean you think you can just put me in jail in secret, and just keep me there?"

"Yep."

"I'll scream. I'll yell. Somebody will hear me. I'll make such a fuss—"

"That wouldn't be smart."

"Why not?"

"Barbara Gregg was messed up in whatever was going on out at Brandon Warner's place, and now she's missing. Donna Smith knew some of what went on out at Brandon Warner's place, and now she's missing, too. Donna told you some of it. Maybe jail is the safest place you could find in the whole world right now. Maybe if I don't lock you up real good, tomorrow or the next day *you'll* be missing, too."

"That's ridiculous," the girl said weakly, without conviction.

They reached the alley that led behind the courthouse. Peabody pulled into the officials' lot and parked close to the basement entrance. Hurrying his prisoner along, he got her down the stairs and into the office hallway without anyone seeing them. Shaw had paid attention to the logic of what he had just told her; she quietly let him rush her along.

Peabody pointed to the old wood bench just outside the entrance to the sheriff's offices. "Sit right there and be a good girl."

She obeyed, again in silence.

Peabody went into the office. Jason Ramsey still was on duty at the front desk and radio. Hesther Gretsch, the secretary, looked up briefly, then returned her attention to the screen of her old Superbrain computer.

"Any news?" Peabody asked Ramsey.

"They found the Smith girl's car."

"Not her?"

"She wasn't in it."

"Where was the car?"

"Copper Creek Gorge."

"Jesus Christ. You mean it went over the edge?"

"Yes. But unless she got thrown out in the tumble down there, she wasn't in it when it went. They've got a couple guys down where the car ended up and the rest of them are searching the mountainside."

Peabody's guts tightened. Parts of the mountainside over the gorge could only be traversed by climbers with the equivalent of alpine experience. Donna Smith might be anywhere in the broken rock and brush over a half mile down to the gorge, and it could take weeks to find her, or verify that she wasn't there at all.

Another card trumped and another lead gone. "No word from Johnnie?"

Ramsey's dark face tightened. "Nothing."

"Shit. Come with me, please, Jason."

Ramsey left the counter and followed him out into the back hallway, where he looked surprised to see the young woman sitting handcuffed.

"I want her processed and held overnight," Peabody said. "Her name doesn't go in the jail record or anywhere else. Anybody here asks anything, you tell them it's a secret operation. Anybody from outside asks if she's here, the answer is no. Anyone want to see her, the answer is no."

Ramsey's dark face creased in a frown. "Not legal."

"She's being put under protective custody until we get some things sorted out. She's cooperating."

Shaw's head jerked up, and suspicion made her eyes hostile. "Maybe this is all some kind of trick."

"They've found Donna's car," Peabody bit off. "At the bottom of Copper Creek Gorge. She wasn't in it."

Shaw went gray. "Oh, my God. I'll cooperate. I'll do whatever you say."

Peabody walked out, leaving her with Ramsey. In the

hallway between jail and office he nearly collided with two of the commissioners, Carl Rieger and Madison Blithe.

"Is Johnnie in the office?" Rieger asked, frowning.

"Not at the moment, no."

"Dammit, Butt, how long has it been since we left word down there that we want to talk with her to finalize some of the plans for Jim's funeral tomorrow?"

"She hasn't been back," Peabody said, holding his nerves tight. "She's out working on a case."

"What kind of a case? Doesn't she realize how important it is for all of us to make Big Jim's funeral a real, moving tribute?"

"Maybe," Peabody snapped, "she thinks her case is important and your public relations are horseshit."

Blithe flicked a microscopic bit of lint off his suitcoat lapel and gave Peabody a steely look. "See here, Peabody. Nobody asked for your opinion. It's precisely that kind of negative attitude that made you lose your office."

"That and the votes you helped buy, you son of a bitch."

"Gentlemen, gentlemen, that's enough!" Rieger glanced at his big, showy Rolex. "Get in touch with Sheriff Baker, Butt. Tell her I want her in my office by three o'clock at the latest. We have to talk about finalizing plans for spacing of county cars in the procession, blocking off several county intersections for the cars to pass through on the way to the cemetery, how to place the black armbands on the uniforms so the American flag patch won't be obscured, and several other vital matters. Three o'clock. At the *latest*. Is that clearly understood?"

Peabody was so fed up with tanktown politics that he felt a strong urge to flatten Rieger's nose. He hung on. "I'll do my best."

"See that you do," Blithe said icily, and turned his back.

Peabody went into the office. Now goddammit, Johnnie, enough is enough, he thought. Where are you? What's happened to you? His worry made him feel sick. He wondered what he was ever going to do if something bad had happened to her. He had accepted this damned job to take care of her. Her disappearance felt like his failure, and he had never realized how much he loved her. He had to find her. Nothing else mattered.

3:00 P.M.

Dave Dickensen had just returned to his office at DD Security Systems after checking out an alarm system that had gone down at a writer's place out in the valley. Usually quick and efficient with the simple electronics components involved, he had fumbled around today because he was so preoccupied by the frightening news about Donna Smith. Boris O'Neal is crazy; he might kill anybody. Dickensen wished fervently that he had never listened to Brandon Warner Wednesday night; now it was far too late.

When the telephone rang, it made him jump. He snatched it up. "Dickensen."

"Dave? Hi. You know who this is?"

The female voice was soft, pleasantly burry, with a west Texas twang. Hesther Gretsch, the clerk at the sheriff's office, his inside source. Dickensen had for three years paid the woman a "consultant fee" of $100 a month. Only twice in that time had she called with inside information that proved beneficial to DD Security Systems, but one of those calls had led to a $37,000 security contract.

"Of course. What is it?" Taut, he poised a Pentel pencil over his notepad.

"I'm on a break, using a pay phone," Hesther told him. "I thought you might want to know this, if you didn't hear it on your scanner. One of our deputies talked to Billy Pratt, out at the northside Texaco. Mr. Pratt said the missing man, Henderson Gregg, asked for directions to Mr. Warner's estate the night he vanished. Since Mr. Warner is one of your big accounts, I thought you should know."

"Thank you," Dickensen said, his pencil lead breaking on the notebook. "I appreciate the information. Have you heard anything more from Copper Creek Gorge?"

"No, not in the last little while."

Boris had done it, Dickensen thought. He had killed her, sent her car off the shelf road. Where had he buried her body? "Thanks for the call," he said. He felt nauseated.

"There must be something fishy about it, though," Hesther went on breathlessly.

Now what? "What makes you say that?"

"Well, we've got a girl named Shaw back in the lockup. No charges, nothing. Just . . . locked up. I understand she worked with this Donna Smith at the Pick & Shovel, so there must be a connection."

The pain of the migraine struck hard into the back of Dickensen's skull. "I see."

"I better get back," Hesther said, sounding nervous for the first time. She hung up.

It was all falling down around him, everything. They had a link to Brandon Warner, and they had a woman who had known Donna Smith. God only knew what this Shaw person might know. Where was it going to *end?*

Dickensen felt like his stomach was eating itself. His heart flopped around irregularly. It was cool in the office, but all at once he was sweating. He had to do something. But what?

Wheeling his chair to the computer on the credenza behind his desk, he entered his password to get into the office network, then typed in another code that ensured no one else was online and that no one else could get in and look over his shoulder while he was anywhere in the company files. Then he quickly called for the employee assignment rosters for the month of September. To his satisfaction, the screen filled with computer garbage and a blinking message that said there had been a vector interrupt, whatever that was. Changing files quickly, he asked for the personnel data on Hinson. The first of three employee record cards came up almost instantaneously. It showed Hinson's termination date as last Monday—two days before the chaos at the Warner house—and it also showed Hinson's permanent mailing address as a fictitious apartment complex in Phoenix.

All the necessary deceptions were in place; no none could prove anything from the company files.

Dickensen closed the files and turned his computer off again. Checking his earlier cover-up work should have made him feel some reassurance. It didn't.

In the corner of the ceiling, where the spider had been building his web, a fly had flown into its sticky strands. The spider was nowhere in view yet. The fly struggled weakly, its struggle only further entangling it. Dickensen knew how the fly must feel.

4:30 P.M.

BUTT PEABODY DROVE back into Tenoclock after watching the wreckers fail in their first attempt to drag the smashed green Mustang out of the deep gorge with their long cables. If they failed again tomorrow, the car might stay down there forever.

Every bone in his body ached, and the big muscles in his shoulders felt like they were stretched so tight they could snap. He felt sick with worry.

Turning onto Frontier Street, the back shortcut to the courthouse, he directed his thoughts back to everything else that had happened today. Such concentration was hard because of the numbing worry.

If Johnnie were here now, he thought, they could discuss it all. He could see some of the pattern now. It didn't make sense yet, but the lines from the Greggs to Brandon Warner and probably to Dave Dickensen were unmistakable.

At the ramp onto Olive Street, fronting the courthouse, he encountered traffic backed up solid from the corner light.

The courthouse was more than a block from Main Street and still farther from most of the old-looking new shops and arcades hawking everything from postcards and T-shirts to truly fine art like Luke Cobb's work. September was not one of Tenoclock's biggest tourist months despite the lure of the turning aspen. Nevertheless, most of the traffic clogging the streets was from out of state: vans, big campers, smaller cars with carriers bolted on top. Stewing while he waited for a break in the line, Peabody noted license plates from Kansas, Missouri, Nebraska, Oklahoma, Wyoming, Utah, Texas, California, and a rare one, Rhode Island.

The Rhode Islander, driving a cream-colored Toyota sedan with a wife in the front and two small kids loose in the backseat, waved Peabody into the line of traffic ahead of him. Peabody waved thanks and got into the line, inching forward toward the light. Damned fool, with kids unbelted in the car, he thought. Too bad the understaffed Tenoclock police had unwritten orders not to waste time or antagonize visitors with citations for such violations, unless flagrant.

Peabody inched along in the traffic, playing little attention to the host of ordinance-mandated old-fashioned signs hanging from rococo balconies: MOUNTAIN GREENERY; BEST ANTIQUES; DUMB DAME'S CANDY; ROCKY MOUNTAIN KNIFE; OSGOOD CAMERA; TENOCLOCK HIGH; BOOKS; THE EVERY-THING SHOPPE. Men, women, and children jostled and sidestepped each other on the crowded board sidewalks. One of them abruptly stepped out in front of Peabody's bumper, cutting between vehicles to get across the street. Hitting the brakes, Peabody gave the man a glare. This, he thought, was what the city-county big dogs had dreamed of, and now they had it. A good time being had by all. Except the people who had spent their lives here because they loved the valley's isolated peace and quiet.

Parking behind the courthouse, he entered via the back way. Hesther had gone home, and there was no sign of the other two male deputies. At the front desk, Ramsey stoically sipped more of his own rancid coffee.

"Don't you ever sleep?" Peabody growled at him.

"Sure. Don't worry about it."

"You better go home."

"Nobody to tend the store if I do."

"Higginbotham out looking for her?"

"Yep."

"Went by her cabin?"

"Yep."

"No sign?"

"No sign."

"Epperly out, too?"

"Same deal."

"Are they following orders, for once, about keeping it off the radio?"

"So far."

"Phyllis Shaw is safe in the lockup?"

"That she is, Butt."

"Anything else?"

"Commissioner Rieger was by. Twice. He seemed real steamed. Said something about a three o'clock meeting."

"What did you tell him?"

"I said Johnnie must have had to go to Montrose for some stuff, and we'd sure get her in touch with him the minute she got back."

"That's as good a lie as any, I guess. All right. I've been out there to where they found the Smith girl's car, and I ought to write up a report. But screw it. I'm going out and start driving some of the back roads myself."

Jason Ramsey's face lengthened. "Do you think—"

The radio blatted, cutting him off: "Unit three to base, priority, over."

Peabody stiffened as Ramsey keyed the mike. "Go ahead, three."

Dean Epperly sounded breathless and excited. "I've found something. I've found something. Over!"

6:05 P.M.

With a final burst of energy, Johnnie crawled the last few feet out of the horizontal crack and dropped sideways to the floor of the old mine shaft. The flashlight slipped out of her hand and rolled a short distance, its faint illumination making little dust circles. Johnnie scrambled after it and turned it off.

Again in total blackness, she leaned weakly against the dank granite wall and waited for her heartbeat and breathing to slow.

She forgot and licked dry, cracked lips. Her swollen tongue felt like sandpaper on them. It hurt to swallow, but she kept forgetting and trying to do that, too. The lacerations on her hands, elbows, and knees stung hotly, oozing blood.

She was back to where she had made the wrong decision and crawled into the fissure. Now she had to retrace more of her footsteps. She wasn't sure she could go on much farther. She didn't have much strength left now, and her thoughts darted irrationally. Everything had seemed unreal and dreamlike during part of the crawl backward.

Her head dropped onto her chest, cracking her teeth together. The sudden new pain shocked her awake. Have to get moving again . . . get myself out of here.

The fork in the tunnel to which she had returned offered no promise of an easy out. To make sure of that, she used a few precious seconds of flashlight battery time to stumble down the other branch and verify that it dead-ended quickly. That meant she had no choice but to backtrack some more.

Whatever memories she might have had about the mine's total layout had fled in a fog of exhausted confusion. Maybe the best thing to do, after all, was go all the way back to the place where she had fallen through. She could just stay there and wait and hope. Maybe she could last a day or two, if she didn't beat herself to death crawling and climbing, as she had been doing, and sooner or later Butt would have people out checking everywhere, even the abandoned mine property.

The idea that her truck would be spotted eventually—soon enough to save her—seemed a lot more reasonable now than it had when she first fell in here and had both physical and mental strength. Then, it had seemed reasonable that she could find another way out, given her knowledge of the mine's layout; her discovery of the two bodies in plastic bags had made her anxious for a quick escape. Now, that kind of hopeful planning seemed only impetuous and dumb. She had worn herself to a nubbin and only gotten herself into worse trouble.

Again wondering what time it was—what day—she realized she couldn't rest any longer; she could already feel tortured muscles starting to stiffen up. Keep moving; that was the only hope.

She got to her feet and used the flashlight just long enough to show her the way back up the tunnel. She held to the right-hand wall going back because her left hand had been hurt worse by all the crawling. Nothing serious, she told herself. You're just missing some skin. Skin will grow back.

She kept moving, stumbling along. She had gotten better at following the wall with her hand, and she knew there were no holes in the floor along this section. She felt like she was making good time.

Her mind wandered. She found herself thinking again about Butt Peabody. She wondered where he was. She could imagine how worried he must be by now. He would figure this all out sooner or later. Would he be in time to save her? If anyone could, Butt could. She realized dimly that she had always counted on him in time of greatest need . . . when her parents died . . . when she came back to Tenoclock and rebuilt the old cabin . . . when the blizzard killed her sheep . . . when she needed a job . . . when Jim Way died and she so badly needed an experienced hand. She remembered the few moments of doubt she had experienced after mentally linking his late-night appearance in town with the sheriff's death. How could she have wondered about him even for a little while?

She thought then about Luke. She wondered why she seemed to think of him so little, and Butt so much.

Time passed. She kept moving. At one point where the tunnel slanted upward slightly, she stopped and used more precious battery to make sure she was taking the correct branch that led back toward the vertical shaft where she had fallen in the first place. Her headache became a constant, thudding entity with a life of its own. She moved to the other side of the shaft, using her injured left hand, when the constant rock-abrasions to her right made it hurt worse.

In another hour or so, she thought, she would be back to where she had started. She was kept moving by the thought of getting back there where someone—she had now convinced herself—would find her and pull her out. That was going to be so nice . . . light shining down from above . . . voices . . . then a rope coming down, and someone—Butt, she was sure, and probably someone else, maybe a paramedic, coming down to haul her out of there . . . give her a drink of water—how wonderful that would be—and let her lie down in the open air.

Put one foot in front of the other. Feel along the wall. Just keep going, everything fine.

Then, without warning, she bumped squarely into some large, hard metal object that made a groaning noise as her impact rocked it. Her hip stung where she had hit whatever it was. She turned on the flashlight to see.

An old ore cart, orange with a heavy coating of rust, sat on the tracks, nearly blocking the tunnel.

Johnnie was so dazed that she started to edge her way around it before her mind caught up with meanings.

She was supposed to be heading back the way she had come.

There had been no old ore cart like this one blocking her way in.

She was not where she had imagined she was. She had

taken a wrong turn somewhere in the dark. She was hopelessly lost.

6:10 P.M.

A CHILL DRIZZLE had started to fall, quick-forming low clouds bringing on premature nightfall. Down at river level, around the old Interocean Mining Company site, portable floodlights had already been set up, making a large pool of light that nearly blinded Mayor J. Maxwell Copely as he pulled his car off the road and onto the slick driveway leading downward. County Commissioners Carl Rieger, in the front seat beside him, and Madison Blithe, in the back, leaned forward anxiously. There were cars and pickup trucks everywhere, men slogging around in the mud, and Copely weaved his way through them.

"Who *are* all these people?" he muttered, braking.

"Peabody put out a call for volunteers," Blithe replied.

"He did?" Rieger squeaked. "Without checking with any of us first?"

"Now, now," Copely said. "This is an emergency, after all."

"Yes, but look at that backhoe over there, and the bulldozer! Who does he think is going to pay for all this?"

"Worse than that," Blithe said, "how is this going to make us look? First Jim Way and now Johnnie Baker."

Rieger's eyes widened, horrified. "No one said she's dead yet. They may find her."

"Well," Copely sighed, "let's see what we can find out."

The three men popped open car doors and got out gingerly in the gumbo mud that was rapidly becoming worse with the steady drizzle. They looked around, confused by the lights and men hurrying in all directions.

"You, there!" Rieger called sharply. "Jackson! Where's Butt Peabody?"

The thickset laborer named Jackson glanced back over his shoulder. "Don't know." And kept going.

"There he is," Blithe said, pointing. At the boarded-up entrance to the mine shaft, Butt Peabody, carrying a big battery lantern and coil of rope, was just climbing back out through timbers that had been partly removed. Luke Cobb, with a flashlight and prybar, appeared behind him. They started across the muddy, floodlit enclosure.

Rieger and his associates met him halfway.

"Butt," Rieger burst out, "what's happened? What have you found?"

"Just a minute," Peabody snapped. Looking beyond them, he yelled, "Willis! Let's get that air compressor going! I want your longest hose hooked up to it and dragged back inside there. I'll show you where. Hustle!" Then, as men scrambled around an air compressor mounted on a truck, he turned back to Rieger. "We haven't found her yet."

"Why," Blithe asked, "the compressor hose?"

Butt Peabody's eyes looked like lead. "Front planks on the mine entrance had been pried loose, a hole about big enough for somebody Johnnie's size to crawl through. We found some of her bootprints outside and inside, too. Luke and I just finished checking it out."

"You mean," Rieger cried, "she's in there somewhere? *Why?*"

"Shaft goes back a couple hundred feet, maybe, and forks," Peabody said, reaching for a cigarette with a hand that trembled. "One fork is blocked. The other had planking over it, covering a vertical shaft to level two. It looks like the boards gave way under her and she fell down there."

"My God! How far?"

Luke Cobb spoke up hoarsely. "There's water down there—a pool. Butt climbed down. It looks like she fell into the water and then climbed out and started trying to walk her way out from the lower level."

"Is that possible?" Blithe demanded.

"I dunno. There used to be vertical air vent shafts, but

most of them have caved in long ago. I'm sending men up and downstream, just in case she got out somewhere."

"Is that likely?" Blithe asked quickly.

"No."

"What," Copely said, "are you going to do next?"

"Get that air line in there and pump fresh air down the hole. Get our boys who know what they're doing inside a mine or cave to climb down to that lower level and start a search."

"Tonight?" Rieger blurted. "In this weather?"

Peabody gave him a look that could have killed. "It's always the same a hundred feet down, Carl."

Rieger wrung his hands. "I knew it was a mistake to name a woman acting sheriff. I knew we should have named Epperly or Higginbotham. A man would have never done something this stupid, and right on the eve of Jim Way's funeral, too."

Luke Cobb said bitterly, "You should have thought of that sooner. God knows I tried to persuade her not to take the miserable job!"

Peabody stood quite still, his big chest heaving with emotions none of them could clearly read. He opened his mouth to say something, but just then two workers hauling a thick canvas air hose slogged by. The air went out of Peabody's chest. Stone-faced, he turned and started after the pair. "I'll go in with you and show you where to put that thing."

No one said anything for a few moments. The engine on the compressor whined and then coughed to life, its racket making all the other hurried activity seem crazier.

"Maybe," Blithe yelled over the roar, "she's all right!"

"She has to be!" Rieger yelled back. His face worked. "We just can't stand any more notoriety right now!"

Steaming, Butt Peabody climbed through the broken planks at the mouth of the mine shaft and held the lantern high, helping the two volunteers, Regan and Scheine, climb through with the heavy coil of air hose. He led them back into the tunnel to the place where the old 2 x 8s had shattered over the vertical shaft. "Let's drop it down there almost to the level of the water, and then get the valve opened for max flow."

The two men wordlessly unrolled the last of the hose, lowering it into the hole. When they opened the control valve, the hose puffed up and the sound of escaping air came reassuringly from down below.

"Okay," Peabody panted. "That does it. Let's get back. The cave guys might have started to arrive by now, and I don't want to waste any time getting them started."

Leading the two men out, his mind filled with fear for Johnnie, clamoring rage at Rieger and his cronies, confused plans for how to proceed, and a gnawing curiosity about what lay beyond the spot where Johnnie apparently had fallen through.

The first two men into the tunnel hadn't noticed it, neither had Luke Cobb, and neither had Regan or Scheine. But Peabody had.

The planks through which Johnnie had fallen had not given way entirely because of aged rot or bad luck. Peabody had seen almost at once that there were some bright, even edges on two of the center boards. The very recent marks of saw teeth.

Somebody had booby-trapped the planking to make sure that anyone crossing carelessly would plunge to their death.

Why? And who? He didn't have any idea. But he knew one thing: As soon as he got the searchers organized and into the ground, he was going to find some stronger boards to put across the broken span, and then go back in there himself for a careful look-see.

8:30 P.M.

HUNKERED UP AGAINST the damp rock wall of the cavern, on the edge of exhausted sleep, Johnnie jumped violently. Had she heard something? A vibration, a subterranean rumbling of some kind, the hint of an echo?

"Here I am!" she yelled hoarsely. "Here!" The sound of her own voice racketed and ricocheted off the walls and cavernous roof, making a deafening roar that made her clamp raw hands to her ears.

Beyond the ringing inside her head was only a profound silence—no response from anywhere else.

She had imagined the sound like a faint, faraway human voice, she thought. She sank back against the rock.

She had followed one of the other mine shafts through several crazy, seemingly senseless twists and turns, and had just about been ready to backtrack once more when the tunnel led her into this natural cavern. It appeared that the miners had blasted straight ahead, but there had been a natural cave formation just to the left of their blasting position. The explosion had torn out the side of the tunnel and opened up this large area.

The big cave was at least sixty feet across, with an irregular rock ceiling that she guessed at forty feet in some places. Her flashlight would no longer probe the outer limits; to one end of the cave, a large, irregular pool of black water seemed to ripple ever so slightly in its last illumination.

Desperate, she had crawled to the edge of the pool, dipped her filthy, blood-caked hands into the water, and tasted it. Unlike any of the other seepage she had tried again and again, this tasted fresh.

Wonderfully fresh.

Flat on her belly beside the pool, she had lapped the water up as fast as she could get it in. Ice cold and sweet, it had hit her empty stomach and started cramps, but she drank more. It took willpower finally to stop.

After resting a few minutes, she felt a little better. Hurting all over, she had explored the perimeter of the cavern, looking for the place where the miners had dug on. She had to go all the way around twice, skirting the far end where the pool seemed to emanate from under sheer granite, to realize the truth: The miners had not gone on from here; the cave-in into this place had stopped them from progressing farther in this direction.

So she had come to another dead end. She had to go back again. She was so tired she cried for a while. But then she tried to tell herself it might be worse: She might not have found water. Count your blessings; wasn't that what her mother had always said at the worst of times?

Maybe it was dawn of Saturday by now, Johnnie thought. Maybe soon they would spy her Jeep and start searching for her. She had to survive—tell them what she had seen in the upper level, breathe fresh air again and see the sun.

Survival was all that mattered right now. She wasn't about to give up or let the terror get the better of her.

She would get out, she thought. She *would*.

With that thought, she curled up as tightly as she could in a fetal position, trying to get warm against the stone wall of the cavern. Her mind drifted with the pain. After a long time she fell into a fitful sleep.

11:00 P.M.

CARL RIEGER RUSHED into the big, chilly back room of Lemptke's Funeral Home. One horrified glance told him that everything he had heard so far was true: There stood a mud-covered Butt Peabody; a rumpled Judge Fred Otterman; police chief Chubby Mayfield; and mortician John Lemptke, looking slightly dazed by it all.

On two gurneylike tables in front of the group lay two sheet-shrouded corpses.

"What is all this?" Rieger cried. "Who are these bodies?

Judge, what are *you* doing here? Butt, what's the meaning of all this? Where did you—"

Judge Fred Otterman interrupted tightly. "It's the missing girl and her father."

"I don't know anything about any—"

"We found them in the mine," Peabody said. "That's when we notified Chubby and he called you."

"This is terrible!" Rieger groaned. "How much more bad luck can we possibly have? What happened to them? Did they fall into some kind of—"

"Not likely," Peabody said. "They've both been shot."

"Shot! Oh, dear lord!" Rieger's mind raced a mile a minute. "Now look here, everyone. We can't have this news getting out right on the heels of poor Jim's unfortunate death. Gadfrey! This has to be kept as quiet as possible, at least until after his funeral tomorrow. Then, perhaps—"

"The judge is here," Peabody grunted, "because I'm asking for an immediate court order for an autopsy on both of these people."

"But of course! That's the law! No court order is—"

"I'm not talking about a routine quickie find-the-bullet. I want a complete post, with a pathologist from Montrose in attendance, bloodwork—the works."

"What does Max say, as our local assistant district attorney?"

"We can't find the sonofabitch. I'm asking Fred directly."

Rieger turned to stare at Fred Otterman.

Otterman solemnly shook his head. "There's no other way to handle this one."

"But then the news will get out," Rieger groaned. "Ten-oclock is going to start looking like the violent death capital of the world."

"I want Jim's funeral postponed," Peabody said.

"*Why*, in heaven's name?"

"While the expert from Montrose is here for these jobs, I want a more complete look-see at Jim's remains, too."

"But that makes no sense! Jim's funeral is scheduled for

the morning! There's never been a suggestion of foul play in his death!"

"Johnnie suggested it," Peabody bit off.

"Oh, maybe so, but who took her seriously? Surely you aren't trying to suggest that there could be some connection between—"

"I want a forensics-type exam on Jim Way, too. If we have to fight it out legally, then the judge, here, can issue a temporary restraining order to block Jim's burial until we get it sorted out in court."

"No," Rieger said hoarsely. "That's . . . just too much."

All eyes turned to Otterman. There was a moment's total, profound silence. He swallowed hard, his protuberant Adam's apple going up and down. At the moment, any resemblance to Joseph Cotton was impossible to see.

Rieger could not think of a subtle way to say what he had to say. "Fred, you must not do this! Think of the notoriety! The rumors! Just remember which side your bread is buttered on, here."

Otterman's protuberant eyes swiveled to Rieger's face. Was he remembering the reelection help, or possibly thinking about the small percentages he owned in three of Rieger's land development schemes? Hoping so, Rieger held his breath.

"Come on, come on," Butt Peabody growled. "Yes or no?"

Otterman straightened himself into the Joseph Cotton configuration. "Any motion—" His throat made a gargling sound and he had to clear it and start over. "Any motion for a second and more detailed postmortem examination of Jim's remains would have to come from a higher authority."

"Then call Gunnison!" Peabody yelled.

Otterman spoke out of a face that had lost all color. "I deny your request."

"Jesus Christ," Peabody said bitterly, looking at the floor.

"Thank goodness!" Rieger breathed.

"You dumb shit!" Butt Peabody said.

"What?"

"You dumb shit! This little girl has been missing since the same night Jim got run over by the train in that freaky, so-called accident. This man—the girl's father—was last seen earlier that same evening, getting some directions to a place where his car was later found abandoned, and he hadn't been seen or heard from since. They died, and Jim died, and it all had to happen within the same few hours. Don't you think there's at least *some* chance all three deaths could be related in some way?"

"I don't know!" Rieger stammered. "I don't c-c-care. We've got to think of our reputation, here!"

Peabody turned to Otterman. "But at least you'll issue the order for a post on these two?"

"Yes," Otterman said grimly. He turned to Lemptke. "Consider this an oral order of the court under governing state statutes. Contact Montrose at once and get a man down her immediately."

"Where does Johnnie Baker's disappearance fit into all this?" Rieger demanded. "Why are you throwing your weight around, Butt? Why aren't you out looking for her?"

"We've got men started down the shaft," Peabody snapped. "I'm heading back out there myself in just a few minutes."

"Then she's still—"

"It looks like," Peabody cut in, "Johnnie found these bodies out at the old Interocean, and then fell through a trap somebody had left."

"But who would do such a heinous thing?"

"It's just possible, Carl, that we'd have a better chance of trying to answer that question if you'd stop fighting a forensics exam on Jim."

"I've told you! That was an accident, and any further damaging publicity is simply out of the—"

The heavy back door, slamming behind Butt Peabody, cut off Rieger's words.

11:40 P.M.

BUTT PEABODY HUNCHED over the desk in the sheriff's office, listening to the distant telephone ring. He had finally gotten through this far, at least.

A male voice answered: "Governor's mansion, Security."

"My name is Butt Peabody. I need to talk to the governor. It's an emergency."

"Sorry, sir. The governor has retired for the night."

"Goddammit!" Peabody yelled. "Get your ass in gear and go tell him Butt Peabody is on the line and it's a life-and-death emergency!"

There was a long pause. Then: "Hold, please."

Fuming, Peabody held. If they decided to give the governor his name, he thought, it would be all right. It had been a long time since he had helped the governor's daughter out of that jam, and Everett Parkman himself hadn't been down for the elk season in three years. But he wouldn't forget.

"Butt? Is that you, old son?"

"It's me, Mr. Governor, and I've got a problem down here that only you may be able to help me with."

There was a slight pause, then: "Butt, you sound strung out, man. And the name is Ev, remember? Now tell me what's going on, and how I can help."

Peabody took a deep breath and began at the beginning. He had to make this good.

▽

Saturday, September 29

HIGH MOUNTAINS TO the east blocked the rainy dawn, keeping it dark in the river bottom. The mine site continued to buzz with activity. More floodlights had been brought in, and a second compressor added its engine note to the earlier one, both sending air down into the tunnel. More volunteers had arrived, with the result that now the road shoulder above the site was lined with pickups.

Near the mine entrance, Butt Peabody faced the second shift of underground searchers. He felt dazed for want of sleep, and his voice sounded thick in his own ears.

"Harmon, Johnston, and Brevart," he said, looking up from his tablet notes, "you're the ones that know this place the best from all your exploring down there, and all. You know what the earlier guys checked out. Any questions about how you're supposed to proceed?"

Harmon, tallest of the gang that would continue the search from this end, shook his head. His two best friends, ruddy-faced teenagers, looked solemn and ready. Wearing miner's hats, they had leather harnesses and all manner of ropes and other gear hanging all over them.

Peabody turned to three other volunteers. "Murphy, Slaughter, Stein—you're the primary backup. One of you stays on the upper level, one goes as far as the number six cutoff where the other guys quit this morning, the third does whatever Harmon tells you. You maintain radio communications at all times. Everybody got that?"

Everyone nodded.

"Turrentine," Peabody told an older man, "you stand guard at the mouth of this shaft. No unauthorized person goes in. I mean it. Nobody. You've got that special deputy's badge I just stuck on you, and you've got that revolver. This is serious. *Nobody* goes in without my okay. Have you got that?"

Turrentine, his gray face worried, asked, "What do I do when somebody like Niles Pennington arrives, and says he's going in regardless?"

"Yell for me. I'll handle it."

"What," Turrentine persisted, "if he just tries to bull his way by?"

"Glenn," Peabody sighed, "if everybody didn't already know you were an accountant before you retired, you would have just told them with that question. I said nobody goes in. I mean nobody goes in. If Pennington or anybody else tries, shoot the fucker in the leg."

Turrentine giggled nervously. "Right!"

"I mean it."

Turrentine's grin died.

Peabody turned to some of the other volunteers awaiting orders. "The Kupplemeir bunch will be going in through the old Arvada vein entrance anytime now, but that's more than three miles from here, and the charts don't even show it links up anymore. You guys are to scour the surface everywhere, looking for old ventilation shafts or natural cracks. Anytime you find something, holler down into it. She might hear you. Jones and Klimer, I want you two to go along the river, listen up, and look for any sign of a sinkhole or something where you might try yelling, too. Jackson, you do the same on the far side. Henthorne, Riddle, you two head up the slope beyond the road here and angle east. Perkins, I want you over on the far side of the hill, over toward Crystal Lake. We know there once were shafts that far, so who knows?"

Peabody turned to Luke Cobb and tried to make his voice sympathetic despite his growing dislike for the man. "Luke, you can stay with me here or you can walk the back side of Calliope Hill, looking for vents and cracks like the other guys."

Cobb nodded angrily. "I'll walk."

"Let's get after it, then."

6:30 A.M.

JUDGE OTTERMAN HAD just staggered out of bed and into the bathroom when the door chimes sounded.

"Who the hell can that be?" he groaned. Raising his voice, he called, "Honey?" No response. Louder: *"Honey?"*

From the adjacent bedroom, a sound came from under the covers: "Uumph?"

"Shit." Otterman got up from what he had just started doing, pulled up his pajama bottoms, and hurried angrily down the hallway, into the entryway, and to the solid oak front door. He looked out through the peephole just as the chimes sounded again. "What the—?"

He opened the door. Standing there on the stoop was the perfect Colorado state trooper: young, tall, handsome under his broad-brimmed hat, splendid in a perfectly pressed uniform.

"Judge Otterman?"

"Yes?"

"Your Honor, I've come from Gunnison. I have an order from the district court." The trooper whipped a 9 x 12 brown envelope out from under his arm and handed it over.

"From Gunnison?" Otterman said, slightly dazed. "At this hour? The district court doesn't even open on Saturdays!"

"Special situation, sir, according to the governor's office."

"Governor's office?"

"I'm on the governor's staff, sir. He ordered me to Gunnison a few hours ago. The judge had this waiting for me when I arrived there."

"What the hell *is* it?"

"I'm sure I don't know, sir. By the way, sir, could you show me on this city map how to get to Mr. Carl Rieger's home? He's the chairman of the county commissioners, I understand?"

"He lives just up the street. Have you got something for him, too?"

"Yes, Your Honor. I believe it's duplicate papers."

"Okay." Otterman stepped out onto the front porch, concentrating with some effort. "You see the curve in the street up there? The big house on the right, with the pines along the driveway? That's Carl's house."

"Thank you, sir." The trooper actually saluted, did an about-face, and walked briskly to the gleaming patrol car parked in the driveway.

Otterman closed the door and carried the light envelope into the living room. There, sitting on the sofa under his mounted moose head, he slit the tape on the end of the envelope and pulled out what was in the envelope. It consisted of two sheets of legal document. Otterman read the two court orders all the way through.

"Good God," he said.

His wife, puffy-eyed and wearing a quilt robe and fuzzy slippers, shuffled into the room. "Who was that at this hour, dear?"

"Court orders from Gunnison."

"At this hour? That's never happened before!"

Otterman carefully replaced the papers in the envelope. "A temporary restraining order, blocking the burial of Jim Way. Another order for an examination of his remains by a state-appointed forensics man. Jesus." Otterman shook his head. "I think I see the fine hand of Butt Peabody in this. Who else around here could get this kind of help direct from the governor's mansion?"

The telephone rang.

Ramona Otterman turned. "I'll get it."

"No. Let me." Otterman glanced at his watch. "That trooper made good time. This will be Carl, having cats. Will you start the coffee, dear? I need some. Bad."

6:40 A.M.

JOHNNIE WAS DREAMING. She was a child and she was stuck in a closet in her house, and she kept calling for help, but no one came. She hurt all over, and she was cold.

Then some sound—a small tumbling rock somewhere—routed her out of her exhausted sleep. As her head jerked up, she cracked the back of her skull against the solid limestone she had been slumped against. She opened her eyes and saw, very faintly, the pale pool of water in front of her, the rock shelf on which she had slept, the vaguest outlines of the distant cavern walls and roof.

Everything came back. She remembered her predicament. It was a very bad moment.

She sat up straighter, rubbing stiff legs and arms. After napping fitfully all these hours, however long it had been, she felt like she hadn't gotten much rest at all. But she had to guard against the kind of lethargy that could slump into despairing inaction.

"Just stay calm," she reminded herself again, aloud. Her voice sounded hoarse and funny in the echo-filled chamber. "People have been in worse jams. You've got to backtrack again, but that's okay, you can do it. You're not dehydrated now, and you slept more than you had any right to. So just think straight and be logical."

She got to her knees. The movement cost her pain in her lower back, shoulders, arms and legs—almost everywhere. She looked down at herself. The front of her jeans was a ragged mess from the crawling and climbing, and she had scabs over fresh wounds everywhere. Her elbows were even worse. When she bent her arm, scabs cracked and fluid oozed out. Her hands were so swollen she could not completely close them.

Well. Get on with it.

Climbing to her feet, she forced herself to stretch, making abused muscles work. Then, in the faint twilight, she limped over to the edge of the pool, knelt, cupped her hands, and scooped up water to drink. It tasted delicious, but its cold instantly hit the bottom of her empty stomach and made it start protesting.

Drying her hands on what was left of her shirt, she looked around and spotted her flashlight on the dirt nearby. That was when the realization hit her like a thunderclap.

She was *seeing*.

There was light in here. Not much, but enough pale, diffused light that her dark-accustomed eyes could make out even small details.

Her heart started to pound as if she had just run two miles. She stared first at the roof of the cave, then along the walls, looking for the source of the light. It was *daylight* she was experiencing, and it was dimmer up above. There was an opening to the outside here somewhere; it was not above, as she would have expected, but down here at the lower levels.

She scrambled around, trying to see where the light seemed to be the strongest. It took her two or three minutes to figure it out. At the far end of the pool, where it seemed bordered by a perfectly vertical wall of rock, that was where the light was brightest. The light was coming *through the water*.

She tried to figure it out. Excitement made her feel crazy. She took several deep breaths, trying to calm down. Then she walked painfully around the narrow ledge that bordered part of the pool, getting as close as she could to the spot where the light seemed to be coming in below the water line, through the rock wall itself.

That was when she understood: There was an underwater hole in this sheer stone wall. Daylight was shining through the water from the other side.

She felt nervous sweat break out all over her body. This explained why the water tasted fresh and good, when everything else she had tried underground was heavy with gypsum, sulfur, and iron. This water tasted fresh because it *was* fresh. There was a source just beyond this rock barrier. Possibly the Rock River itself, possibly some pond or lake.

Which it was made no difference. It was *there*, not far away. If light could penetrate through the water with enough intensity to provide this faint illumination here in the cavern, then the distance to the other side could not be too great.

She didn't have to think any farther than that. Trembling, she managed to peel her boots off swollen feet. Her fingers fumbled clumsily at her belt buckle, and then she got her jeans pulled off. She ripped the filthy remains of her shirt getting free of that. Standing on the edge of the pool, she braced herself for the cold, then without hesitation swung her bare legs over and lowered her body into the water.

Even mentally prepared for the cold, she lost her breath from the shock. Her lungs spasmed for a minute or so. Clinging to the crumbling rock edge of the pool, she got herself under control and took several deep breaths, loading up on oxygen. Her feet would not touch bottom. There was no way to gauge how deep the water was.

Letting go of her hold on the side, she took a few strokes to reach the place close against the sheer wall where the light seemed the brightest. Gulping in one more lungful of air, she jackknifed her body and dove, open eyes aching with the cold, feeling along the wall with her fingertips and moving toward the spot where the light seemed brightest.

Her movement took her under the stone wall. Knowing she was swimming under solid rock, she kicked forward, pushing herself hard toward the light ahead. Then the light source began to be more specific: a small, single spot of brightness surrounded by the impenetrable dark of more solid limestone or granite.

She reached the underwater hole in the wall. The light here was very bright, almost painful. She could feel a slight current flowing in against her. The water coming in felt marginally warmer. She concentrated on the bright hole that meant escape and freedom.

She reached it. It was irregular, slightly oval, with jagged edges all around, and no bigger than the face of her TV set at the house. It looked impossibly small for anyone to slip through. Oh hell, oh no. She probed the edges of the small opening, feeling the rough edges. She could see that it wasn't far through the hole to even brighter light on the far side and freedom.

She was beginning to need air, but she wasn't finished yet. Putting her arms together in a diver's position, she kicked into the small opening. Immediately her shoulders scraped on both sides. Maybe if she kicked hard, and pulled herself, she could get through. But maybe not.

Abruptly she was out of air. Pushing away from the hole, she braced her bare feet against the stone and kicked herself back in the direction she had come. Her lungs began to spasm again.

She tried coming up and banged against rock with no air space between it and the water. Sinking lower, she kicked hard, moving with the slight current toward darkness ahead. She sensed, rather than saw, the rock overhead vanish. Lunging upward, she erupted into the dark, cold stale air of the cavern. Gasping and coughing, she swam to the bank and managed to heave herself up onto the stone fragments littering the shelf that surrounded the pool.

Was that narrow hole of light an escape, or a death trap?

6:55 A.M.

PACING BACK AND forth in front of the mine entrance, Butt Peabody went cold when Bill Harmon, his underground crew leader, climbed back out of the mouth of the shaft, covered with chalky powder from head to toe, his hat light still aglow.

"What is it?" Peabody demanded. "You didn't—she isn't—"

"No, we haven't found her." Harmon turned and spat. "There's been a collapse down in there sometime in the past eight or nine months. Dusty as shit. The old Wimberly section is completely cut off."

"Well, that ought to make it easier, then. Cut down the amount you got to explore. Right?"

Harmon removed his hat, mopped sweat off his face with his shirtsleeve, and spat again. "I'm afraid not. The cave-in doesn't make it easier. What it did at the same time was open a big horizontal faultline crevice back in there. We found her tracks all over the place. We can't tell for sure, but it looks like she must have tried to crawl back into it, looking for a way out."

Peabody's insides sank. "She could be stuck back there."

Harmon's eyes were bleak. "I know."

"Well, you've just got to crawl in there after her."

"Lennie has started already, and George is staying back in the shaft. The other guys are going around another way. We've got Lennie rope-tied in case he slips or gets stuck, so we can pull him back." The dust-stained sweat coating Harmon's good-looking face formed little cracks as he grimaced. "I told you at the start that we couldn't explore all of this in a week. Finding this faultline complicates it worse. I thought you ought to know. We might be in for a real long siege."

Peabody's eyes stung. "We've just got to do our best."

"Here's a suggestion," Harmon said. "Let a couple more of the backup guys come down as far as where we're exploring the fault. They could poke around down several more side shafts that branch out from there." He looked at Peabody and read his mind. "If they stay roped together, and go real slow, they're capable of handling it. I've had them in caves before. They're not idiots."

Peabody thought about it. His fright yammered to get out. He didn't like the idea of sending more men into the lower level, because he knew how dangerous it could be. But how long could someone like Johnnie survive without food and water down there?

"Take anybody you want who'll volunteer," he said.

"I won't have any trouble finding volunteers." Harmon turned and clinked toward a grimy collection of workers standing near the air compressor trucks.

7:15 A.M.

SHIVERING BESIDE THE pale pool of water in the cavern, Johnnie fought the fear and considered her options.

She saw now that she had been foolish almost from the beginning. She should never have come out to the mine property alone, or at least without notifying the office. Of course she had been excited, but that was no excuse.

Once she had seen the marks around the mine entrance, she thought, she should have driven all the way back to Tenoclock, if necessary, to get help. But she had been so darned sure she was about to solve the riddle of Jim Way's death that she hadn't been cautious enough.

She could have gone on, beating up on herself. It had been stupid to forget caution once she found the two bodies, no matter how shocking the discovery had been. Then, having fallen, she should have elected to stay put.

All of that was behind her now. But *this* time, facing the most crucial decision of all, she couldn't afford another error of judgment. Make a wrong decision now, and it was all over for her.

Should she dive again, and risk everything on trying to squeeze through the jagged hole in the rock to the freedom that lay just beyond? Or would it be smarter to start backtracking again or even wait right here in hope that searchers would be capable of finding her before it was too late?

A deeper shiver went through her, making her teeth chatter. It came from a combination of her nerves and the bone-chilling cold. And it made her see that she couldn't stay here. And how could she backtrack, as thoroughly lost and disoriented as she was now?

She had only one choice, unless she wanted to sit here like a mouse in its hole, waiting for rescue that might never come. She had to dive again, risk it all on squeezing through that hole.

She dreaded it. She really didn't know if she could squeeze through. She had no way of knowing exactly how long she might have to hold her breath on the other side even if she did manage to get through. Her fear said to pull the rags of her clothes back on, hunker against the wall, and just wait. But wait to die, knowing you might be turning your back on a chance to find blessed fresh air and sunlight just a dozen yards away?

She thought about it, and saw she could never make the fear go away. She had to face it or back down.

Perhaps, she thought, she should wait an hour or two. Just in case rescuers might be close. But the longer she waited now, the weaker she was going to become. If she was to act, it had to be now.

A thought that might have come right out of her father's mouth lanced through her mind: If you're man enough, you'll try.

She felt a flush of heat through her bloodstream. I'll never be a man, Daddy, and I know that's what you always wanted. But I'll be woman enough—for once—or die.

She wouldn't cower another minute.

There was nothing more to think about. Kneeling beside the milky pool of fresh water, she breathed deeply several times, loading up on oxygen again, making herself slightly dizzy from hyperventilation. She tried to relax her muscles by flopping her arms loosely and flexing her aching legs.

Allee allee in free!

Now.

With one more deep breath, she slipped into the frigid water. Part of her said to wait and breathe more, or even turn back. *No!* With a last deep breath, as much air as her lungs could possibly hold, she ducked under the surface and kicked powerfully toward the vague splotch of brightness that meant escape.

Knowing her way now, she kicked hard, boring straight through the cold water toward the light, going slightly deeper to avoid brushing her head on the rock ceiling again. She reached the hole in a matter of seconds. It looked even smaller than it had before. Her spirits sank and fear struck again. Then she filled with anger at herself for her weakness, and pushed ahead.

Kicking, she stretched her arms ahead of her body and into the open. Her shoulders brushed painfully against rock protrusions on both sides. The light was so bright—she was so close! Wriggling, she twisted her body sideways and scrunched up her shoulders. They squeezed through.

Now her hands encountered the outside lip of the thin rock wall that stood between her and escape. She grabbed both sides and pulled her body farther. For an instant she knew she was going to make it. Then her hips stuck in the hole at its tightest point, the spot where only a contortionist's act had gotten her shoulders through at an angle.

She could not twist her hips out of line with one another as she had her shoulders.

New fear gusted. She pulled hard with her hands. Her lungs began to scream for breath but there wasn't any air, only the frigid water. She was more than halfway through, but stuck tight at the hips. She realized that she couldn't slide back the way she had come; she couldn't hold her breath long enough to get back to that black cavern even if she found a way to contort herself in reverse.

She lunged again, feeling the rough rocks tear flesh on her hipbones. My God, if she had just lost that five pounds when she said she would!

Consciousness began to ebb. There was nothing but the cold and the panic and the need for air. Bubbles burst out of her mouth and over her face as her lungs began to spasm. She lunged with everything she had left. Bright pain came

from where her skin was tearing on the rocks that held her.
Maybe she gained an inch. Had she gained an inch? She had
to get through *now* or it would be too late.

She pulled with all her strength again. The effort forced
more air out of her mouth, the bubbles tickling her face as
they exploded upward.

With another convulsive pull and thrust, she felt her body
slide forward. More flesh was scraped off both hips. But she
really moved forward this time—felt her hips break free, her
thighs bang against the rough rock. She clawed the water.
She was *out*.

Her heels smashed painfully against the inside of the rock
tunnel as she kicked wildly, propelling herself out and
upward. She shot up through the water. The surface seemed
no closer. This was taking forever. Was she far deeper than
she had thought? Was she going to drown here, for God's
sake, this close to the—

She burst to the surface, erupting in a geyser of brilliant,
sparkling droplets. Her momentum failed and she fell straight
backward, going under again, seeing a shower of bubbles all
around. She stroked frantically, fighting with diminishing
strength, and got back to the top again.

Blessed air gushed into her lungs. Shaking, she cleared her
vision. She had come out in a lake, close to the shore, barren
rocks and pebbles along the shoreline. She recognized it.
Crystal Lake!

It wasn't far to the shore. Feebly she rolled over onto her
side and swam toward it. After two dozen endless strokes
she felt her knees and feet bang painfully against the rocky
bottom. Staggering, she got to her feet and waded the last
few feet, dropping exhausted onto the small shore rocks.

She lay facedown, listening to the hammering roar of her
own heartbeat, gasping in more air. She had no strength left.
But she had made it.

She had made it.

11:00 A.M.

A NURSE POKED her head in the door of the examining room at the clinic. "Doctor, is she going to be able to see some of these people in a little while? They're driving us crazy out here."

Dr. Georgia Packard flipped a wisp of dark hair from her forehead and continued putting stitches in Johnnie's left hip. Numbed by exhaustion and whatever Packard had injected into the IV, Johnnie felt nothing as the needle went in again and Packard pulled the fine gut through.

"Same bunch caterwauling?" Packard snapped.

"Mr. Peabody, prowling around like a bear. Mr. Cobb, saying he's her fiancé and he has a right to be in here. Mr. Pennington, from the paper. A man from the radio station. Two of the county commissioners and the mayor."

"My, my," Packard murmured ironically, snipping off a knot. "Well, just tell them all to hold their goddamn horses. I'm busy. I'll talk to them in a few minutes."

The nurse hesitated in the doorway. "They all want to talk to her."

"Well, she's going upstairs to a private room, and I'm ordering no visitors."

"Yes, Doctor." The nurse started to back out.

Johnnie raised herself on one elbow. "Nurse? Wait a minute. Hey, Georgia, I can't go hide someplace now, of all times. I need to talk to them, and then I need to get out of here."

"Dammit, Johnnie," Packard said, cross. "Hold still or you'll yank that IV out and then we'll have a real mess here."

"Georgia, I'm not checking into this place."

Packard looked at the ceiling in exasperation. "Listen, dumb-dumb. Just because I've stitched a few lacerations and stuck on some Band-Aids, that doesn't mean you have any business tooting out of here like Dale Evans or Wonder Woman. These X rays show a couple of hairline cracks in your ribs, and I'd like to get some more shots of that thick skull of yours. You're dehydrated. Your left lung sounds like it's got a little fluid in it. You've been through a hell of an experience. I insist that you stay in bed here at least overnight, and then tomorrow we can talk about it."

Clutching the white cotton drape around herself, Johnnie sat all the way up. Everything reeled dizzily for an instant, but then straightened out. "Georgia, you play a mean golf game, but you're a flop as a curmudgeon. You don't scare me. Finish the bandages and I'm outta here. I mean it."

Georgia Packard rolled her pretty gray eyes. "If you insist on taking out that IV and walking, I can't be responsible."

"Take it out," Johnnie ordered, looking down with distaste at the tape-crusted intravenous needle and loops of clear plastic tubing. "I'm okay, I tell you!"

Packard leaned over to pull the tape from the back of Johnnie's hand. "This is not a smart thing to do."

"I'm sure you're right, Doc, and I appreciate your concern."

The needle came out hotly and a small piece of plastic tape went over the puncture wound. "I'm going to give you a shot of antibiotic, and then a prescription for some pills to take. I want to see you again tomorrow."

Johnnie swung her bare legs off the side of the table. "Is there a robe or something I could put on until my deputy gets back with a change of clothes? I mean a real robe, not one of those darned backless things."

Packard smiled. The smile softened her face and showed the nice person she was. "Modesty? I am deeply moved. Wait a minute." She left the room, closing the door firmly behind her.

Johnnie took several deep breaths, gently testing the level of her pain and her strength. The IV, or something they had put in it, had made her feel much better than she had any right to feel. She felt hectic and twitchy; probably running on adrenaline again, she thought.

Swiveling slightly on the table, she looked toward the big X-ray films still stuck on the vertical light table against the wall. She couldn't see the hairline cracks that Packard had found in her ribs. But when she breathed deeply—despite the tight tape job the doctor had done—she could feel the pain sharply enough.

There was nothing like almost dying to make you feel intensely alive, she thought ruefully. After the searchers had found her, she had been wide awake and mentally hyperclear for several minutes. She had passed out during part of the wild truck ride in, but then had come around, microscope clear again. Butt Peabody had tersely filled her in on things that had happened while she was playing journey to the center of the earth.

She still felt fully alert despite the odd mental sensations created by the stuff in the IV. She thought she saw a lot of what had been going on as far as the Greggs were concerned. She shuddered, remembering what she was certain must have been Barbara Gregg's blue face staring out of the black plastic wrap in the mine shaft. And Jim Way's death had to be connected to the Greggs. But it wasn't at all clear exactly how. But she knew enough now to be able to imagine some things that could be done to try to clarify everything. There was no time to waste in following through. She could rest and recuperate another day.

The door of the examining room popped open. Johnny turned back toward it, expecting Georgia Packard. Instead, Carl Rieger bustled in, his face sweaty and blotched by strong emotion. Johnnie clutched the drape more tightly around her body.

"I'm glad you're all right," Rieger fumed, pointing a pudgy index finger at her. "But that was a *despicable* thing to do!"

"What was?" Johnnie asked, bewildered.

"Going to the governor! Getting that order to send a medical team down all the way from Grand Junction to tear up the remains of poor Jim! My God, they're already over at the funeral home, doing that gruesome business! And when it was obviously a drunken accident that we've all tried to cover over for Myldred's sake! How do you think this has made her feel? She's over at the courthouse right now, hysterical! All our plans for the funeral have been canceled. She's talking lawsuit. What kind of woman are you, anyhow? Don't you care about anything but playing Dick Tracy games at the expense of—"

"That's enough!"

Rieger stopped in midsentence. His eyes widened. "What? How *dare* you—"

"How dare *you!*" Johnnie shot back, instantly as outraged as she had ever been in her life. She began to shake with anger. "You . . . you asshole! You officious piece of . . . piece of . . ." She stopped long enough to gasp air. "Look, Carl! I didn't contact the governor and get these court orders you're talking about. I guess I wasn't smart enough to think of trying that. Butt Peabody did it. And God bless him for it! We've had two gunshot murders—we already know that much about the Greggs—and anybody who wouldn't see the possibility of a link with Jim's crazy death has got to be brain-dead. Another girl—a friend of Barbara Gregg—is missing, too, her car down at the foot of a mountain. Maybe it's time you stopped thinking about town and county PR and started making sense for a change!"

It was a long speech, and she stopped, suddenly light-headed for want of air. She was shaking uncontrollably, pumping adrenaline giving her a hot flash.

Rieger, at first slack-faced with shock at her counterattack, had gone slit-eyed and cold as she pounded him. His lower lip trembled and his voice went hoarsely ugly with venom: "You'll never serve out the month as acting sheriff, you pushy bitch."

"Get the fuck out of here!" Johnnie yelled.

The door flew open. Georgia Packard and the nurse rushed in. Packard, a large white plastic bag in her hand, gave Rieger an acid look. "You were asked to wait outside!"

"I needed to talk to this . . . this young woman. I . . ."

Packard pointed at the open door. "Out."

"You can't talk to me like that!"

"Out, goddammit, or I call hospital security! I mean it, Carl!"

With one more hate-filled glare at Johnnie, Rieger stormed out of the room.

Packard closed the door none too gently. "Shithead." Then she noticed Johnnie's shakes. She came over and put an arm around her. "Hey, what's all this?"

"He just made me so damn mad," Johnnie said, and felt her eyes go wet.

Packard stroked her back. "Yeah. Well, I suppose I'll hear about throwing him out, but sometimes, honest to Christ, some of these guys . . ." She motioned to the nurse. "Go get one of our security guys. Tell him I said to stand in front of this door."

The nurse hurried out. Johnnie pointed to the heavy-looking plastic bag. "Is that a robe?"

"No." Packard handed over the bag. "Your deputy just got back with your extra clothes."

"Great." Beginning to steady, Johnnie reached for the bag.

"You insist on leaving?"

"Yeah." Johnnie slid off the gurney, experienced another moment of weakness, and slipped out of the hospital gown.

The doctor eyed her professionally. "You're white as that sheet. Are you sure about this?"

"Dead sure."

Packard sighed. "I hope that phraseology doesn't turn out to be more accurate than you think."

Hanging on to the gurney for balance, Johnnie managed to get into her underwear and reached for her Levi's. "Can I talk to Luke and Butt in here for a minute?"

"Sure. No problem. What about the others? Niles Pennington is still out there. When last heard he was lecturing our counter nurse about the First Amendment."

Johnnie hesitated. She realized quite suddenly that she no longer cared at all what Niles Pennington printed in his rag, what Carl Rieger threatened, or anything else of that nature. She felt a gust of self-confidence that put new strength in her. Something had happened down there in the mine, or some other way she didn't yet understand. All at once she was free—really *free*—of worrying what other people might think and even whether she was fit for this job. It was a heady feeling, great.

She giggled and said, "Screw Niles, too. Just Luke and Butt, okay?"

Packard watched her button her blouse. "Ready to see them now?"

"Please."

Left alone again, Johnnie finished zipping up and was just pulling on her socks when the door opened and Butt came in, followed by Luke. Butt's eyes devoured her as Luke hurried to her side and grabbed her in a bear hug.

She winced. "Take it easy on the rib cage."

"Sorry! Sorry!" He looked at her with X-ray eyes. "Are you *okay?*"

"The doc wanted me to stay overnight, but I'm fine." She turned to Peabody. "Butt, have you heard anything more from the autopsies going on over there?"

Peabody nodded. "Just talked to John Lemptke. The boys from Grand Junction are working on Jim's remains, and then they said they plan to go right back and redo John's work on the Greggs. He's mighty pi—upset about that. They say they'll have an oral report on Jim by noon, latest."

"What did John find on the Greggs on his first exam?"

"Both of them were shot to death. I already told you that."

Luke stroked Johnnie's hands. "Can't we talk about this later? How do you feel? Can I get you anything?" His eyes filled with pain and worry. "Listen, I'm taking you to my place when we leave here. I won't take no for an answer. You need rest and quiet."

"Hush, Luke," Johnnie said. She turned back to Peabody. "Same gun for both, or did he establish that?"

"Not the same gun. The girl was shot once with a .45-caliber slug. The daddy took three 9mm copperclads right in the chest from close range. Two killings, two different guns, and none of that tells us anything about how and why Big Jim laid himself across the railroad track."

"He didn't lay himself across that track, Butt."

"I think that's pretty obvious by now. He went by the old mine, saw somebody messing around, checked into it, found whoever was trying to hide the Greggs where nobody would ever find them, and got himself killed for his trouble."

Johnnie nodded. "I'm going to the office from here. We can talk on the way. If we use the back exit, maybe we can duck Niles and the kid from KTCK."

Luke protested, "Honey, you need rest! I want you to come home with me."

"Luke, there's work to be done, dammit. I'm sorry, but that's the way it is."

"But you're not well!"

"I'm well enough. Look. I've got a theory I want to check out right away. Maybe I can get the job done with some local calls. If not, I still might be able to track down a couple of old friends in Hollywood who could help me with what I need to know. This can't wait, Luke!"

Luke stiffened. "Okay, then. Nothing I can do to change your mind?"

Johnnie wished she could make him understand. "Honey, it's my job."

"Yes. Of course." He bent to brush his lips across her cheek. His smile seemed stiff, forced. "Hey, I'll go look in at the studio and make sure it's still there. Call me if there's anything I can do, okay?"

"Okay," she said gratefully.

He managed to make the smile a slight grin. "See you guys later."

The treatment room door closed quietly behind him. Johnnie looked at Peabody, trying to read his expression.

She said. "He's a good guy, Butt. Really."

"Sure," Peabody said quietly. "He's tired. We're all tired. He just wants what's best for you."

"Will you drive me to the courthouse?"

His eyebrows arched in surprise. "Why, hell yes. Whatever you want from me, you got."

That made her feel better. "Let's get after it, then."

1:35 P.M.

IN THE SMALL, barren back waiting room off the mortuary area, Butt paced back and forth, puffing a cigarette, while Johnnie sat on the hard folding chair and listened to her body hurt. She had had good luck with her second telephone call to California, and it had verified her guesswork. But she had begun to realize why Georgia Packard had wanted her to stay in the hospital: Fatigue had come with a vengeance, her left knee had begun to swell painfully, and the prescription-strength Motrin wasn't putting much of a dent in her other aches and pains.

Waiting for first results on the total tissue examination of Jim was hardly conducive to relaxation.

"How much longer, do you suppose?" she asked Peabody.

He shrugged. "I expected word before now."

"What do we do, Butt, if they don't find anything?"

Peabody's left eyebrow canted. "Punt?"

"I'm serious."

"Me, too. If those boys don't find some other cause of death, we're out of work and maybe in for a lawsuit from Myldred."

"What about the Gregg part of it?"

"We don't have all the answers yet, but the stuff you just got on the telephone makes part of it pretty obvious, doesn't it?"

"In theory, yes. But where's our evidence?"

Peabody scratched his head. "Maybe we can locate a gun—get a ballistics match."

"That's a long shot, Butt."

He rolled his eyes toward her. "Tell me about it."

"Then we're back where we—"

The outside door swung open. Carl Rieger, trailed by Mayor Copely and Chubby Mayfield, walked into the small room, bringing chill wind that swirled Peabody's thick cigarette smoke.

Grimacing, Rieger waved his hand in front of his face. "Do you have to smoke in here?"

Peabody, stone-faced, stabbed his cigarette into the aluminum ashtray. "Sorry."

Rieger turned to Johnnie. "Any report yet from this wild-goose chase?"

"Not yet," Johnnie said icily.

"I don't have to remind you of the consequences if this preposterous embarrassment doesn't *fully* support whatever harebrained theory the two of you seem to have."

Johnnie refused to flinch from his stare, and glared right back. "No, Carl," she said softly. "You don't have to remind me."

"What are they doing in there? Why is it taking so long?" Rieger strode toward a small, wire-reinforced window high in the steel door that led to the mortuary rooms. "They're right in here?"

"Yes," Johnnie said.

Rieger went on tiptoe to reach the window.

"You don't want to look in there, bub," Peabody grunted.

"Why wouldn't I?" Rieger demanded. He peered through the glass. "I can see—oh!" He dropped back off his toes and turned quickly from the little window. His facial color vanished. "Yes. No. I mean, I don't." He put his hand over his mouth and hurried out of the waiting room.

Five minutes passed. Rieger came back, gray-faced. Peabody sat beside Johnnie. Mayor Copely paced the floor. Chubby Mayfield thumbed at a two-year-old issue of *People*. A few more minutes dragged by. Johnnie's nerves stretched tighter.

At two o'clock the steel door swung open. John Lemptke, wearing a floor-length latex apron and white surgical gloves, came out carrying a small, half-circular white porcelain pan. One of the state-ordered forensics experts had followed him as far as the doorway, but waited there, expressionless. Lemptke was pale.

"You didn't find anything, right?" Rieger said nervously.

Lemptke walked over to where Johnnie and Peabody sat. He held the surgical-type pan down so they could look inside.

"What is it? What is it?" Rieger demanded, pushing up to his side to get a look.

In the bottom of the pan, wet with a thin, brownish liquid, were two small, lumpy, dark metal objects about an inch long. Slightly misshapen, they were still obviously identifiable as large-caliber bullets.

2:30 P.M

W HEN DAVE DICKENSEN drove back into the rear parking lot of DD Security Systems and saw Butt Peabody's battered pickup truck there, his uneasy lunch, half a tasteless BLT that had stuck in his throat, turned over in his stomach.

Dickensen had heard the chatter on the scanner early this morning, and had had two informative calls from Hesther Gretsch. He knew Johnnie Baker was out, and he knew about the bullets found in the Greggs as well as the special experts coming in to do a new, minute examination on the body of Jim Way. Dickensen did not really know about Way's death; he had fought to keep from thinking about it, speculating about what must almost surely be the story. Now that events on all sides were coming together, everything was far worse than it had seemed even in the middle of a sleepless night. He had been a fool. Now it was too late. He felt dazed, paralyzed.

Peabody's appearance now could only mean disaster. Dickensen felt an urge to turn back to his car and run—anywhere—and never stop running. But he couldn't do that. Maybe . . . somehow . . . he could brave it through.

Peabody, long legs outstretched and battered felt hat tipped down over his eyes, sat in the straight chair against the wall outside Dickensen's office, looking for all the world like he was taking a quick snooze. Dickensen wanted to yell obscenities and kick his booted feet out of the way. Don't play mind games with me, goddammit. Don't you know I'm smarter than that?

His foot scraped the floor. Peabody tipped his hat back with an index finger and straightened up. "Oh. Glad you're back, Dave. Want to have a little chat with you."

"What is it?" Dickensen demanded. To his dismay, he could hear the tenseness crackle in his own voice. "Is this official business?"

"Well, you might say that, yes," Peabody said, and yawned. They went into Dickensen's office.

"What is it this time?" Dickensen grated.

"Well, Dave, it's like this. It seems like both those bodies we found out at the mine had bullets in them. Preliminary report says death by gunshot wound in both cases. Little girl and her daddy, both. Sad."

"What does that have to do with me?"

"Seems like . . . you know . . . when a couple of people are shot to death, there's got to be a perpetrator out there someplace."

"Are you trying to be funny? You're wasting my time! What do you *want?*"

Peabody's eerily calm eyes never left his. "Strange thing. They weren't shot with the same gun."

"So what? Why should I care? What do you want from me?"

"He was shot with a 9mm Luger-type bullet, she with an old army-style load: a .45."

Dickensen felt like screaming and going across the desk at him. "So? So?"

"Then," Peabody went on in the same maddening, sleepy tone, "there's the matter of Big Jim."

He's trying to trap you somehow. How? "What about him?"

"Nice enough man, Big Jim. Of course, I didn't appreciate it, the way he beat me out of office. But he wasn't such a bad person."

"Are you going to get to the point? I'm sick of this! State your business or get out of here! I've got work to do!"

"Old Jim didn't die as a result of that train running over him."

"Didn't?" Dickensen croaked.

Peabody's eyes looked like mercury, totally unwavering as they watched. "Two bullets found."

The information speared Dickensen's gut like a frozen knife. "Bullets?" My God, it was just what he had most feared, had tried to convince himself could not be true. Panic rioted. But Peabody was watching—watching with those quicksilver eyes, waiting. Say something—anything. "Jim was shot?"

"Yep. That surprise you, Dave?"

"Hell, yes, it surprises me! Doesn't it surprise you?"

"Yeah, and there's another real funny thing. Except not ha-ha funny, just strange funny. Bullets dug out of Jim don't match either of the calibers found in the other bodies. He was shot with a .357 Magnum, looks like." Peabody sighed. "Three murders. Three different guns. Puzzling, wouldn't you say?"

Dickensen's thin cords of self-control began to fray. He could feel them going. "It's not for me to say, is it? I don't know anything about law enforcement. I just run a little security firm, here."

"Odd, though, wouldn't you say? Shoot a man and then go to all the bother of hauling his carcass down to the railroad track to make it look like an accident?"

"How should *I* know? Why are you telling me all this? What do you want from me?"

Peabody produced a bent cigarette and lit it with a wood match. The smoke swirled, making Dickensen almost gag.

"Dave, a year or two ago you bought a couple of those pretty Taurus PT99 AF's, didn't you? And a couple of Glocks, I think I remember. Both shoot a 9mm Luger cartridge, your standard 124-grain metal case bullet."

"I got—" Dickensen began, but his words came out a wet gargle. He cleared his throat and started again. "I got them for some of my people. Every one of them is registered. You know that."

"So I guess," Peabody said slowly, "you wouldn't mind if we wanted to mess around with this, play detective, you know, have the state boys do some ballistics tests—sort of compare the markings on slugs fired from all your 9mm with the slugs dug out of Daddy Gregg?"

A gust of relief, hot as orgasm, coursed through Dickensen. Peabody was fishing! They had nothing on him! Hinson's Glock had been his own, not company issue, and it was so deep in San Juan Lake no one would ever find it. "It will be a nuisance, Butt. But if you insist, I can produce every registered weapon we've got."

Peabody nodded as if satisfied. "Any old .45s or .357s you might have laying around, too, ten-four?"

Dickensen made his voice angry. "You don't think any of *my* people had anything to do with any of this, do you?"

Peabody smiled and spread his big hands, palms up. "Lord, no! We just want to cover all the bases, you know? I mean, I'm just a has-been who wasn't even smart enough to get reelected, and Johnnie is just a girl. But something weird happened around here the other night. *Real* weird. If there's some way we can get to the bottom of it, we ought to try, don't you agree? You, of all people, with your security business, want law and order."

Dickensen got shakily to his feet. "We'll cooperate, Butt. You bring a court order, we'll cooperate."

"Need a court order, do we?"

"You're fucking right! I'm beginning to resent this!"

Peabody rose and stretched as if just waking from a nap. "Oh, one more thing, about your man Hinson—the one you had on the Sky Estates gate the night all this stuff happened?"

"Hinson? Hinson? Where did you get an idea like that? Hinson had already left the company. I was on the gate myself that night. I've *told* you people that!"

"Yeah, so you said before. But isn't it funny how people remember things different!"

Dickensen's guts had drawn tight again. "What do you mean by that?"

"I talked with a couple of your boys who say Hinson was supposed to be on the gate all this week."

"They don't know anything. I don't go around issuing handouts every time somebody leaves us. Our computer duty rosters can back up everything I've said."

"Yes, uh-huh. But your receptionist tells me you've had some computer system problems. Wiped out a lot of valuable personnel and assignment records, she says."

"Yes, but I know what the truth is!"

For the first time, Peabody looked directly into Dickensen's eyes with none of the pretended laziness. "Johnnie has gone out to Brandon Warner's place, Dave. We don't know exactly what took place, or how, or what the three different guns mean, or a lot of other things. But she's got a theory about part of it. And after hearing what she dug up on Warner from some friends in Hollywood, I'd say her theory starts to make quite a bit of sense, even with all the holes left in it."

The shock that jolted through Dickensen's nervous system made everything that had come earlier feel like nothing. "Brandon Warner? Jesus Christ! She's gone out there to *confront* Brandon Warner? She can't do that!"

Peabody's thin smile was mirthless. "She's headstrong, Dave. When she gets an idea, there's no stopping her." He paused, heaved a sigh, and moved toward the door. "If what we think is true, I guess after she gets him behind bars we'll have to be asking more questions of you too, Dave. I guess I was hoping you might be a little more forthcoming right now, but I see I was wrong. See you later, pal."

Peabody pulled the office door open and walked out.

Dickensen stood behind his desk, ice running in his veins.

Three guns.

Three deaths.

Jim Way killed with a .357 Magnum.

Dickensen knew he should have guessed as much. But he had been desperately denying reality every moment since that night.

That night—Christ, only last Wednesday, and it seemed an eternity since then! How could he have been so stupid? How could he have panicked the way he did, let himself get caught in front of this avalanche? He was going to be ruined. He might go to prison for the rest of his life. Why couldn't he have seen how hideous this could become?

Standing at his desk, he flashed back to Wednesday night. His mind blanked out the reality of his office, and he was back there again, in the chaos of it.

Going into the Brandon Warner house . . .

He would never forget his feeling as he saw Hinson at the head of the great staircase, read his expression, took the stairs three at a time and followed his guard down the long hallway to the door that led into the master bedroom. That moment of shock would live with him forever.

Brandon Warner, buck naked, staggering around the room, tears streaming down his face. Warner, drunk or drugged or both, stoned out of his mind, hardly in control enough to stand.

At the far left corner of the bed, sprawled faceup on the floor in a puddle of blackish blood, a woman—a young girl, actually, she couldn't have been much more than eighteen— the front of her slender, almost spindly nude body splashed all over with blood from the gaping gunshot wound in her lower chest.

Closer, almost at the shocked Dickensen's feet, *another* body, this of a man, dark-dressed, facedown, arms and legs akimbo, and another spreading soggy red wetness on the carpet beneath him.

And Boris, great, hulking, beetle-browed Boris, looking for

all the insane world like something out of an old comic
horror TV movie, standing just to the side, watching
everything, swaying on legs as thick as wharf pilings, the
overhead light gleaming on his wet, slicked-down black hair,
his piggy eyes unreadable. Calm. Mad.

It was a scene from hell. Brandon Warner began moaning
incoherently.

Hinson plucking at Dickensen's sleeve. "I came in behind
him and I was too late and he'd shot her and he turned on
me and I had to shoot him first. It was self-defense, honest
to Christ, boss! It was him or me!"

"We'll have to call the sheriff," Dickensen remembered
blurting at once. "We'll have to—" He had stopped then, and
confronted Warner. "Who are these people? How did this
happen?"

"Happen?" The word seemed to penetrate Brandon
Warner's drugged stupor for a second. "She's just a girl,
someone from town. She and another girl—I can't remember
names—I don't know who this man was. She said something
about her father looking for her."

"We'll have to call the sheriff. It was self-defense. We'll
have to just tell everything the way it happened."

That had been when Warner's eyes suddenly took on
genuine awareness. "Tell everyone what happened? Have
this scandal dragged through every tabloid in the world?
Ruin my career just when I'm ready to make a comeback?
Impossible! No one must ever know about any of this!"

"But how—" Dickensen had begun in confusion.

"Get out!" Warner had yelled at him. "Just get out, both
of you, you and your man! You don't know a thing! You were
never here!" Warner turned to Boris, standing unmoving
against the wall, watching, listening, taking in everything.
"Boris! You can fix this. You always fix everything. You can
take their bodies away somewhere, can't you, Boris? You can
take care of this for me, can't you, Boris? Tell me you can fix
this bad thing!"

Dickensen could still remember how Boris had blinked,

nodded, turned toward him and Hinson. "You leave. I can take care of everything."

"But—"

Warner had rushed unevenly to a tall antique armoire against the far wall. Flinging the doors open, he rummaged in a drawer, turned, careened back across the room toward Dickensen and Hinson. Naked, bloated, whale-blubber fat beneath coarse black body hair, he stank of liquor and dope and sweaty sex. "Here! Take this! It's a bonus for your trouble! Now for God's sake, just go! Go!"

The thick package he thrust into Dickensen's hands had been a bank-type bundle of money. Hundreds. Hundreds and hundreds and hundreds.

And at that moment the fear had knifed into Dickensen's own bowels in a way he had never known before. He could report all this. He should report all this. And the scandal would roll over him, too, and his ruination would be far more certain than Warner's. He had imagined the talk: "Dave Dickensen? DD Security? Oh, yeah, right. The one that had the deal where the two people were shot to death when he was supposed to be providing security, and I hear there was dope and booze and every other goddamn thing involved. Right. Hire his outfit and buy yourself a murder or something!"

That instant's horrific vision had made the decision for him. He didn't need this. He hadn't had anything to do with it. It had all been an accident. Warner was a millionaire many times over—world famous. If he said Boris could handle it, then Boris could handle it. If anything goes wrong, let them take the hit for it. Just get out of there. He had grabbed the gaping Hinson's arm and dragged him out of there.

It would be all right, he had told himself then. Maybe the other girl could be a problem, but he could find her. Warner could pay her off, too. And then nothing more would ever come of it.

And until now, Dickensen had tried to convince himself that it really all had been just a horribly unlucky accident, and that big Jim Way's death had no connection.

But now he knew better.

Three guns.

The father of the girl had rushed in, tried to shoot Warner, and had shot his own child instead. With a .45. Hinson, coming in behind him, had fired reflexively with his Glock.

Jim Way had died by a third gun. A .357 Magnum.

Boris owned a .357. Dickensen had seen him lovingly cleaning and oiling it once in the hallway while he and Warner talked.

Dickensen had never known how Boris tried to "fix" everything last Wednesday night. But now he could imagine. Boris must have put the bodies of the girl and her father in the estate van and then taken them to the old mine. Why he had done that rather than bury them, Dickensen would never know. Maybe he hadn't thought there was time to bury them, or maybe he couldn't think of a place less likely to be disturbed than the old mine—perhaps for decades, perhaps even longer.

So he had gone there to finish his grisly mission. Then by the worst accident, Jim Way had bumbled by, probably a little crocked as he often was on his late-night drive-arounds. Boris had had his .357 with him.

A .357 Magnum had killed Jim Way.

Boris had killed the sheriff.

Boris had killed Donna Smith, too. Now that events had begun to domino, he might kill anyone who seemed to threaten Brandon Warner. He was a madman, and Warner had no control over him.

And Johnnie Baker was on the way out there now.

The hollow cough of a starting truck engine hurled Dickensen back into the present. All his thoughts had taken only seconds. Butt Peabody was just leaving the rear of the building.

You can just stand here in the office, a voice in Dickensen's head told him.

The thought made something putrid burst like a pus pocket inside his mind. He could not let it happen again.

Peabody had just backed around to drive out of the lot,

and his eyes widened in surprise as Dickensen ran out in front of the truck, waving wildly for him to stop.

Peabody rolled the window down. "What the hell?"

"You've got to stop her," Dickensen choked.

"Stop—?"

"Johnnie! Call her on the radio! Stop her! She mustn't go out there alone and start asking Warner a lot of questions. You don't know what you're dealing with here!"

"What are you talking about? I was running a bluff when I acted like she planned to bring him in. We don't have that much yet. I was trying to jar something out of you, just like she's going to try out there."

Dickensen reached through the open truck window and frantically shook Peabody's shoulders. "You don't understand! The estate's gate is on automatic during the day. There's no guard. You call and they buzz you through, and it's just going to be her up there, and Warner, and Boris!"

"So what? So *what!* Goddammit, man, spit it out!"

"Boris! Jesus Christ, Butt! He *must* be the one who killed Jim. He has to have killed the Smith girl, too. He's crazy!"

Peabody reached for his microphone. "You're telling me a lot here, Dave. I guess you know that."

"Just stop her! Do you want *more* people dead? *Stop her!*"

2:35 P.M

FATIGUE GNAWED AT every muscle in Johnnie's body as she parked in front of Brandon Warner's soaring stone-and-redwood chalet. Only her nervous excitement kept her moving briskly. This was a showdown.

Turning off her walkie-talkie, she left it on the seat of the Jeep and carried her notebook up the broad front steps of the mansion. Magpies swooped and chattered across the lawn and squirrels and chipmunks scampered. She pressed the doorbell button and waited.

She felt slightly foolish and uncomfortable in her light-weight gray gabardine uniform blouse and slacks, with the sheriff's badge gleaming on the left breast, the Tenoclock County emblem on one shoulder and the American flag sewn on the other, and even the ridiculously heavy .357 Magnum service revolver belted on her right hip. Her hurried change before coming out here might, however, give her the smallest psychological edge; even the high and mighty sometimes felt a twinge of intimidation at the sight of the uniform and artillery of the law, and she needed every possible advantage she could get if this was to have a chance of working.

The heavy front door swung open and a handsome, middle-aged Chicano woman wearing a blue work dress and white apron stared out at her.

"Sheriff Baker to see Mr. Warner," Johnnie told her.

The woman just stared, not comprehending. A figure moved in the relative dimness behind her, and Brandon Warner, wearing a black dinner jacket over faded Levi's and a lumberjack shirt, came into view. "She doesn't understand a word of English, Sheriff!" He unleashed a brief burst of Spanish at the woman, and she bowed and rustled away somewhere. Warner swung the door wider. The smile was only on his lips. He looked anything but friendly. "You said on the gate telephone that you were here on official business?"

"May I come in?" Johnnie asked coolly.

"I'm very busy."

"This won't take long."

Warner heaved a martyr's sigh. "Come in, then."

Johnnie entered. He closed the door, then wordlessly led her to the left, through two doorways, and into what might have been called a parlor or sitting room in an older house. Smaller than most rooms in the mansion, it was furnished in Spartan black and white contemporary, with sun-washed windows looking out onto a grove of changing aspen. A hummingbird who should have long since flown south buzzed around a feeder just beyond the glass.

Boris O'Neal was already in the room, sitting rigidly still in one of the large white leather chairs near the windows. His eyes followed Johnnie like slowly turning ball bearings.

Brandon Warner walked to the sleek white leather couch and draped his thick body across its length. "Sit down, Sheriff," he said with distaste. "If you must."

Johnnie took a chair facing him across a long coffee table. She could feel Boris's eyes on her. Under the material of her shirtsleeves, her arms prickled with bumps. Something primitive radiated from Warner's bodyguard, something unimaginable. Instinct was shouting warnings below the level of cognition.

Warner placed a cigarette in a holder and Boris moved quickly, with surprising grace for a big man, to produce a small Colibri lighter. Warner inhaled and studied Johnnie through the smoke. "Now. Your business?"

Johnnie spoke as she had planned: "Had Barbara Gregg often been here before, Mr. Warner? Or was Wednesday night her first visit?"

Warner's hand, in motion with his cigarette toward his mouth, hesitated just an instant. His face showed absolutely nothing. "Barbara? Barbara who? I have no idea what you're talking about."

He was good, Johnnie thought ruefully. Dammit, he was far too good. Her verbal leap for the jugular, intended to take him off his guard, had accomplished nothing: He hadn't so much as blinked an eye.

Nothing to do but go on with it. "I'm talking about Barbara Gregg, the young woman whose body we found in the old Interocean mine. She had been a houseguest of yours."

Warner stabbed the cigarette into an ashtray. Red sparks flew. "Nonsense! How ridiculous! Barbara Gregg? What kind of a little nobody was she? Good heavens! Unless she happened to crash one of my infrequent parties, I'm quite sure she would never have been allowed to set foot on my property!" He turned his head. "Boris? Have you ever heard of this Gregg person?"

Boris's mouth opened like a trapdoor. "No. Never."

Warner gestured in the air. "There you are. As my bodyguard, Boris has taught himself to have an encyclopedic memory for names and faces. You may think he's a lout. Admittedly he looks and sometimes acts like one. But his loyalty to me is unflinching. He has taught himself this facility with names and faces the better to protect me from sensation seekers."

Warner got ponderously to his feet. "Is there anything else, Sheriff?"

She hadn't laid a glove on him. She pressed on: "You remember her, Mr. Warner. She was a friend of Donna Smith. And you certainly remember Donna Smith; she had been out here several times before."

For the first time, Warner's fleshy face colored with anger. "I think that's about enough! I don't know any—what was her name?—Barbara something-or-other, and I certainly don't know any Donna Smith. If you want to prove otherwise, Sheriff, I suggest you produce testimony from this Barbara whoever, or this Donna nobody. Otherwise . . ."

A light on the small, ivory telephone at Warner's elbow began to flash. She waited.

Warner waved airily. "The machine upstairs will get it. I've already picked up *one* too many calls today. Was there more, Sheriff? Or shall Boris escort you out?"

"You know Barbara is dead," Johnnie told him, "because I just told you we found her body in the mine. I think you also know about Donna Smith."

Warner waved the question aside. "What are you trying to do? Are you implying *I* had something to do with all that? What is this? The cheap tabloid game? Make up any wild story and try to pin it on a celebrity?"

"You would be better off to answer my questions, Mr. Warner."

"I've had enough of this. Boris, show the lady out."

Boris moved ponderously. Johnnie got quickly to her feet. "We have a witness, Mr. Warner. If you don't cooperate now, we'll be back with a warrant."

Boris O'Neal took a step closer. Johnnie backed up. "I'm leaving."

"You bet you are!" Warner snapped.

Johnnie backed toward the door. "We have some mutual friends in Hollywood."

"What?"

Johnnie played her last card. "Your reputation goes far and wide. How fascinated you are by young women—by *very* young women—girls. How often the police even in Tinseltown have almost been forced to seek criminal charges for those little parties you like to get minor children into."

Warner's face contorted. "This is outrageous!"

"That's why you have all the video equipment upstairs, isn't it? To make a record of your fun and games? Did you make a tape with Barbara Gregg Wednesday night, Mr. Warner?"

"Get out!" Warner roared. "Boris!"

O'Neal reached for Johnnie. She danced back from him, moving into the foyer. She called back, "Don't try to leave Tenoclock. I'll be back."

Boris made a guttural sound in his throat. Johnnie turned and hurried out the front door, half ran down the steps to her waiting Jeep. She climbed in fast, started it up, and drove away from the house.

She was drenched with nervous perspiration. Maybe it had worked, she thought. *Maybe* he would crack and do something foolish, or even decide his best course of action was to explain what had happened. At any rate, she had not been bluffing. He hadn't cracked, but she could get search warrants now, and come back.

The air was cold, not more than fifty degrees, but she jerked the window flap open and let the wind rush in on her. It felt icy and good.

The rushing wind riffled the pages of her notebook on the

empty seat beside her along with the walkie-talkie she had forgotten to turn back on.

2:50 P.M.

BUTT PEABODY THREW the microphone across the seat of his truck. "Goddammit! First they don't answer the phone and now she doesn't answer on the radio!"

"Do something!" Dave Dickensen said thickly. "Do anything!"

"I'll be back for you." Peabody slammed his truck into reverse and backed away from the building, leaving Dickensen standing there in a cloud of gravel dust.

Laying on the horn, he terrorized about a dozen motorists as he wheeled across Silver Street, cutting through to the highway. Once on the pavement leading north out of town, he scrambled for the microphone again to call the office and issue some orders. But he knew he was far closer than anyone else to Sky Estates, and if he couldn't get there in time, no one could. He put the accelerator to the floor, and the rebuilt 450 V8 under the hood began to sing as the speedometer swung up toward 100.

2:50 P.M.

BRANDON WARNER LISTENED to the fading sound of Johnnie Baker's Jeep. Turning from the window, he strode angrily up and down the length of the white room, waving his hands over his head, letting himself have a fit.

"Damn, this is terrible! How much more does she know? How could we ever convince anyone now that it was all just bad luck?" He turned to confront Boris, statuelike in the foyer doorway. "What do you think she'll do, Boris? Was it a bluff? I don't think so. This is ghastly! I don't know what to do!"

Boris suddenly turned and started away from the doorway.

"Boris? Where are you going?"

Boris lumbered straight on, robot legs making his lumberjack boots thud on the floor with each stride. "She won't hurt you. I will fix."

Warner stared for just an instant, not understanding.

Then he did.

"Boris! Wait a minute! *Boris!* No! Good God, *no!* There's got to be some other way!" He ran into the foyer. "Boris!"

Ignoring him, Boris shambled across the staircase. He started up, taking the steps three at a time.

"Wait!"

Boris ignored him and disappeared into the upstairs hallway.

"Christ," Warner groaned, so upset he spoke aloud. "If he hadn't bumbled into the sheriff Wednesday night, none of this would have happened! The girl and her father would be hidden in that mine for years, maybe forever. I should have asked if it all went well when he came back. If I had known at once about the sheriff—that stupid trick of trying to make it look like a train accident . . ."

A sound above interrupted him. Looking up, he saw Boris coming back down the stairs, his big revolver in his hand.

"What do you think you're going to do with *that?*"

Boris reached the foyer and brushed past him without a word. Going to the priceless Queen Anne desk, he opened the key drawer and pulled out the keys to the van.

Everything had spun out of control. Frantic, Warner rushed across the tile floor, losing one of his shapeless loafers as he grabbed Boris by the arm. "Jesus, man! Stop! You'll only make things even worse!"

Boris rumbled, "I can fix it."

"*No,* damn you!" Warner tried to swing him around.

Boris jerked his arm, tearing loose from Warner's grasp. It

was a gesture a man might use to flick away an insect, but it made Boris's hand hit Warner with blinding power. Warner was knocked backward like a doll. Arms windmilling in a vain attempt to regain his balance, he smashed into a glass tier-top table stacked with his darling dead mother's collection of little Hummels and gleaming pale Lladros. The table went over. Warner went with it, hitting the floor with shocking force. Shattered glass and pieces of pottery showered down around him and he felt sharp, hot pain in his mouth.

Struggling dazedly to his knees, he saw that Boris had vanished outside. He raised himself, cutting his hands on shards that covered the floor with a crystalline glitter. He staggered to his feet and careened to the open doorway.

Boris was nowhere to be seen.

Then Warner heard the sound—an engine. He reeled onto the vast front porch. From the side of the mansion—from the garage area—the estate van slammed into view, engine screaming. Warner got just a glimpse of Boris hunched over the steering wheel.

"Boris! No!"

There was no way Boris could have heard. The big van rocketed down the driveway and vanished behind the trees.

Warner sagged against a massive redwood support post. He was ruined, he thought. He was finished. Nothing could help now.

2:53 P.M.

DOWNSHIFTING AT THE sharp switchback curve that marked the start of the steep grade down the mountain, Johnnie took a deep breath and started thinking about her next step. A fat brown marmot, sitting high beside the road, distracted her by suddenly deciding to dart across the pavement in front of her. She braked more sharply and the animal made it into the brush on the high, upslope side of the road to her left. On her right there was no guardrail, and the terrain dropped off precipitously into tumbled boulders, brush, and a dense stand of spruce intermingled with a few golden aspen. A hawk sat on a stump, ignoring the Jeep's passage. A team of magpies dive-bombed something unseen in the high grass, then swooped sharply upward against the sky, turning on one another. Far off and below on the right, through a slight haze, lay the river valley and the distant clutter of Tenoclock.

Another sharp turn in the road took the town out of view. Ahead were several more sharp switchbacks, nothing but jagged rock on the uphill side, steep declivity and trees on the right. Driving automatically, Johnnie tried again to sort things out in her mind.

She was sure now that something unbelievably bad had happened at Brandon Warner's mansion last Wednesday night. Proving it was going to be another matter.

Warner might be a great actor, she thought, but the hidden side of his life was as black as the caverns she had crawled through only hours ago. She had not set out to learn this, or even to solve the riddle of the disappearance of a father and his daughter. But fate had brought her this way, and now she knew that the bizarre attempt to hide Jim Way's murder by placing his body on the railroad track was directly related to the other horrors. She thought about Dave Dickensen, and what Butt had told her about his name on the Gregg man's notepad. How he was involved was not yet clear.

Movement in the big outside rearview mirror caught her eye for an instant: a full-size van, taking a curve a hundred yards behind, higher on the curving downhill road. The driver would be on her within a minute at the speed he was coming, much too fast for this section of the road. Under other circumstances she might have slowed further, then reached out and stuck her flashing red light on top of the Velcro sewn onto the canvas top of the Jeep. As it was, she intended to let the idiot go by.

She returned to her worries about the deaths, and Brandon Warner. Her ideas were all fine and good, she thought, all excellent theory as far as they went. But they didn't go far enough, and she had no proof of anything. Her bluff hadn't worked. Bluffs never seemed to work in real life the way they always did for Perry Mason.

In her rearview mirror she caught sight of the oncoming van again. It had closed fast, was rounding the switchback just behind her. She edged closer to the shoulder to let him pass.

Ballistics tests were the next stop, she thought. And there was always the faint hope that continued work on the autopsies might develop a new bit of information. Also, despite what Dickensen had been saying all along, she would put Butt onto the job of trying to track down the now-vanished DD guard named Hinson. They had to redouble their efforts to find Donna Smith's body, too. And question Phyllis Shaw more intensely in case they had missed some angle with her.

The van filled her rearview mirrors. She edged even closer to the shoulder, the Jeep's right wheels biting gravel at the edge. The van pulled out to pass. Johnnie instantly eased off the gas. The guy was a maniac! Another sharp inside curve lay just ahead, nothing but sheer rock on the far, or left, side, and a steep gravel slope downward on the right to tumbled boulders, heavy brush, and scattered small aspen. Johnnie's nerves tightened. If someone came around the curve ahead just now, it could be a mess, and . . .

The van loomed beside her, and then with shocking suddenness veered closer. Metal crashed against metal. The impact knocked her sideways against her shoulder harness and the Jeep slewed to the right, two wheels already in unstable shoulder gravel. She glanced angrily at the other vehicle, and just as she did so, it slammed sideways a second time, hitting her even harder.

Across the slight space between the rushing vehicles, for a split second, she saw and recognized the giant form behind the wheel of the van, eyes flicking her way with murderous intent.

Hell, but too late for recognition to do her any good. The van swerved toward her a third time. The impact this time rattled her teeth and she felt herself losing control. Her right front wheel went over the edge of the gravel and dug into softer loam, sliding. She fought to regain control, but couldn't. The Jeep slid farther right, going half sideways, dirt and gravel flying over the windshield. Then it left the roadway entirely, shooting down at an angle toward the trees and boulders ahead and below.

Fighting the steering wheel, Johnnie slammed down into second gear and got her weight on the brake. The Jeep bounced over something and tilted at a crazy angle and then slid through mud and loose dirt. She could feel underlying rocks and stumps jolting the wheels and frame. I'm going to roll over! No, she wasn't; the careening vehicle slowed, and then half-turned around as she spun the wheel and got it going almost straight in line with its inertia again. The noise was deafening—rocks hitting, pieces being torn off underneath, metal screaming.

She sideswiped a small spruce, bounced over a two-foot boulder—hell, there went the transfer casing—skidded again, and plowed into a dense stand of small aspen. The windshield checkered with the impact and the hood buckled and a cloud of steam whooshed up and a tire blew. Then the Jeep bucked twice more, pitching wildly, and came to a dead rest in the middle of the aspen grove, wildly swaying trees and branches on all sides.

Something else blew under the ruptured hood and water spurted over the spiderwebbed windshield.

Dazed, Johnnie had only one thought: to get out in case it caught fire. Punching her seat belt buckle, she got free and lunged against the flimsy ragtop door. The latch gave way suddenly and she sprawled out, falling through flimsy aspen branches onto the hardscrabble earth. She scrambled unsteadily to her feet and managed to stagger a dozen paces away from the mangled vehicle. She stepped on something that rolled under her foot and went sprawling, her left ankle feeling like fire.

Rolling over, she looked up toward the roadway thirty or forty feet above. Her eyes followed the raw wheel-torn ruts in the gravel and weeds where she had bounced along, losing speed, fighting for some control. She could see the road. She looked for the van.

She didn't have to look far. It had stopped a hundred feet or so on down. As she located it, she saw the driver's door pop open and Boris appear. He scanned the embankment, but apparently couldn't see her sprawled in the weeds. He ran back down the shoulder toward the Jeep, moving with frightening agility for such a big man.

Johnnie hunkered lower. She saw that any movement on her part would give her position away at once. With numb fingers she clawed at the flap of her holster.

Boris came down the side of the gravel embankment, head down, watching his feet in the sliding shale and gravel. He had something in his hand, and ice water dashed through Johnnie's veins as she recognized it.

Getting her own revolver free of the holster, she tugged the hammer back to full cock. Was she capable of using it? She remembered the last time she had range-fired the weapon. Early in the spring, well over six months ago. All she had come away with was a pair of ringing ears and a paper silhouette target with tattered edges.

Gravel peppered down toward her hiding place as Boris plunged on. She heard his labored breathing, like a big wild animal's. He hadn't spotted her yet, but she could see him clearly against the rocks and the sky. He loomed as big as a house. His face was terrifying, not because of his expression but because there was simply no expression there at all—*nothing*. He was working hard, coming down fast, hurrying to finish her if necessary. He was not afraid, not angry, not anything—simply intent.

My God, can I fire this thing right?

Boris stumbled around some larger fallen rocks and moved nearer the Jeep. He saw the side panel popped open. Then, as if notified by some animal instinct, he started to turn precisely in Johnnie's direction. Her insides shriveled, and time seemed to stop.

His eyes found her. His right hand—holding the .357 revolver she had already spotted—started to come up.

Steadying her right hand with her left, by the book, Johnnie fired. The big revolver bucked hard against her hand, leaping up off line with the recoil. She went instantly deaf from the explosion. The bullet hit him. He staggered backward. But then, with a terrible slow intensity, he regained his balance and started to raise his right hand again.

Johnnie fired again. Again. *Again.* She saw the bullets hit.

Slowly, like a lightning-struck tree, Boris started to fall backward. Johnnie's gun exploded one more time without her consciously willing it. Boris went down. He didn't move.

Stunned and deafened by the gunshots, Johnnie knelt in the harsh gravel, sobbing and trying to get fresh rounds out of her belt to reload. Her hands wouldn't function and she kept spilling bullets onto the ground. The sharp stench of cordite filled her nostrils. She thought she was crying but she wasn't sure. The deafness made everything crazier.

Boris had fallen over backward. She was staring across the tire-torn ground at the bottom of his boots. They were very big boots. They didn't move. Nothing moved. Johnnie gave up trying to reload, and just slumped over and began shaking.

She was still shaking uncontrollably when Butt's truck appeared on the road above and he slid to a halt, jumped out, and came ass over teakettle down the embankment to grab her in his arms.

4:25 P.M.

A COWBOY BLUEGRASS band was playing to a fair-sized crowd in the tree-lined park across the street from the elk antler monument, and two of the chamber of commerce's hired cowboys slowly walked their nags up and down Frontier Street, nodding to children and occasionally doffing a sombrero to a lady. Chubby Mayfield, resplendent in full dress uniform that included a beautiful fawn-colored Stetson and gray lizard cowboy boots, strolled along Main Street, beaming at everyone and giving them a happy howdy. A cool breeze swept out of the distant San Juans, making the aspen tremble and live up to their Colorado nickname, "quakers." To all outward appearances, it was a perfectly splendid fall day in Tenoclock.

In the basement of the county courthouse it was a different story.

"The people have a right to know!" Editor Niles Pennington yelled, striding back and forth in front of the desk Johnnie had taken in the deepest corner of the sheriff's department. "This high-handed suppression of the news is unconscionable! It's . . . it's . . . unconstitutional! On behalf of the citizenry of Tenoclock County I demand a prompt and complete explanation!"

Trembly, Johnnie bit into her Quarter Pounder and wondered how she could eat. But maybe the food would make her stop shaking. She refused to answer Pennington. A million work details to do and yet-unanswered questions flooded her mind. But the feeling overwhelmed all of them. *I killed a man.*

Pennington drew himself up to his full height and shot an indignant finger toward the water-marked ceiling. "You won't get away with this! I'll file a formal complaint with the board of county commissioners, and ask the district attorney in Gunnison to file criminal charges for failure to maintain open records as required by law."

Johnnie reached for a french fry. If she spoke at all, she

knew she could not trust herself to refrain from a choice cowboy obscenity.

Pennington glared once more and turned away. Johnnie took a deep breath and scanned the room.

The young morning disk jockey for KTCK stood nearby, nervously fingering some folded copy paper and a Flair pen. He had come in moments earlier, asking if Johnnie had a handout on what was going on. On the far side of the room, near the reception counter, Jason Ramsey sat quietly, watching a red-faced Maxwell Copely have a shouting match with Butt Peabody while Carl Rieger and Madison Blithe stood by, awaiting their turn. The continued ringing in Johnnie's ears mercifully muted the noise. She still wasn't hearing very well except when someone was up close and shouting, as Niles Pennington was.

Near the back of the long room, Deputy Dean Epperly grabbed up one of several jangling telephones, listened with a stunned expression, replied, listened again, and furiously jotted notes on a memo pad. His face twisted by a worried frown, he trotted through the maze of vacant desks and said something Johnnie couldn't quite hear as he handed her the notes. It seemed that the Denver Post was holding on line one, two Denver TV stations had crews en route, and CNN's Charles Jaco (himself!) was now holding on line two. Johnnie crumpled the memos and tossed them into the wastebasket.

Another kid from the radio station rushed in, dragging a couple of battered metal boxes with black crinkle finish, some tangled wire with a small suction cup on one end, a microphone, and what looked like a small toolbox. The disk jockey hurried to meet him, and after a moment's consultation the technician dumped all his gear on an empty desk and started hooking wires together.

At the far back end of the room, Deputy Billy Higginbotham hurried in, found Johnnie with his eyes, and gave her an OK signal. She nodded. Higginbotham ran back out the way he had come, returning to the jail.

Johnnie put down her burger and watched her hands shake.

The disk jockey came up the aisle between desks, dragging his microphone on a long cord. Behind him, the technician had red and green lights aglow on the boxes he had just plugged in and hooked together with one of the telephones. The jock reached Johnnie's desk and waved frantically at his helper, who said something into a boom-mike headset, threw another switch or two, and gave him the go sign.

The disk jockey started talking into the mike. By leaning forward and straining, Johnnie could make it out.

"Good afternoon, friends and neighbors in the Tenoclock Valley," the boy intoned. "We interrupt regular programming to bring you this live, on-the-spot news coverage from the courthouse. This is Charles Ducharme, speaking to you *live* from the office of Acting Sheriff Johnnie Baker." Ducharme paused, his Adam's apple bobbing, then resumed in his best Ted Baxter tones, "*This* . . . is what we know at this hour.

"Less than one hour ago, the famous actor and Tenoclock property owner Brandon Warner was taken into custody by Tenoclock sheriff's deputies and placed in the Tenoclock County Jail. We are unable at this time to secure any information on what if any charges are planned against Mr. Warner. He was arrested at his Tenoclock home.

"In another development, Mr. Warner's longtime friend and personal bodyguard, Boris O'Neal, was killed in a high-speed chase and running gun battle with Acting Sheriff Baker. The connection between this incident and the arrest of Brandon Warner is unknown.

"Still bringing you up to the minute on developments that have shocked our vacation wonderland, it is understood that David Dickensen, well-known civic figure and operator of the DD Security Systems here in Tenoclock, is also in custody in the county jail. No formal charges have yet been filed. County Judge Fred Otterman cannot be reached. Assistant District Attorney Max Shoemaker is reportedly on a fishing trip to Blue Mesa Reservoir, and whether he has been notified of these developments, we do not know."

Ducharme, who had been getting slightly red in the face, paused to gasp some air. "We are here with Acting Sheriff Johnnie Baker, reporting live at this hour." He rolled his eyes toward Johnnie, who had a mouthful of french fries. "Sheriff Baker, what can you tell us about the bizarre series of incidents?" He thrust the microphone at her.

Johnnie looked up into his wide, stupid, pretty eyes, and couldn't come up with any reply.

"No comment at this time." The ringing in her ears made her voice sound funny to her.

Ducharme's boyish, nervous smile evaporated. He swallowed and tried again. "Sheriff, you shot and killed a man named O'Neal a while ago. Was that the first man you ever killed? Tell us how you feel about using your gun in the line of duty."

Johnnie's nerves cracked. Reaching out angrily, she grabbed the microphone out of Ducharme's hand and swung it down just as hard as she could against the edge of the desk. The loud cracking noise made everybody in the room look sharply toward her. The young technician at the other desk hurled his headphones off and put his hands to his ears with an expression of sheer agony. Pieces of the microphone fell to the floor.

"You broke it!" Ducharme cried, aggrieved.

Johnnie handed the pieces back.

Carl Rieger and Madison Blithe had broken off their heated conversation with Butt Peabody across the room and headed in her direction. Rieger's face looked as red as a traffic light.

"We have to talk, Johnnie," he rasped. "In private."

"Now," Blithe added.

Johnnie put down the remains of her burger. She thought it would be quite a while before she felt solid inside again, but the food had already begun to make her feel a bit stronger. "There's an interrogation room back yonder. Follow me."

The two commissioners trailed her as she walked toward

the back door, going into the narrow back hallway and then opening the door of the room they were supposed to use for questioning suspects. The light was already turned on. Windowless, with a low concrete ceiling, three of the room's walls were ancient limestone, glistening with gypsum seepage. There was a rusty utility table inside, and four rusty metal folding chairs. To Johnnie's surprise, her opening of the door caught Luke Cobb sitting bent over on one of the chairs, despondently holding his head in his hands.

Luke looked up sharply at the sound of the door. His eyes glistened with tears. "I was just taking it easy a minute."

"Sure," Johnnie said quickly, recovering from the surprise. "I guess I need the room now, though, to talk with these gentlemen."

Luke got up quickly and hurried out, brushing past her and the two men in the hall behind her. She let Rieger and Blithe enter the room, then swung the warped door closed. Before she could turn to face him, Rieger was all over her.

"My God, Johnnie, this is terrible! You can't be serious, arresting someone like Brandon Warner! You have to release him at once and issue an apology!"

"You don't know the story," Johnnie told him.

"We don't need to know any story! Do you realize who you've put in jail? We'll be the laughingstock of the world! We want that poor man released instantly!"

"I suppose," Johnnie said wearily, "you'd like to have Dave Dickensen released, too?"

"Of course we would," Blithe replied. "He's one of our leading businessmen. He couldn't be guilty of any serious infraction."

Blithe's cellular phone beeped, interrupting. He pulled it out of his coat pocket and extended the antenna. "Yes?" He listened. "That's right. Immediately. At the courthouse. Right." He snapped a switch and shoved the antenna back into the telephone case.

The interruption had given Johnnie enough time to collect her thoughts. "Dave Dickensen has signed a statement. Max Shoemaker is in Gunnison right now, conferring with Red Plechton. Charges against Mr. Warner and Mr. Dickensen will be filed anytime now. It's way too late to talk about pushing this under the carpet."

Blithe's eyes narrowed. "Do you want to tell us what all this is about?"

"In a nutshell, yes. But it doesn't leave this room."

"Of course not!" Rieger exclaimed. "Do you imagine we would be a party to anything that might hamper an official investigation?"

Johnnie let that one pass. "Brandon Warner has an appetite for young women—the younger the better. He had two girls up at his house Wednesday night, Barbara Gregg and Donna Smith."

"But the Gregg girl—" Rieger began.

"Be quiet, Carl," Blithe snapped. "Go on, Johnnie."

"Barbara Gregg's father had just come to town to look for her. Our latest information from Mrs. Gregg is that the mother of a girlfriend of Barbara's down in Texas had found a letter Barbara sent the girl down there. In it, she said she was going to have a date with Brandon Warner. When Barbara's folks heard that, they knew enough about Warner's reputation to make the news the last straw. Gregg rented a car, leaving the family van at home for his wife to use, and hightailed it up here. When he got here, no Barbara to be found. He figured she might be with Warner right then, last Wednesday night. He went out there, got through the security, and burst in on them. Donna Smith ran for it. We think Gregg accidentally shot his own daughter. Then, according to Dave, his guard, a man named Hinson, came in on Gregg and shot him in self-defense."

"But if it was self-defense—" Rieger began eagerly.

"Carl," Blithe cut in again, "will you please shut the hell up and let the woman talk."

"Warner panicked and paid off Dickensen and Hinson," Johnnie resumed. "Boris was to dispose of the bodies. Now. This part is supposition, but what must have happened was that Boris took the bodies to the old Interocean mine to bury them deep. Don't ask me why he didn't dig a six-foot hole in the garden somewhere; maybe he knew how animals dig stuff up around here or maybe he just panicked and it was the only thing he could come up with."

Johnnie paused, swallowed hard, and took a few deep breaths. Talking with Boris O'Neal made the picture of his dying come back into her mind. I killed a man. She was never going to be quite the same.

"But what," Rieger asked impatiently, "did any of this have to do with Jim's death? If anything?"

"I think Big Jim just happened by on his way back home, and caught Boris at the mine site. Boris killed Jim and drove him in his Bronco to the place where he faked the wreck and put Jim—already dead—on the tracks."

"Incredible," Madison Blithe said so softly Johnnie almost didn't hear. "I can't believe it!"

"We're pretty sure of most of it."

"But if Boris did kill poor Jim, why didn't he hide the body in the mine, as you say he did the others?"

"I don't know if we'll ever know that," Johnnie admitted. "Maybe he had already reboarded the shaft entrance and was on the way out when Jim saw him. Maybe it was a time factor, or maybe Boris panicked a little. Or maybe he was smart enough and fast enough on his feet to realize that the Greggs might never be looked for seriously, but there was sure to be a big search for Jim if he turned up missing, so his body had to be accounted for."

"My God!" Carl Rieger said, dazed. "And you say Dave Dickensen was a party to all this? My God!"

The silence in the little room was tomblike.

It was Carl Rieger who finally spoke again. "So this man Boris O'Neal actually did the killing?"

"Yes."

"And you killed O'Neal! Good! At least you did that part right."

Johnnie didn't trust herself to reply.

"And," Rieger added, "Brandon Warner himself is an innocent man!"

Johnnie stared at him, stunned. "Innocent?"

Rieger spread his hands. "What did he do? He was an innocent bystander! He couldn't be held responsible for whatever this man O'Neal might have done on his own!"

"You've got to be kidding!"

Someone knocked on the door and Butt Peabody stuck his head in. "Everything okay in here?"

"Fine. What's up?"

"Telephone. Red Plechton."

Johnnie hurried into the office and picked up the line that was blinking. "Yes, Red?"

Plechton's nasal voice tensely clipped off the words: "I'm here with Max, Johnnie. We've got the copy of the signed statement from Dickensen. I'm filing multiple charges. I'm sending a couple of deputies from here to come collect both suspects."

"I'll be glad to turn them over," Johnnie said, breathing relief.

"Hell of a mess, Johnnie. I've already got TV people in the outer office."

"Welcome to the club, Red. I'll call after your guys get the prisoners out of here, and we can talk about anything else you need."

The connection broke. Johnnie looked up to see Jason Ramsey hurrying up the aisle from the jail. He looked worried.

"Now what?" Johnnie asked.

"Mr. Wesley is back there, saying he wants to see his client."

"Our biggest lawyer? Who does he say is his client?"

"Brandon Warner."

"How the hell did Wesley get drawn in so fast? We haven't even given Warner his telephone call yet."

Ramsey's dark face smoothed the way it did when all his defenses went up. "Blithe contacted him."

"Madison Blithe? Why, that skunk!"

"Do I let him in to see Warner?"

"Yes. You have to do that." Johnnie thought with dismay about the things she had just told Blithe "in confidence." If Blithe hadn't yet told T. Thomas Wesley all that was known about the case, it wouldn't be much longer before he did. She wondered what connections Blithe and Wesley had on a regular basis, and why. She wondered if she would ever really get used to this kind of stuff.

5:33 P.M.

FILING OF CHARGES in Gunnison against Brandon Warner was the lead item on the evening news out of Denver. Johnnie sat in her office with Butt and Luke and watched the tape of a nervous Red Plechton being interviewed by more reporters than she had known existed on the western slope.

"David Dickensen, a Tenoclock businessman who operates a home and business security company, has been charged with three counts of conspiracy to conceal a felony and two counts of accessory to homicide," Plechton told the gaggle of microphones thrust at his face. "Brandon Warner has been charged with two counts of failure to report an accident and one count of withholding evidence relating to the commission of a felony."

Johnnie jerked upright. *"What?"*

"Listen," Butt growled.

"No bond has been set in the Dickensen case," a sweaty Plechton was saying. "Bond for Mr. Warner was set at fifty thousand dollars."

Johnnie hit the mute button. "How can they *do* that? Warner had a hell of a lot more to do with all of this than Dave did!"

Peabody kept staring at the silent tube. His voice was sepulchral: "Warner is a lot more important."

"Are they scared up there, or what?"

"Hell, yes, they're scared. They're going to have press from everywhere watching every move they make. If they file something and fail to get a conviction or plea bargain, they'll look like morons. Not to mention the kind of damage suit a man with Warner's money can afford to come back at them with later."

Johnnie had no words.

Peabody shrugged. "Boris's death helps them quite a lot, you see. Your defense lawyers can say Boris was the villain who did everything, and Warner didn't know most of what went on. Dave can use that defense, too. I'd say they've got a fair chance of beating the whole thing, or maybe working out a plea bargain for some high misdemeanor."

Johnnie stared at the TV, now showing file footage of Warner at a resort in the Bahamas sometime in the past. "So they'll beat us. Just like that."

Luke said, "It's just another reason to ditch this job. Who supports you? Why should you care when no one else does?"

Johnnie studied his expression, one of sympathy and bafflement. "If you stop caring, Luke, what have you got left?"

"Besides," Butt growled, "we're not *quite* beat yet anyway."

"Of course you are!" Luke shot back bitterly.

"Nope. Next round in Gunnison Monday morning. They got to have a filing and then a hearing. We can go up—demand to put on some testimony."

Johnnie studied his weather-beaten face. "Will that do any good?"

"If there's any justice it will."

"*Is* there any justice, Butt?"

He looked down at her, his face showing the tiny furrows carved by thousands of days and nights under the sky. "Of course there is," he said, his voice gentle. "You have to believe that, Johnnie. Or else you have to quit this job."

Johnnie shook her head, and again Boris's dying formed

stark pictures in her mind. "If I ever quit, it wouldn't be because of losing a case, or any amount of hassle people like Rieger can give me."

Butt studied her expression for a moment. He leaned back and fished for a cigarette. "First and only man I ever killed wasn't much more than a boy, really. Long time ago. I pulled him over for speeding and driving over the center line, and when I leaned over to ask him for his driver's license, he grabbed a cheap old little revolver out from under the seat. I've always thought he was high on something; he managed to miss me at point-blank range. I hit the ground and got my piece out and fired twice. Both of 'em took him in the—" Peabody's voice had begun to quiver, and he stopped dead for a long moment. Johnnie saw his face working.

"Well," he said after a while.

"So you never really get over it?" she said.

He looked at her again. "Not unless you're the kind of shithead who should never be in law enforcement in the first place."

7:10 P.M.

T HE GROWING HORDE of cameramen and reporters scrambled for position as Brandon Warner, handcuffed and flanked by two Gunnison deputies, emerged from the front doors of the Tenoclock County Court House. Warner, wearing jeans, a dark sweatshirt, a leather bomber jacket and a dark stocking cap, looked calm and confident. His local lawyer, T. Thomas Wesley, followed close behind him. Johnnie's deputy, Dean Epperly, followed behind with Dave Dickensen in tow, and two Tenoclock policemen helped form a wedge through the milling crowd as they went down the steps toward a Gunnison sheriff's car parked at the curb.

Johnnie stood alone in the darkened offices of the county assessor on the second floor of the old courthouse, watching.

Warner, surrounded by his protective cadre of officers, reached the open door of the cruiser. He turned and waved like a man off on a grand adventure. The brilliant TV lights showed a purplish cut on his mouth, a souvenir, Johnnie knew, of his last encounter with Boris O'Neal.

Reporters yelled questions, but the deputies helped Warner into the car. Dickensen went in next, and the back door was closed. The two Gunnison deputies climbed into the front. The cruiser's headlights came on. It moved away from the curb, slowly forcing surrounding press corps out of its path. Then the TV lights began to die, and Johnnie spotted Wesley hurrying through the night gloom toward the parking lot to get into his own car and follow.

She closed the old wood-sash window and groped her way across the dim expanse of the unlighted office. At the glazed hallway doors, she stopped a minute and struggled with some of the feelings going through her. There were so many she couldn't sort them out.

"Well," she breathed after a few moments, "shit."

She opened the door and went into the hall. Luke sat on the old wood pew-type bench there, waiting.

"I thought I'd take you home now," he told her, standing.

She studied his face. She thought he looked awful—ten years older, totally stressed out.

"I've got to write a report," she told him. "I've got to call the DA in Gunnison again. We need to follow through on all the forensics reports. Then we have to decide what to do tomorrow, and in what order."

Luke's forehead wrinkled. "Haven't you done enough? You need rest now!"

"It's going to be hours yet, Luke. There's no way around it."

His face twisted. "You were almost killed today."

Johnnie moved close to him. "It was bad. But I got out."

Luke held her. "When you get through this case, are you going to step down?"

"Step down? It hadn't entered my mind."

"I don't like the hours you have to keep. I don't like the

thought of your being in danger. And you know the commissioners aren't going to forget the way you embarrassed them proving Jim Way's death was murder after they had written it off."

"My God, Luke, they can't hold it against me for doing my job!"

"They'll hold it against you for investigating, for hiring Butt Peabody, for everything. All they think about is the town's image. They thought they were getting a cute girl who wouldn't rock the boat. You've been a—I almost said bull in a china shop."

Johnnie chuckled. "I'll fight 'em regardless."

"They'll get you. Just like they got Butt."

"That's crazy!"

"You're too strong a character. Don't you see that? They weren't able to control you through this deal and they won't be able to control you in the future. They want a nice, quiet, stupid, low-profile law officer. You aren't that. You need to quit before they fire you, or drive you away."

"I won't quit, Luke. How can I, when I've just learned I can *do* this kind of stuff?"

Luke groaned and turned away. "I'm a modern man. I've worked hard to get sensitized to the things women need. I had a marriage fail, but now I've *learned*. I know you want tenderness and caring and understanding. I know you have to have your space. But I have needs, too, you know. You don't have to have this kind of shitty job. You could teach singing lessons, or have an acting studio or something. You could even be a clerk in my gallery. Think of it, Johnnie! You wouldn't ever have to face danger or political pressure again. We could be together twenty-four hours a day—you could wear makeup and pretty little dresses and high heels."

"Luke," Johnnie groaned, seeing at last. "I'm already doing what I want to do. This is the kind of life I want."

He stared at her. His eyes seemed to sag in their sockets. He was a good man, she thought. But this difference between them could never be resolved.

Finally he said, "You won't go home with me now?"

"Oh, Luke," she said sadly. "No. Not now. Not ever."

"Yes. I see. Well, then."

"Luke. I'm sorry. I'm truly, deeply sorry."

"Yes." He tried to smile. "Me, too."

He turned and walked away, heading for the stairs. Johnnie did not move until he had reached the first floor and she heard the door open and close, signaling that he had gone.

10:50 P.M.

JOHNNIE PUSHED THE report file back away from her on the desk. "I can't do any more tonight, Butt."

Butt looked up from his desk with a gentle, probing expression. "About time you said that."

She rubbed her aching eyes. "I feel like there's so much more to do—all the damn paperwork. But I've had it. I'm so tired I can't see straight."

"Well, I wonder why," Peabody said with a crooked smile. "All you've done lately is get lost in an old mine and almost drown yourself and get run off the road and damn near killed by an eight-hundred-pound gorilla, and shot somebody, and arrested the most famous actor in the world, and got double-crossed by half the cowards and brown-nosers in two counties."

"I'll feel better after I get about seven hours' sleep."

"Sleep twelve. I can handle the pressing stuff in the morning."

"It's Sunday. You don't work on Sunday."

"I'll make an exception. It's not like I'm a churchgoer."

Johnnie got up and double-checked the wall clock against her watch. It was far too late to call Luke's studio. But she realized that she wouldn't have called earlier, either.

Butt pulled on his heavy coat and jammed a ski cap on

his head. Bushy hair stuck out all around. He caught Johnnie looking. "What?" he asked, forehead wrinkling again.

"Butt, I know it's way out of your way, but could you drive me home? I know I could take the county truck, but I think I may be too tired to handle it tonight."

"Why, hell yes," Peabody said instantly. "I'd've offered, but I just naturally figured Luke was waiting somewhere, and you'd want him."

Johnnie studied his dear, weather-beaten face, and realized how long she had known him, how central he had been in so much of her life, and how long she had taken him for granted.

"I don't want Luke to take me," she said. "I want you. If you don't mind."

"Why, Johnnie," Peabody said gruffly, "I surely don't mind. Let's get outta here. Maybe you'd like to stop at Taco Bell on the way and grab something more to eat?"

"It sounds great," Johnnie told him, feeling the grin spread all over her face.

He held out his arm. She linked hers with his. How long, she wondered suddenly, had she dismissed the fact that she always felt good around him?

They walked out together.